# PRAISE FOR BLUE EARTH

Psychologically and politically penetrating, *Blue Earth* portrays the frailties and quiet triumphs of contemporary individuals coping with their own loss of land, family, and culture against a historical backdrop of unacknowledged violence and theft. Characters that are often both victim and perpetrator operate with complex humanity amidst the wide scope of Achtenberg's vision. This book is, put simply, magnificent.
— Christine Stark, author of *Nickels: A Tale of Dissociation*

In *Blue Earth* generations repel and embrace one another, and individuals are people you want to know. The characters in this novel dance with loss and despair, rage and hope. We are seduced by their historic burden and contemporary doings and undoings; see our own lives reflected in the book's dark mirror, even as we learn a tragic history kept from us by those who would forever erase our origins. Achtenberg takes the reader backward and forward in time, through the lives of people who are violently split open and cleave to one another in a desperation and relief that leap from the page. Memory is the thread that binds and finally lets them loose. This is a brilliant novel by one of our truly intuitive and accomplished writers.
— Margaret Randall, author of *Ruins*

*Blue Earth* is the story of the United States, a country that has yet to own up to its past in order to move on and heal. Achtenberg's passionate, brilliantly crafted language, combined with her profound ethical imagination, makes this one of the most important books to appear at this moment in our history.
— Demetria Martinez, author of *Mother Tongue*

Anya Achtenberg's *Blue Earth* is a thoroughly absorbing narrative, rich in both lyrical grace and historical depth. Farm and city, past and present, life and death converge on the land, lost by both its original and later inhabitants. Using dream, vision, and memory to enhance her compelling story, Achtenberg creates morally complex and culturally diverse characters whose lives are affected by loss, poverty, disease, and war, but whose ultimately redemptive encounters with one another take the book far beyond its Midwestern setting.
— Martha Collins, author of *Blue Front*

In the great tradition of Willa Cather and Wallace Stegner, Anya Achtenberg writes of the violence, both past and present, that shapes the people of the vast American Midwest. It is a story of bloodshed, loss, despair and the search for redemption. Deep and searing, *Blue Earth* is perhaps one of the best novels of the past decade.
— Kathleen Spivack, author of *With Robert Lowell and His Circle: Plath, Sexton, Bishop, Kunitz et al.*

# BLUE
# EARTH

*A Novel*

## ANYA ACHTENBERG

Reflections of America Series

MODERN HISTORY PRESS

Grateful acknowledgment is made to the editors of *Harvard Review*, for their Fall 2000 Issue, in which a section of this novel first appeared as "More Than The Wind."

Library of Congress Cataloging-in-Publication Data

Achtenberg, Anya.
*Blue Earth* / by Anya Achtenberg.
pages cm. -- (Reflections of America Series)
ISBN 978-1-61599-147-1 (hardcover)
ISBN 978-1-61599-146-4 (pbk.)
ISBN (invalid) 978-1-61599-148-8 (ebook)
 1. Life change events--Fiction. 2. Self-actualization (Psychology)--Fiction. 3. Minnesota--Fiction. I. Title.
 PS3551.C418B58 2012
 813'.54--dc23
                              2011053525


Published by Modern History Press, an imprint of
Loving Healing Press
5145 Pontiac Trail
Ann Arbor, MI 48105

www.ModernHistoryPress.com
info@ModernHistoryPress.com
tollfree 888-761-6268

Distributed by Ingram Book Group (USA/CAN), Bertram's Books (UK)

# ACKNOWLEDGMENTS

I want to thank many people, including Meridel Le Sueur, who opened up the story of Minnesota to me.

Marilise Tronto, whose full vision of the book and her profound belief in it have made an enormous difference in an often lonely work, and carried me through.

Kathleen Spivack, who has given me the gift of believing in the value of my work, and supported me actively and lovingly throughout the very long process of finding publication for *Blue Earth*.

Sharon Doubiago, whose comments and suggestions were of profound use, helping me come out of that place of too much dreaming to communicate from within the dream of it all.

Victor Volkman, publisher of *Modern History Press*, whose irreplaceable support has been deeply respectful, solid, and real; and all those at the Press who have helped on *Blue Earth* and as well on *The Stories of Devil-Girl*.

Margaret Randall, who encouraged me with crucial publishing decisions, and supports this book and all my work with her belief and her generous spirit.

Christine Stark, who helped me tremendously with final revisions to bring false notes into their true sound, and who has been powerfully supporting me in bringing this book into the world.

The Writers Workshop at the Joiner Center for the Study of War and Social Consequences at the University of Massachusetts / Boston, where I worked to move more fully into fiction from poetry. Larry Heinemann and Stratis Haviaras especially supported this book's beginnings, and Fred Marchant's general support was always a gift.

The organizers and participants of the Dakota Commemorative March, including Chris Mato Nunpa and Waziyatawin (formerly known as Angela Cavender Wilson), who welcomed me in my brief participation, which gave me some very important knowledge.

The Minnesota History Center, for the staff's kindness and generosity during my visits. My research there helped open the worlds to me.

The New Mexico writers who studied with me, and taught me, and treated my work with honor and love, among them, Amy Fisher, Phyllis Johnson, and Annie Lewis.

Michigan writers Rachel Diem, Lee Sayles, (and Leaven Directors -- ) Karen Bota and Melanie Morrison, as well as many others who for 8 years at the Leaven Retreat Center on the Grand River spent summer days and nights with me, along with my co-teacher Demetria Martinez, in rich writing workshops which helped sustain my spirit all year.

The Harwood Art Center in Albuquerque, where I wrote through the dark season, windows rattling with the winter wind, and which gave me the respite of the mountain view down the corridor when I got up from the folding table, the computer sitting on the magical cloth.

The many people who helped me to name the book, and make final decisions on the cover and its stunning collage painting by Margo Ray.

The readers of earlier versions of the book, including Marilise Tronto, Sherry Quan Lee, Donna Olmstead, Bronwyn Mills, Kathleen Spivack, Demetria Martinez, Martha Collins, Amy Fisher, and Gary Jefferson, who all took my manuscript seriously, and gave me many reasons to keep on.

Maya Gonzalez, Paulette Tabb, and Mehrzad Araghi, for everything, always.

And the two tornadoes I have known personally, who found me and left me blessedly alive, with books and papers, computer and stories, intact, thank you.

All praises and all thanks to the blessing of the home of the body that has sustained my work, and to the invisible presence of those from my scattered history. Praises and gratitude, always.

Anya Achtenberg
May 22, 2012

## ALSO BY ANYA ACHTENBERG

*The Stories of Devil-Girl*

*The Stone of Language*

*I Know What The Small Girl Knew*

# BLUE EARTH

"Little by little I will drive them out from before you, until you are increased and possess the land."

— *Exodus*

"You shall not oppress a stranger; you know the heart of a stranger, for you were strangers in the land of Egypt."

— *Exodus*

# CONTENTS

| | | |
|---|---|---|
| Prologue | Blanket Over Blue Earth | 1 |
| Book One | Journey Out | 3 |
| Book Two | Birds in Flight | 29 |
| Book Three | How Far From the Garden | 61 |
| Book Four | Walking the River | 113 |
| Book Five | Sun and Moon in the Afternoon Sky | 147 |
| Book Six | Floor Plan of Paradise | 195 |
| Epilogue | Dream of Home | 209 |

# Prologue

## Blanket Over Blue Earth

Sioux, this sliver of sound on the tongues of French trappers, was a name that hung on. Sliced clean from *nadewisou*, as the Ojibwe called the Dakota, their old enemies. Little snakes, treacherous snakes, they said in their language. But snake across the land is what the settlers did, the French along with Scandinavians, Germans and Dutch, the line of settlements like a jagged spill of flour, white thunder come to earth.

Twenty-four million acres were taken into white hands in a quick no-frills signing at the crossing of a river, Traverse des Sioux, in 1851, then eleven million more, grabbed to build up the territory's broad shoulders and lengthen her western hip.

This was Minnesota, land of water, soon to be the heartland of America. Her dairyland, too, her breadbasket, her fragrant lumberyard, her blooming fishery. She birthed pipestone from her generous quarry, forged iron from her belly of earth.

This new land wanted workers. She opened herself to miners in their rush for wealth. To farmers and loggers and men who drove the railroad stakes into the earth. To churchbuilders. She gave them deep cold nights when liquor would sell, and children be conceived to work, the girls like the boys, the frail and the sturdy, the talkers, the silent ones and the ones who could not read.

Minnesota, achingly green, fertile with the bones of the buffalo and dollars from the trade in their bones and hides, air trembling with the breath of Dakota murdered and starved, became an altar to work.

"Let them eat grass or their own dung," one trader had said, as he stood, arms folded, in front of a locked warehouse stacked with food.

"We are only little herds of buffalo left scattered," Dakota Chief Little Crow had said, before he gave an order to attack.

Trader Myrick was found in August of 1862, the year of his Lord, in a dead sprawl against the warehouse steps, grass stuffed into his mouth.

On the day after Christmas, thirty-eight Dakota swung from a scaffold built in Mankato, their death chant rattling the branches of bare trees. One chop of the ax brought them all down.

The soldiers forcemarched Dakota women, children and elders a hundred and fifty miles through the spreading farms to Fort Snelling on the Mississippi River. Thousands were imprisoned, killed, exiled to the western plains.

Once Blue Earth County was all birdsong mixed with the language of trees. Its colors the vibrant notes of wildflowers, its dance soft, its cry spinning around tepees and cooking fires, its hunt celebrated with feasting, its children carried everywhere when they were too young or too tired to walk, but that was before the singing was in German; the land, named in English.

By the time seven generations of one German family had labored on a corner of Blue Earth, lived in their farmhouse and prayed in the church nearby, it seemed to them they were the first people there. After so many births on that farm, so many deaths. Deathbeds in the house, deathbeds in the fields.

Now Carver, the only son left, was selling.

The banks had laid interest like a plague over the land. Soon the brilliant-edged patchwork of fields would be blanketed by one color, one crop, one invisible owner. Some farmers sold early. Some hung on till their purses emptied out. That's what Carver did.

But he could not face them: the girl, with her bracelets made from daisies, and his wife, who refused to become a wisp of flax in the storm coming up.

# *Book One*

## *Journey Out*
### *Fall 1985 - Fall 1986*

"Sometimes I go about pitying myself,
and all the time
I am being carried on great winds across the sky."

*— Ojibwe*

"Those who give up their farms without a fight, without seeing if they could have kept it going, always live wondering what might have been. ..."

*— The Haymakers: A Chronicle of Five Farm Families*
Steven R. Hoffbeck, p. 138

"On December 6 [1862] President Lincoln notified [General] Sibley that he should 'cause to be executed' thirty-nine of the 303 convicted Santees. ... Execution ... was the twenty-sixth day of December in the Moon When the Deer Shed Their Horns. That morning the town of Mankato was filled with vindictive and morbidly curious citizens. ... At the last minute, one Indian was given a reprieve. About ten o'clock, the thirty-eight condemned men were marched from the prison to the scaffold. They sang the Sioux death song until soldiers pulled white caps over their heads and placed nooses around their necks. At a signal from an army officer, the control rope was cut and thirty-eight Santee Sioux dangled lifeless in the air. ...
A spectator boasted that it was 'America's greatest mass execution.'"

*— Bury My Heart at Wounded Knee*
Dee Brown, on the Dakota Conflict, pp. 9-10

## *Chapter One*
### *Fall 1985*

No, boy, Carver heard in the wind moving over the land that sprawled out behind the old church. When the words struck him, he knew he was turning hard, like the old man had, but his own good bones were still covered in flesh warmed by the golden air of autumn, while his father's were laid out in the black soil, his arms crossed over the Book of God's Word.

Carver felt nothing when he left the hospital that night. They'd stood over him to tell him of his father's last moments. He was sitting right outside the room, facing the glass, watching people race in and out when it happened. He could do nothing but lower his head, and that was the way he walked back into the house, where his mother was wailing and rocking, finding the rhythm of her own death. "Carver," she said when she saw his face, "it's over, then."

She leaned on him after, and on Katie, and he did what he could, working through the night on the acres she still had left. In that night daze, in the hush of silver light that made it seem he was moving through the negative of a photo, his jacket glowing and his face in darkness, he saw his work disappear, though he knew it went back into the land.

His mother did all of the milking herself. She always had. She'd been pretty good, too, at getting the tractor up the rise without it stalling. She wouldn't go near it anymore.

Carver brought over a pot of tea each night, and sat with her before he went to tend to the alfalfa in the front acres. But then she went into the great silence of the farm.

"What is it, Mom?" he asked her one night.

She looked up and put her hand to her ear. "They're laying the tracks to Heaven for me. Can you hear it, the tracks getting set down? I could always hear it, the pounding of the spikes, ever since I was a girl, though the trains were already coming on through each day."

"No, Ma, I can't hear it."

"That's good, Carver. Each person should hear their own sounds inside, not what a mother tells them to. Not what a father says."

It was then that he heard again the shots of the salute at his brother's funeral. He heard the twenty-one bursts, but the firing didn't stop. He kept on hearing it, or maybe it was the cracking of trees in the wind, or his mother making a small humming sound as she turned to him, and a sharp grunt as the hammer fell ringing against the spikes.

"Go, get out of here, son. Go to Katie, now. I'm alright," she said, and sipped her tea.

He touched her hand and was shaken by the small explosion in her throat as another spike was set, then went back out into the moonlight and got to work again. He could at least try to make it right.

No flowers pushed up from the grave where his father slept, turned into silence. Carver knelt by the headstone that said, "Beloved Mother." He wanted her arms around him as so many times when she'd tried to protect him from his father, or comfort him afterwards. But it wasn't his father who had lost the farm. What could he do now, but go on and be hard, if that's what it took.

He stood up and flung a rock at the sun, then walked away, weak-kneed, not certain of the path out.

As he read the notice in the papers that night, Carver understood it for a moment, how men could not own the land, the same way they could not own time. With the farm each day closer to auction, a few hairs fell out of his head whether he brushed hard or not at all. His beard grew in gray if he did not shave it, his stomach rumbled if he did not feed it, and his heart, well, that ached more each day, as he thought of his faraway girl, his perfect Rose, and of his wife, no longer his because of some legal paper, and maybe some misguided notion she had. Or, maybe, and his heart seized up at this, because of his rough ways.

But the seasons would keep on their coming and going, there on the land, even after he was gone to the Cities. The field mice and rabbits would feast there, unless the company that bought the place got rid of them. The land would yield or it wouldn't. The sky would bless it with rain, or would not. The earth would keep on turning, like those speeded up films of night into day, and day fallen to night. And his own wife and daughter would be living in another town, his land under another's plow, the rest of his folks dead and buried, and there was nothing he could do about any of it. That's what everyone said, anyway. Or whispered.

He stopped wondering what it was that had broken him down, made him so hard sometimes. He knew the hand of his father. The loss of his brother. The grief of his mother, and he useless to do a thing for her. Just dig and bury: seed, family, his own sorrow.

He'd already asked every question he could think of. In the silence, he made up his own answers.

Those nights after Kate left and took Rosie with her, Carver figured it out. He knew that they were coming for the farm, and for the things he'd bought and the things he'd made, and this woman, who didn't know the meaning of the word wife, left and took his girl, the flower of his flesh. He packed up all through those days and read the Bible every night, for three or four hours. Then he lay down in the stillness, down in the dirt, and smelled its truth, its giving. And he figured it out, just like he was told by the stars and their pretty pictures, here a great gourd full of water, full of blessing; over there a warrior, and circling his powerful waist, a belt to hold a man together in the darkness to do whatever he had to in the light.

Look to the land, the sky told him, that last night before auction. Own its beauty, the Bible said. Know that its wildness defies God. Walk upon the land, and with your long step, make it yours. It lies beneath you. It needs you to work it, to know it, even to force it, in the harshest weathers, in the plagues of insects, in the dust of drought. In the ice of loss. In the green knowledge of harvest. Plow here. He had heard all this many times. Plow deep in the earth and turn the land to opening. Seed it. With all manner of your needs, for bean and grain and the green tops of the vegetable world, seed the land. Make the rows straight. Water and water until all beauty floats up from the belly of the land. Make it give forth the pink buds from its violet furrows, and eat here, eat what you made flower. Then feed your village, and in harsh times feed no other. Become master of the land in God's image.

Own beauty, he repeated.

It's them that work it, have a right to it. He was told this by the old man, an upright old man in most habits, who stood over his son each evening at dusk and asked him what he did that day, what he accomplished that could be done by no other, just him and the sons he was to have. And he'd wanted a son, always. When Katie told him a child was coming, he was proud and took himself to the fields each day a better man, sure to be echoed by a boy working at his side, full doubled someday by a grown son to leave the land to. He had dreams of the wind coming up to bring that boy to him, and he was strong, fair-haired and strong, and looked to his father with clear open eyes, the land trembling around them as they made their plans—which fields to give what crops, which machinery to fix up and drive through—writing their dreams together into the land. In his head, Carver was seeing the rooms to add on for the little ones who'd come after the first, and he didn't think once that Katie might not give him the child he needed.

She was upstairs for so long with the midwife and the neighbor, and he knew she was strong and clean and wouldn't have any kind of trouble, like some women did. It was the polio that had worried him, but that was a long ago thing. After all, Katie was a farmwoman and knew how to grow a world inside of her.

Imagine, he thought, by lying beneath him, this woman goes on to grow a whole new world within her very flesh.

Well, that day he does what the man should do. He drinks some whiskey, not too much, and sits in the parlor room. He gets up and walks around the house and stares off into the fields, into the burning sun that comes right into the room and sits with him as he waits, the sun glowing fiery and the yells come down the stairs to him like his ears are antennae. He's used to listening for birdcalls and angry sky, for the cough of machinery, the yowl of sick cattle, the sound of plow when it catches rock, when it grabs old bone. But now it's Katie's yells that burst right into his head like his own when he got it as a kid, and he's remembering some of those times and seeing that other face of his father, who loved this land and every stick of God that grew here, died here, and got reborn into nourishment. A hard man with his sons, to show them what was necessary, pushing at Eli till he ran off to the war before he was taken, so when the footsteps come down to tell Carver the wife's okay and the child is here, he falls to his knees and prays, and his heart is so full it leaves no room for embarrassment, until the neighbor says it.

"Carver, it's a girl. Healthy. Perfect."

And then he knows the cruelty of God because he knows he would have to work to love it. He needed a boy. The Heinz family needed a boy and the land needed a boy and when she turns to go back to tend to Katie, he lays his head on the sofa and beats his fists there, pounds till the stuffing comes up through the worn upholstery and flies around his head till he can't raise his fists anymore, and the sofa cushion is flat and empty now, the heart of it flying around the room like a storm of milk.

But they don't hear him. How could they not hear him, when he is calling out his pain? They must think it joy, women who don't understand what sits on a man's shoulders. They stay upstairs a long time, without even coming to look at him there on the cold floor next to the sofa, and then, after the night has moved him through its belly, after he sees his father turn away from him again at the grave of his brother, and his mother stay there weeping and not getting up, the shots of the salute still in the air like steel birds falling for the rest of that year, he runs the fields like a starving rabbit. He sleeps under a tree until something warm moves close to him and raises him up, and takes him like waves up the stairs to the room where they are.

There in bed, Katie is smiling under her tired eyes, and the baby is a little flower she gives him to smell and hold and he knows it is right. This child is given him to feed and protect, the boy will come later, and he can prove that he is a good man now with two females at home, a man that feeds the whole family from right out of the earth spinning under them. Stars in her, she buzzes like a cat in his arms, and he shakes her just gently so that she will know him. Then she opens her eyes and that's when he falls in, forever. He leans down to kiss Katie, but she's asleep, so he puts the baby on her chest and tries to make her suck while Katie still sleeps, and she does, his flower, she sucks, as he holds them both, and knows that he is their protector, their big prairie angel. Then he whispers to his flower, "Grow," and he keeps whispering to her, "grow, grow."

# *Chapter Two*

No patience now for packing. He'd been King of the Land, or at least Mayor of the Little City, a city of silos and four-legged citizens, landscaped with soybeans and wheat, and the good timothy grass he'd bale and leave around the fields, like giant cattle curled over on their sides until he had need of them.

He loaded up his car, not enough, what he took, to keep things from rattling around. He took off down County Road 14, wanting to stay off the bigger roads until he was sure he could see over the loose piles of his possessions in the backseat.

It was the beginning of September, and Rosie would be starting school. He reached back behind him to check for the pink knapsack he'd bought for her. Something stirred and was caught up in the wind, and fell before he could see what it was. The clouds stopped moving. Something behind the white face of them was opening into darkness, and maybe his suffering, alone as he was now and without land, had much to do with the dark eye that had caught him in its gaze. Then he saw a bird stumble like it was earthbound, its wings dragged down, and fall back like a child at the side of the road listening to the sounds of the earth. Something like hair flew up now and whirled, raced until it weakened and lay flat on the black earth. He jammed on the brakes and sat in his car in the middle of the road for a moment. He wanted to take a breath and gather his bearings, but then it seemed like the road was disappearing, as the sun struck through and blinded him at the wheel. Someone laid on the horn, and he put his foot on the gas.

As he drove, he saw the fair hair of his girl enter his vision, as if it had slipped through a tear in the day, but it flew blackened under the glare of the sun, and reddened with his straining toward it. It was red cloth now, like a flag ripped up by wind, by time. He slowed down to go through another town, and was distracted by a group of teenagers, boys and girls together, different colors, looking like they were aiming to get into trouble. The light changed, but he stared out at them without moving the car.

"Hey, Mister, what are you looking at?" and it was that harshness of voice that made Carver jump back to attentiveness, and stab the gas pedal. He imagined these kids laughing at him, projects brats, he figured, none of them with a solid root anywhere. And now as he flew down the road, speeding on his own dare, he saw red, red cloth whipping about in the wind, marking each mile he drove away from his roots in the land, from the knowledge that was surely his of how to make things grow.

The numbers kept clicking on his odometer to carry him further from his farm. Something red sliced across his vision. Something soft in him pleaded to go home.

Renter, he was to check that box on the employment application, but wouldn't say all he could afford for now was a shabby motel room. Renter, not owner, same as those kids in the projects, same as the faces he walked past each morning to get to the gas station that would be his place of employment. His place. Paycheck in his hands Friday night. Nothing to put it back into, he thought at first, but a good drunk. Those first few checks, gone as quick as the bartender could pour. But then he began saving to buy back his land, saving every cent he could, for Rosie and Kate, for the farm, and he sat in his small room and watched from the window, the sky and the trees, the children going to and from school, and the awful traffic down the avenue.

"Red light, green light, one, two, three," he heard the children calling in their games.

## *Chapter Three*
### *June 1986*

When the wind picked up the child to dance her through the green air, her end-of-the-school-year dress caught on a splinter of the door. A jagged mouth was ripped in the fabric as the other children were guided to the basement. But Carver had been sitting steady across the road, watching her among the others, though the twister was but a parking lot away. He ran to her as he had dreamt, to carry her to safety, her soft arms around his neck, she like his own sweet girl.

It was more than luck that he was there. It was more than luck that he had dreamt all night of the winds carrying off the farm the bankers had stolen from under his feet. It was more than wind that carried her to the safety of his room, beyond the motel sign that now swung sideways on a dead cord.

Carver set her down and wiped her tears away with his handkerchief. She ran to the window where the rain had spilled through, and pressed against the glass to find the school across the way.

"It's okay, Angie, I know your mom and your pop."

"You do?"

"Sure, they come to my gas station all the time. They show me pictures of you, and I show them pictures of my little girl, and that's how come I know you're Angie."

"Oh," she whispered, and the roof shook, and there was no light in the room as the worst of it came to pass over the motel.

"I have something for you that's very nice," Carver said in a lull in the battering of hail.

The girl looked up, and Carver saw the northern sky in her eyes, and was dazzled again. He pulled out the cedar chest, where the new dress floated on top of layers of old things. He held it up in the dim light and prayed she would see its beauty. Lace, those puffy sleeves, a blossom at the belt and more roses, fine ones, rosettes, the store lady would say, at the collar. He turned to her, soft in his love even as the hailstones struck the tinny roof, ugly but strong, that lay under the raving sky.

"Come put it on," he had to speak up so she could hear him. "Please," he remembered to say, hearing his wife's annoyed cough at his abrupt ways. And what would he do with the dress now, anyway? Kate sent back each package he had mailed to Rosie.

Angie came closer, but when the sign swung at the room and sent the pebbles of plexiglass and the shards of window glass in a cascade through the frame that had given him a view of the school, she screamed and flung herself under the bed, scooting to the middle of the darkness and rolling up. Didn't she know he would never let anything hurt her?

They stayed this way for a while, their breathing tight in the sudden quiet, until the siren went off again, by mistake he was sure, since he could feel the storm breaking.

"Come, Angie, put on the dress. Think how happy your mom would be to see you in such a pretty thing," he said. "Think how proud your pop would be."

She stuck her head out from under the bed and saw the full peach dress swaying in front of her. Then she saw the slit of light entering from under the door and ran to it and wept again, combing the light with her small fingers. She lay there and heaved out sobs for some minutes, and he waited, remembering that he had been told he was not patient when the planting was going or the crops were being taken.

A great sneeze came from the child on the floor, and with his worry that she would catch cold or worse, he said, "Think, Angie, think about your dress all torn up. Think how they'll feel to see what the storm's done to you."

She looked up at him and then he knew he could lift her into his arms, slide off what was torn and drenched, rub the one clean towel over her till her skin warmed and the room warmed, and lower the new dress over her fragrant head, her sleek arms come through each bowl of sleeve. He zipped the long zipper tooth by tooth up to the back of her neck, careful not to catch a thread of gold from her head.

"Oh, Angel," he said in his softest voice, as her neck lifted up from the collar of rosettes, and all he could think was swan, white swan in the garden. "Spin around, spin around, twirl your skirt," he said, and she smiled a bit in the dry clothes and turned like a ballerina as she did in the backyard under her father's eyes. He didn't know what to do next, when she stood still in front of him, to make her feel safe.

"Now come sit here, on my lap, and rest with me till the rain stops," Carver said, patting his thighs, and she did, both quiet then as the storm settled back down into the earth.

# *Chapter Four*

"Lord," said Barb to no master in particular, as she stared trembling out of the window that had held strong that afternoon, and would again. Soon her husband would come down the street with their girl, so small yet, in his arms. She strained for the sight of them, got up from her sickbed to walk through the rubble, and knelt before an enormous elm wrenched up from its broken circle of green and laid down on its side. Even the concrete slabs of sidewalk could not hold the growing thing in its protection. She saw the long entwined roots dying in the air above the road. She wished for a wind to pull the tumors from her, wrench from the root each one, and then pass over her, pass over.

The radiation, just this morning to follow up on the surgery, held her in its grip. She put her ear to the trunk and heard its struggling, or so she thought, as she used to hear the corn struggle their heads upwards from earth and wrap themselves in silk and strength.

No man down the street yet, no child. And no one would find Barb until a light rain had washed a thin strand of hair down across her eyes, and her arm had fallen over the curve of the bark, and she'd slept for a while, pillowed by the dying tree.

Always the trees here danced their leaves around the house, and chanted low songs of the seasons. Even hooded by snow they had voice, if only there were listeners, and Barb was a listener. In waking and in sleep, she listened to the life around her, even that passing beyond other people's hearing. And that afternoon she went into the tree, into the very marrow of it, beyond the faces whirled into the grain, perfect faces of wood hidden by the thick cantankerous skin that had cracked and yet held to the living trunk until this moment, this severing from earth.

It was the dream of the tree she went into. She drifted in its soaring and its staunch embrace of earth, and it was this she sensed in her family, in her angel-daughter and in her man August, though no one called him that but Barb. Now she heard her own voice calling him to her that first time, "August, August, my late summer man," who held her flesh as he would a sacred book, the wings of the pages flying open in his breath as she wrapped herself around him, there beneath the tree that was canopy and light, that was precise entrance into the blue of Heaven.

"You are perfect," he said then, beginning to quiet the voices of home that had shamed her for her mask of earthly toil and her imperfect garment of flesh. She was perfect, and young, and had just entered this world in its fullness of sorrow and loss, had just come to be on the line and put her hands to the making of things that would lodge themselves everywhere in the world to do the work of killing. She had for the first time held the shiny baubles of parts that, assembled into cluster bombs, would explode in the hands of a child attracted to the pretty sparkle of it under the sun, but she had not yet met the truth of her labor in the magazine articles that named her bosses, pointed to the factory that pulled her from bed each morning for her early shift, and described how such a thing worked.

She was a good young girl, nice looking as some, though not so much as many, but August came off the line every day and rushed to her. In the summer they met at the lush place by the hip of the lake's wandering body, and she took the evil out of him, the work of war that he ate from, and slept under the roof of. She took the evil out of him and he swore he would hold her this way for all his time on earth. She listened, and she believed him, and celebrated him when he left the line, some time after she did, that line of blood spreading over the map of the world like a conqueror's diagram of attack. River of blood, she heard it singing those nights after she'd quit and before he had, and then they both found work that left not so much in the pocket, but much more in the heart. They rejoiced then, truly rejoiced, and drank a fancy bottle of wine out back beneath the two old apple trees, before they went upstairs to his small apartment to make a very quiet kind of love that would wake no one, but remain with them for all of their days.

"Come in here, Barbara." She heard it like every summoning by the stern voice of her father when she had forgotten one of her chores, or had been careless, and the animals had suffered for it. But this was the doctor, stern also in his white coat and his knowledge of illness, which he seemed more to dispense than to treat. She tried to see him in the light of day, in the harsh, brilliant sunlight that fell from the window above his desk. She tried to read his face for judgment as she had learned to do at school, and wrapped her arms around herself to protect her belly and her breasts. She watched his mouth. She could not hear him. She fled to the edge of the fields, where the trees grew in a tangled grove. He tapped his pen on the blotter, as if to get the ink to flow, as if he would not tell her to her face but instead write down the name of her disease, draw the paper up between two fingers, and turn away from her. But then, there it was. He said it.

"Well, Barbara, it is cancer. Melanoma. The biopsy confirms it. Surgery, radiation, should take care of these," he tapped his own chin and pointed to the back of his neck, "but this might be a sign of something happening deeper in your body. We couldn't rule out the beginnings of a systemic cancer here. Barbara, do you understand what I mean? A spread of cancer cells into the lymphatic system. Not always easy to isolate and treat, to cut out or radiate. That's why we cut into some of the lymph nodes, and so far they're clean. Of course, we'll be looking again to make sure. Whatever it is, we'll do our best."

She looked at him without a word, returning from the grove of trees where she had fled. What joy to finally know her enemy.

Her husband brought her inside and made frantic calls for help with his search for their little girl. The winds had quieted down to sleep with each other against the curve of earth, closing the bright eye of Minnesota summer. The woman slept, needing to dream her daughter safe out of the storm. She woke to see her husband getting the flashlight from the closet.

"I'll call soon as I can," he said, and turned to go back out.

Carver had known it would be a good thing to follow Mopstick home the night he'd stopped for gas at closing time, and now, here it was, paying off, getting the girl home safe and sound, though he was loath to let her go. He hadn't done anything wrong, but he wasn't a fool. He knew what people might think. He lifted her down from the boss's truck just a ways up the street from her house, in the darkness and damp green air. He led her around deposits of broken glass, tree limbs and splintered boards. They stepped over somebody's laundry pulled into a tangled trail and caught on the branch of a great fallen elm. They stood still for a moment, while he searched the sky to find the North Star.

"There it is, Angie," he pointed, "the star of heaven."

She looked up, and clung to him in her dizziness under the sky and its moods.

He bent to her, and could feel her straining toward the house. She twisted her head away from him. "Listen," he said, and she looked at him, "remember, we have a secret now, a secret just for us."

And she remembered that he'd been nice to her, and had taken her out of the angry howl of the winds. "Okay," she said, "I remember."

"You want to keep your new dress, don't you?"

"Oh yes," she smiled at him, and he tousled her hair and kissed her on the crown of her head.

"So, I'm going to wait right here behind this car, like we're playing a game, while you run across the street to your house, and I'm going to watch and see that you get inside all safe, and then like a little cat I'll disappear without a sound."

"Okay," she said, and they each put a finger to their lips, watching each other, and let their breath escape in the shush that meant secret.

"Just remember, the winds took you, and the winds brought you home, and don't worry your folks about how scary the rest of it was, how close the tornado came to hurting you."

"The winds," she repeated, "the winds," and hugged him a bit before she twirled across the street under his gaze. A dancer, he thought, just like Rosie.

Oh Mama, Barb kept hearing in her ear like god's truth calling to her, until the sounds of the girl at the front door sent her husband, flashlight gripped like hope, crashing down the steps. He flung open the door to see her, whole and clean and her hair only a bit damp.

"Daddy," she cried, and it made Mopstick's blood flow again. He picked her up and ran with her to Barb. Some moments passed before they realized Angie was wearing a dress they had never seen before.

"She looks like death warmed over," Anita said under her breath, as she carried in the soup.

"It's the radiation." Mopstick pushed his thick black hair back behind his ears, and propped Barb up on three pillows. He pulled the worn comforter up to her chin with its small field of lesions, and fed her, one arm under her back, the other hand guiding the spoonful of soup the neighbor had brought.

Barb swallowed and gasped. "How are your boys?" she managed.

"Driving me nuts, eating me out of house and home. They're so damn cute, though. They think flushing my cigarettes down the toilet is going to save my life."

"They're good boys," Barb said, "good hearts."

"I'll give them that. Now, I'd better go have a smoke before my lungs clear up. I'll check you tomorrow."

"Thanks for everything," Barb said, and Anita shrugged and leaned over to kiss her damp forehead. Barb couldn't hear her say to Mopstick as she left, "Those doctors, they're doing her no good," but the taste of the soup's spices on the sides of her tongue stayed with her, and pushed some of the poison to leave her. When Mopstick returned to her side, she had already gone to sleep, calming as she saw Angie smile in the green air, still but for a boa of leaves dancing around her neck.

Barb would sleep that night as she would sleep for years, with her sickness and its journey through her body. As she dreamt, she saw her illness banished, her skin healed back over her bones, fine and smooth, a skin of pure pleasure inviting her man to run his hands over her. She wanted what she had once heard the men talk about at the table when she was close to being a woman—flesh as smooth as a field without a rock to stop the plow.

She was dreaming of how he would touch her, when the girl climbed up into her arms, and the three of them rocked each other in the stillness after the storm. When the girl leaped from the bed and spun around to make the wind move the fabric of the new dress this way and that, Barb remembered to ask.

"Angie, now tell us what happened. Where were you? Where did you get this dress?"

"Oh, the wind blew, it blew so hard the door to school banged shut and no one came to open it, and then, Mama, the wind picked me up and I flew, and the

15

glass was breaking and the trees were crying all around me, and I was crying too," and she did then, she sat on the bed and cried so hard it seemed that nothing could stop her, and reached for the woman and for the man who looked at each other and smoothed her hair and kissed her fingers, and wrapped the blankets around her.

They whispered, over and over, "Baby, you're safe now. It's all right now." But each time they brought it up, asked about the dress and begged her to tell them what had happened, her words would not come, and she would not stop weeping until she was exhausted by her promise to keep a simple secret.

So they left the dress on a hanger in her closet, put plastic over it to keep it clean, and let her wear it for special occasions, or whenever she asked to. They thought, yes, the tornado, the tornado has frightened her, the tornado has the power to do anything, to take anyone. They were so thankful it had given Angie back to them, that they asked her no more questions.

As Barb slept that night of the storm, she let her dreams sweep up the broken glass and lay down the roofs that had flown away, back over the gaping houses and their chilled and fearful inhabitants. The girl fell asleep next to her, while the man watched them and dozed in the lamplight with the drumming of his heart.

## *Chapter Five*

The tornado raced well to the south of Carver's poor room, zigzagged through the towns of Shakopee and Prior Lake, over to Assumption and down along the river to St. Peter. Then, well-fed and losing force, it bore down on its tapered limb toward Mankato, where each man and woman and their brood were waiting with their heads covered best as they could, until the winds collapsed into a hollow of earth between the blankets of wheat of one old farmer who lay panting on his bed. He was seeing the fields cleared once and for all of his small labors and making ready for a great Caterpillar combine that would roll over his land, join his farm to those of his neighbors and beyond, and make food for a starving world, or money for the greedy.

But the sky relented and the winds put down in place all the things of this world, although the arrangement was now exactly as it must have pleased the one whose harsh breath was the tornado. Barn roof made a tent in the neighbor's field to the south. Hay once bound in bales fell like manna from heaven for many hours, feeding animals in the next county. Laundry rinsed itself off in Circle Lake, dipped once more into the dark waters of Buffalo Lake, southeast of Mankato, and decorated the trees from Chaska to New Prague. The plaster-of-Paris Paul Bunyan from the miniature golf course was driven headfirst into the concrete pumped-in pool, his boots up to God. His blue ox Babe was gone without a trace, and his ax now lay on this same old farmer's welcome mat, which hadn't budged an inch from where its dark straw was pushed up against the front door, waterlogged. He was marking time anyway. He knew he was disappearing into the land and would sow it with bone before long.

Carver tacked up the extra blanket over the broken window, catching a glimpse of the moon in the angle of night sky before he unfolded the right-hand corner and thumped at a stray nail he was lucky to find. He finished sweeping up the glass and sat on the side of the bed to suck at a gash in his finger. With Angie gone back home, he saw how dreary the room was, and got jumpy in the dazed fluorescent light that fell everywhere he looked.

The mound of glass in the corner sparkled like eyes. He grimaced at the notion. "What else," he said, "can they take from me?" He leaped up and hit the power button on the TV, leaving a smudge of blood there, and settled back with the finger in his mouth as the screen crackled into a picture of a great black funnel ripping up the patchwork of fields in its path.

The camera swept from town to town, home after home smashed by the hammer of the storm. Cattle lay dead wherever the winds had tossed them. Poor dumb animals, he thought. Two picnickers dead, right at Lake Harriet, their basket of sandwiches swinging from the gracious limb of the tree above their car. "Just like that," he said, "in one night. Just like what happened to me. Everything torn from my hands," and he closed his eyes to see the land in Blue Earth whirl away from him, the animals, the machinery, the house and barn. The woman and the girl had already left before auction, gone to live in town, and he could not remember their faces as the sound of the rising winds outside the motel tugged at him.

I will stand there and not move, he remembered thinking on auction day, not even a twitch. Let them sell the farm out from under me. Dirty bastards. They'll go down the list of everything I have, and run their hands over it all. Curve of the tractor's wheel. Boards we placed edge to edge. Perfect fit. Best barn around. And that window I put in over the kitchen sink, with a half circle of shelf jutting out from the house for Katie's plants.

They'll feel the heft of the tools, one by one. The good balance of them. They'll check the edge of the blades. Draw some blood, I hope. Walk their dirty feet all over the oak floor. Run the engines, drive through the land, like it was something easy to buy and sell.

Sell the land. He shook his head. He had to, before it was taken.

So he did. He stood there at auction day and did not move a muscle in his face, but watched as each thing was carried off, as it all fell away from beneath him.

"This land is the flesh of my fathers." He'd heard an Indian say that once in a bar, before some drunken white guy punched him hard in the eye. He got back up, that Indian, and said he wasn't finished.

"I'll finish you," said the drunk, and pulled back to put some power in another blow.

"And it is the flesh of my mothers," the Indian said, and ducked just right as the other man came at him, the speed of his own fist pulling him down into a heap on the ground.

Carver didn't much like that Indian, but he had no use for a sloppy drunk, either, so he sat up on his stool and watched the show, ate a few peanuts and ducked around it when he needed to use the men's room. When he was finishing up at the sink, the drunk staggered in and stuck his face up close to Carver's.

"That Injun's got a lot of nerve," he slurred, "don't he?"

"Guess so," Carver said, and tried to move away from him in the small space.

"This land belongs to us, the farmers, the people who know what to do with it. What's an Indian do with the land? A little hunting, a little fishing. Not much else.

But this is a great country, isn't it? We know what to do with the land. We know what to do when we want a mess of fish." He laughed. "And we know what to do with a damned Indian."

You don't even know what to do with yourself on a Friday night, Carver thought, and got out of there with the man still talking into the bad air of the restroom.

The flesh of my fathers. The flesh of my mothers. Carver had never thought about the land like that, like flesh, like body, but he knew for certain that it held bones, generations of bones. And now these men were stomping all over his land like he'd wanted to do to that drunk. Lay him down on the dirty tiles and stomp him to silence. He was stupid and dirty and drunk, and maybe right as rain, but he was no man the way he fought and drank, the way he couldn't stand up straight and say his piece. The way he leaned in close, and smelled like an old nightmare.

The idea of someone like that carrying off his farm like a force of nature made Carver queasy and unsteady, but he fought it. He listened to the droning, show-off voice of the auctioneer, and the bids, one slap after another. Like selling a person. Selling a river. They were selling the stream that cut through the land. The pond, the birds, the rabbits, the earthworms. The moss on the trees. The rocks. The shady place near the fields, where he loved Katie.

His knees gave way. He had to get out of there and he tried to walk. He did it, ankles half turning, but he did it. He walked out of there, the auctioneer's voice continuing like the pain inside his head which burst into a kaleidoscope of colors on the right side of his vision so that he couldn't see. The world was a shadow in flimsy color beneath the diamond-edged shapes that whirled over the land and the buyers hungry for its flesh. He groped his way around the wall of the barn and heard the sound of his feet striking the path on his way to the house. The colors kept tumbling around and he remembered the carousel that spun through Blue Earth County each summer. His stomach was heaving up and down with the horse he rode that forever stretched her hooves in desire for flight over the plains, though she went only in circles in the great red tent that sat on the prairie, below the dreaming of the stars.

He found the step, and pushed open the door. He knew he only had a moment, and stumbled fast by two men, two strangers sitting at his kitchen table drinking beers from dark bottles. They stared at him and said nothing, and he held his hand over his mouth and pushed his way into the bathroom by the back stairs. He slammed the door and turned the faucet hard, for a moment refreshed by the spurt of clear water from the well he had dug with his own hands, and then he grabbed the hard circle of the toilet and let go, wanting everything sick in him to leave his body. There, in the dark cramped space, his system was turning inside out, and he let wave after wave cleanse him, take the good food turned bad and leave him empty and hot on the black and white tiles.

19

"Good Lord," he said out loud, and realized that he could see again, the flashing shapes before him settling into the walls. He washed his face and rinsed his mouth, and walked over to the barn. He pushed past the men standing around by the open door, a few patting him on the back however they could to say they were sorry, and found a place to stand.

"Sold," the auctioneer sang out as Carver looked up, "to the man in the fine suede jacket." Carver turned to where the red-faced man directed, and saw the jacket, but did not see the man. The carousel began to whirl again, and the stars over the faraway red tent were shining in Carver's eyes. The jacket walked up to the podium, took a sheaf of papers and shook the auctioneer's hand. Carver breathed deep the fragrance of hay and approaching night, and saw the man's face and understood. He was just a man, a man in a suede jacket, who owned his farm now.

Luck turned around him like the carousel. The stream of diamond mirrors embedded in the cupola above the riders reflected a new sight with every degree of its turning. The next man, the next woman, a child shouting with exhilaration, all holding on to the poles that jabbed into the stars as the chase sped up and took Carver along. As one shining eye shut above him, in a blink the next would find him, then blink again and open onto the man with the suede jacket, the banker who would not bury the bones of his family on this land, but would harvest all that he could, and raise his roof beams high as a cathedral's little heaven over the green crop of money.

What could Carver do? What could the house do but bow to such a man? What could the birds do? What could the stream do, but continue to run by the house, its waters singing, until there was no more house, no more song.

"Sold," Carver heard the word sing out all through that last night. "Sold."

And just when he would refuse it, just when he would step forward in the dream and claim the land again for his own, the window frame spit out the nail from its upper righthand corner and the blanket fell away from the onslaught of moonlight that woke him, the taste of blood still in his mouth.

## *Chapter Six*

This is power, Carver thought the next morning, as he walked through the damage strewn in a circle around the corner of Lake and Chicago, the power of God to rip up the earth with His Holy Breath, the power to deliver my angel into my arms. He went over it in his mind for weeks, over gas fumes and dull nights, in the burger joint and at the bar: that sudden moment of power, its grand acts of theft, its surprise gifts. He made up his mind to go back to church, feeling his life touched by something holy, by the return of his child in the body of another.

But even with his head bowed down, he could not hold the thread of the minister's voice, and instead fell to thinking, Angie, angel-girl, how you flew into my arms, though I had to give you back after the storm. He coughed at the "Amens," mumbled through the hymns, and almost called her name out loud. He raised his eyes to the brilliant stained glass window of the Resurrection and saw her there above him, the bold leaden lines sealing her warmth away. He wanted to hold her again, just like his own little girl.

He thanked his God for that storm, but heard not a word of the sermon as he went further back to the darkness of the tornado, and to that great crossing back into blessedness that came with saving Angie.

He breathed in her name like the song that rose sober and steady around him. He breathed her in, her fair skin and golden crown, like he breathed in the night when it was good. He tightened his hands in prayer. "She's my girl now," he mouthed, "my perfect fruit, no death in her. We are one flesh, flesh of God."

I got the picture, he thought. I can look at someone and see whether they're blessed or cursed. Whether God's with them or has abandoned them. I can see the Hand of God at work in this. Angie's the balm for my troubles, the reward for my labors. Like a sweet song of forgiveness, her voice. Paradise in a new dress.

His time in church became his time to be alone with Angie, to let her brilliant light wash over him. To be family again. But when he thought of his own daughter, he could not lift his head.

## *Chapter Seven*

### *Autumn 1986*

For all the next year, Carver sat in same pew each week, and prayed to know his place in Angie's life.

He came to know that his job was to comfort her from the harshness of life, and show her, her own beauty, instead of letting her stay filled up with the ugliness of her folks. That couldn't be her lot, in a sad house like that. No, sir. Her place was with beauty, and he could show her that. He had to. She was nothing less to him than the pure breath of God, and princess of his heart. Worth more than all the rest. Except for his own stolen daughter. Except for his Rose.

A woman in a full skirt moved down the aisle and brushed Carver's shoulder. He glanced at her, then looked away. Angie was like his own daughter now, and there was nothing wrong with that, nothing meant to go against the order of things.

Anyway, family's more than blood, he thought. And I love her like a father, holy and complete. I love her child's mind of obedience, her body of perfect daughter. I love the future that waits inside her, that needs tending. Oh, Angie! A blessing to the farmer without land, without home, without woman and child.

He looked down into his palms, stretched his fingers and studied the scar left from that night. Nothing's been the same since, he thought. How could it be? Like with Mary.

After months of movies and car rides and talk, small talk, nothing special, he decided to try. He loved how her dark hair fell over one eye. How her eyes were more golden than brown. He loved kissing her, holding her. But when he took her to his room and undressed her, lay her down across his bed, he saw that she was not perfect. Not near it. She was scarred, as if someone had mined her, dug there. The marks on her legs were not golden, but purple, pools of darkness. She could not swim free. There was no rising with him. No graceful wings, but heavy footsteps leading away from the night, clumsy and timid, before the sun.

He came to see she was nobody's daughter. A bare land that belonged to no one. She had no song, though she screamed when he went into her. But then, and each time, he touched her warmth. And each time, he covered her up when he was done. She was not one to look at, scarred like she was. But then he knew he couldn't keep on with it, not even for that release a man must have.

He didn't look at her face when he put her out. It was cruel, he knew, but it's not against the law to want what's perfect. To want beauty. It was her own fault, anyhow. If she'd stayed on the farm, eaten from the earth, bathed in its waters and run through its grasses, she would have stayed a beauty. He could tell it. A real heartland beauty.

He thanked his God right then, that he didn't get caught up in her hurt eyes but did what he had to do. Pushed her away. Then the congregation rose to its feet and he did a moment later. He shuffled out with the others, giving a smile here and there, a nod of his head.

He wanted to go to the bar. He wanted to find a place to lay down his burdens before the workweek took over. He wanted a woman who would know what he needed, but he went straight home, read the Sunday paper and the Bible, and drank the spring water he bought in big bottles, trying to taste the sweetness that had flowed through his own well back on the farm.

He ate nothing, left the television playing, and slept on and off with the ache in his body.

He lay there on the hard bed in his gray room, curled into the stillness in his good Sunday clothes. He let himself slip away, back to the land. He dreamt of Katie, he dreamt of the farm, he dreamt of his people taking the land, and saw the Indians signing it away, generations before he was a boy there. His body stiffened in his sleep with the power of owning the land, sowing seed, making harvest.

But then he went back into the old nightmare. The farm would be taken from him and there was no hope to stop it. And in the nightmare fluttered the edge of Rosie's dress, her church dress, the good one. It was the edge of that cloth in sunlight, burnt to black, that was the last thing he saw as she followed her mother, her own dear hand lifted to the woman and clutched in that one's angry heart of a hand as she was pulled out the door.

"Why? What is it? I'm talking to you!" over and over Carver had yelled out, following them through the house.

Then Kate screamed, she turned around and screamed out with her eyes closed, like it was to the whole plains, her voice spreading there like water through the rows of grain, coming toward his feet with that straight rush, "No more of this!"

Carver did not wake then, but his hands shook with remembering how Katie's voice cut, and he saw, as if it were happening, the girl turn back to him once more, her tiny face like the moon, distant, glowing pale. Then the flash of the cloth, and, an instant later, the wind of her turning away passed over him.

In the stillness of that last night he spent on the farm, he was an empty man. He had lain down and tried to sleep, so he would be ready for the auction. It was then, there was laughter at the edge of the fields, distinct it was, laughter that was not the crows, not the play of rabbits rustling through the rows to gather the nips of crops due them, but human laughter, and it was coming from the border of willow and sumac.

He grabbed the heavy rope from its nail and ran out to thrash the trees with it, spinning with his rage. The laughter came on quicker and louder and he fell onto his knees beneath one tree, the grandest, maybe the grandest one in all the county, and let it reveal its secrets. He saw it all then, the darkness and the fruit that each tree holds and shakes above men in temptation and mystery. He saw it all clearly then, the history of this very land where he had fallen, and knew he was blessed that God Himself would speak to him in the message of the tree.

He heard whispers then, but could not make out the talk, and knew somehow that it was an Indian way of speaking. The sounds moved all around him, as in a game where a message is passed from person to person and changes with each whisperer to arrive at the beginning of the circle. He lay there with the wind blowing hard through the leaves, and tried to understand the words. Then the wind began pelting things at him, and he covered his face with his arm as the darkness swam up, voices chorusing like the voice of Judgment Day that made a man search his own guilty heart. The voices went low, like the sound that comes up from a man's feet, and rose and gathered power and music, a new kind of music for Carver but music all the same. There were many voices and then one voice, and it repeated like a prayer, the prayer of the tree, the prayer of the land and sky, the prayer that sang in his heart when he looked upon the land.

It was funny, he didn't get one word, but he would always remember the way it rumbled in his stomach, like news of war, the way it felt like his very own prayer.

And so he looked up, with thanks to God that he had this place one more night, the prayer breaking open in his belly, but everything was dark above him, dark and blind, heavy and eternal, and then came a horrible sound, louder than shotgun at his shoulder, louder than thunder, than tornado barreling toward him, the hardest noise he'd ever heard, like the crack of the Whip of God.

Something broke. The darkness broke into light but it was an ugly light, a murky light, a hooded light, except for the clear shafts illuminating the bottom of men's feet dancing in the air above him, swaying from the tree in the breath of the wind.

The song had ended with that great noise, but then a band of crows flew overhead and perched themselves on the limbs of the tree, and their calls were sweeter than a person would expect. Others joined them, meadowlarks, thrush, mockingbirds trailing whatever songbirds they still had out there, and he didn't understand it all, but he knew then that he was right. The land was to be fought for, because the land was precious. The land was to be taken back by force, and no price was too great. He saw that in the lifeless feet of Indian men risen above the earth, as he lay in his motel room and dreamt of what would happen: the return of the land to him, of his rights;

the girl skipping back in through the door; and the woman, contrite now, cradling his head in her lap, and kissing his forehead.

"Oh dear God," Carver called out in his sleep, "she must know that's what she is meant to do," and the laughter from the trees stopped as she caressed him, as the rope in his hand fell from it, and the green twilight held them, the land held them, and whatever was swaying above them went back to live in the land. Then they rose and walked to the house, a good house, with a good door that swung shut as Carver let it go, while back on the motel bed without her, he gazed up to see the stars come in through the open window, Orion's Belt there above him, and the blazing North Star leading him to the edge of his dreams.

## *Chapter Eight*

It was a Sunday morning, too early even for church, there on the south side of Minneapolis. The wind entered this house through a small crack in the doorframe, and rose up the stairs on its soft breath. The wind was the bearer of dreams in this house of sleep, but other voices entered too. Some pushed in with the newspapers slipped through the slot each day, or leaked out of the blue drone of the TV. Others burst forth with judgment from the creased foreheads of some of the neighbors.

As with each house, each body of dwelling, this one was not only surrounded by voices from the world of the living, but rocked above the voices that lay within the earth, and came up through whatever grew there, whether girl or flower, fruit or memory, illness or love. And, as with many houses, this one held its groaning in its floorboards, in its doors and beams, in its windows opening, in its faucets weeping with desire, in the grip of its roof hanging on through storms.

This was a house of laborers, a house that got plenty of notice up and down the street, though it asked for none.

And here was the family inside it, living a puzzle of ugliness, and bringing forth beauty.

This was Barb: skin the color of dried wood, or of moon bleached in fall lake water. Her hair: colorless tufts some bird did not snatch from her head and make off with for a plump nest, or a ragged one. Hardly a patch of skin free from the moles and dark raised growths big enough together to feed an army of insects, if she were to have the misfortune to be abandoned in the desert, or tied to one of those logs rent by lightning that seem dead but hide the very beginnings of a fully populated world and its six days of coming into being. It would be on that seventh day the creatures rested, as did the God that created them, and fed on her, as did the God on nectars, his rib splitting at the sight of their feasting, feasting on the moles and tumors of this unfortunate woman too ugly to love, some might say, even for God.

Only one angel, a daughter, could.

And only one man could, a mopstick himself, barely existing as Barb lay dying year after year without having the decency to slim down as she did it.

This was Mopstick: bones coming out of his yellow skin, and not much more than bone himself. Hank of coal black hair; teeth like a bad fence; thumbs like hammerheads; skin pitted like mined land. His looks earned by long years of labor: farmwork—wheat, corn and soybeans; factory assembly lines—parts for weapons, though he was everywhere peaceful in his soul; and putting in his time variously—dishwasher, ditchdigger, schoolbuilder, mechanic. Labor wearing him down to the angles of bone. Or was this an ugliness decreed from birth? This might take inquiry, but when his teeth outgrew their mouth, his fate was sealed. Saved by his maleness from too much commentary. And also by the child, who clung to him and saw him as the first man, and was without complaint.

This was the daughter, Angie: growing infant to woman as the neighborhood watched, and keeping, as the prize of beauty her folks no doubt paid for with their ugliness, her perfect skin of peach, and that fragrance as well. Hair so golden, it called up that substance that made men run off to dig their madness out of the earth, trying to satisfy their greed for light. Each bone and slope of cheek straight from God. Her eyes the blue that banishes storm. Her legs so perfect, it made anyone with sight dream on where they led to. (God only knew, and her ugly folks.) She was, beyond her physical beauty, decreed as well to possess sweetness of disposition and deep wells of devotion. None could lure her from the side of her family. A child almost saintly, evidence of which is that when she was but five, it could only have been God who plucked her from the vicious side of nature, saved her from a twister, and left her floating about in a perfect new dress.

It must have been storm and God ripped the old cheap one off her, all the family could afford, and made more perfect what was already whole and would never have asked for more. It was said she had no memory of where the dress had come from, the twister shook her up so. Reasonable enough. So the story went that she was raised aloft as the storm whirled off the old bargain dress and gave her the horse of the wind to ride. Then the steed turned gentle in the blessed eye of tornado, and somehow lowered her toward earth and into the cloth pinned by God's Hand to a nearby clothesline.

She was a wondrous child, it was clear, and unquestionably good.

This was the way it was in South Minneapolis—some of the neighbors, just getting by after losing their farms, had come to know that if the world could take what had their names on it for generations, there wasn't a thing could be fair in it. A very few, though, began to remember the Indian names for things. Like *Mde wakan*—Spirit Lake, broken now into a thousand lakes, Mille Lacs. Maybe after a century and more of working the land that wasn't ever really theirs, and calling it theirs, writing it up and measuring it theirs, some kind of justice had prevailed, or had at least continued its trajectory, its mysterious workings seen before in drought and infestation. But now, much of the land was in the hands of the slimiest banking men a farmer could imagine, not returned into the hands of the ones who, it was said, moved through the chant of wind and tree before the River was crossed, the Treaty of Traverse des Sioux was signed, and the old century was broken in two.

There were a few neighbors down the street who had a terrible view of the fate of this one poor woman Barb. She must have deserved it, for crimes of all the generations before, they came to believe, as they must have deserved the visit from the sheriff and the shame of the auction and the farewell to the land they had always had their hands in, and loved life out of. This woman must have deserved to be this ugly, and her sickness must have come right from the old guilt living in her heart. Must have.

She'd come from a good farm family, but had left. Left her home. A crazy woman, you'd think, bringing her curse of a face out into the Cities when she could have hid it there on the land, helping out with the planting and household chores, in the bosom of family accustomed to her looks. And, sure, God blessed her with Mopstick and Angie, God made a miracle, but it was up to God to take back what He had given, and so the curse showed up and her ugliness grew like a crop of weeds, virulent and wild. This plague of tumors marked her as one who'd left the land before it was taken, and broadcast to the bankers that the folks around there couldn't stay the troubles and stand firm on their farms. She was a curse to all her neighbors, a few even said, except maybe the Indians. And God was nothing if not symmetrical, bringing her Mopstick with his coal black hair and Dakota grandmother.

True, other neighbors didn't judge and didn't care, and came to Barb with fresh breads and stories and a couple of hours of normal porch sitting, as neighbors do. And they kept right on as Barb went through her bouts of illness. But even they wondered how she still gave out light from the warm voice laughing behind those crooked teeth. How, they asked themselves, did that mopstick of a man bathe her and comfort her, when, though he was no looker, he was a working man and entitled not to be a magazine picture? They noticed the muscles in his otherwise scrawny arms, and the blackness of his hair, though too black for some, and his joking through a chewed-up set of teeth in the dim light of the bar at the entrance to the highway, and figured all that would have gotten him some willing and loving arms to fold him into the hope of beauty, and remind him that pleasure in the darkness is pleasure for all. How, ugly as she was, did Barb have it that he stood by her?

How, in the name of all that is beautiful? How, in the name of home?

# Book Two

## Birds in Flight
### Fall 1990 - Easter 1991

"The wind is a living force. ... It enters us all at birth and stays with us all through life. It connects us to every other creature."

— *Power*
Linda Hogan, p. 28

## *Chapter One*
### *Fall 1990*

The years passed, and Mopstick stuck by that woman. Didn't leave her side except to work hard and bring home the bread to feed her and the angel daughter who was the mystery in this puzzle of ugly, as Carver liked to call it. And Carver, he did what he had to do. Half lived in that gas station, and salted away a few extra dollars every paycheck to put toward buying back his land.

One day his boss pointed out with a jerk of his chin a good-looking redhead at the magazine rack, waiting for her husband to settle up for the gas. After they left, Hanson said to Carver, "I don't know what it is she's got, but she sure has got it."

"It's not beauty that's the mystery," Carver instructed, and leaned over the counter. "Look at God's earth. Look at the beauty of most every child. And beauty in a woman partakes of what is everywhere a comfort to the eye"—he swept his hand around and looked through the front window—"and maybe echoes the seasons." He counted off on his fingers—"beauty that's hot, beauty that's cold, beauty coming into being"—he saw his angel tucked into his mind's eye—"and beauty turning into memory, like a long gone spring."

"You sure are getting particular on the subject of women," his boss said, and popped open a can of Pepsi with a flick of his thumb.

"Well, I am a man who knows these things, having made beauty and ugliness my evening study at the farm, along with the Bible." He shook his head. "With all that I lost packed into my heart, I come to live now in the gas fumes down at this fine station. Dark stains on my work pants, dirt on my hands not from planting and harvesting, but from the fruit of creatures long dead, making of their bodies what men go to war over."

"Oil, you mean."

"Oil," said Carver. "From food to fossil fuels, my work history reads. And my hands show it." He stretched them out and looked down. "Some may call them ugly, but in the night, I've got to say, in the night, beauty opens to them like the earth used to. Now, I can't own this beauty like I used to own the earth. Or so they say," he added. "But if I make it open, make it give forth with the work of my body, it's mine. You know what I mean? This beauty is mine."

The older man looked at him hard. "I'm kind of jealous," he said. "Not that I'm unhappy. I'm not. My wife is beautiful in her own way."

Carver smiled.

"And we're good together. But I'll tell you one thing, I sure wouldn't let you near my daughter," and he wagged his finger at Carver.

"It's only this—I know what to do with a woman, like I know what to do with the land. And not everyone's as lucky as you, Hanson, to have a good fit with a woman. And if you don't, maybe you got to look around. Try on a few more. Some men get stuck and refuse to move on and find what's theirs by rights."

"I don't know about rights."

"Oh, no, it's a right. The right of a man to have the woman that best serves his needs. Now, I got a buddy, not to gossip, but you know him. Mopstick. Frankly, I don't know what the heck is wrong with him. Maybe he's too long gone from the land and his rightful place on it. But he lives like a slave. Serving that woman—you've seen her, sick on and off for years. Staying away from any other. A nod to the next-door neighbor, that's all, and that one is, I tell you, a fine woman. I admit, I think about her myself sometimes. A redhead too, the beautiful Anita, but she's hardheaded. Talks too much. Been without a man for a while, since that teacher with the glasses, quiet spoken, left out of there, and I can see why. That smart mouth on her."

"I think I know who you mean," Hanson said, and they both chuckled and nodded.

"So, anyway, this boy runs to work, runs back home, cooks and cleans and takes care of the daughter Angie, and sits by Barb's bed, hoping for a word. That woman's too selfish to even try, I bet. She ain't dead, after all. But I tell you, he ain't either, and God knows it's not right for a man to be without a woman in the private ways, so I intend to bring him to it. He'll know it's his right, when someone's there before him," Carver winked, "and he stirs."

Hanson was silent until a car pulled up, then waved to Carver to relax. "I'll get it," he said, "you sit."

"She looks like a witch," said one child in a blue sweater with a pink plastic knapsack a person could see through.

Angie turned the corner and stepped right into the bowl of their laughter, laughter so loud it hurt her ears, and tinctured the dust in the hall with something raw and cruel as she passed by.

"Angie's old lady's so ugly, the moon won't rise when she's looking out the window!" said one bright-eyed boy into a chorus of guffaws, kids holding their stomachs to ease out the belly laughs.

She heard it all. They spoke as if to make sure each word hit a particular spot—her flushed cheeks, her heart's ache, her burning eyes.

"You better shut up," it was Angie threatening.

"Gonna make us, little girl?"

31

"Your mother's got so many bumps on her face, the air can't figure out which one's her nose!"

"She's so ugly, the army classified her a secret weapon!"

Angie struck out at one boy after another, flailing, kicking the pink knee sox of the girl with the pink knapsack, and they howled, the group of kids, some from her very own block, and pushed her from one to the other. "You're It," they hollered, "and the Daughter of It! Your mother's Queen of Darkness! Mama of the Mask!"

"Our Lady of Ugly," added another boy in a calm voice, and pushed her hard to the ground.

The other girl bent over to pull up her knee sox and said, looking down at Angie, "And your daddy's an Indian."

One of the boys looking on said, "Watch your mouth. It's enough now." And then he walked away.

"I hate you all," Angie cried, "I hate you," and she got up, collected her books and ran down the corridor, laughter again bursting out behind her, hard and brittle, like firecrackers on the wrong night.

A couple of teachers came out of the staffroom, noticed the group of children talking and giggling among themselves, and smiled at them.

That night Angie dreamt of her mother with many noses, and sat up and stared at the moonless night. She got out of bed and walked the cold hallway in her bare feet, slid through the shadow of the doorway and stood by the bed to watch her parents sleeping. Maybe it was starlight that came into the room then, but her mother's brow was lit, and her hair flew about like breath in the night air.

"Mama," Angie whispered.

Barb stirred and saw the girl there, pale and shivering, and folded her into her arms under the covers. Mopstick coughed a few times from deep within his thin frame and settled down into his dream again, the empty line passing his still hands, nothing to do but rest and watch the conveyor belt carry the blue air of peace off to the silenced war at the end of the line. Angie warmed in her mother's arms, and all were beautiful there, all felt good as they breathed together into the morning.

## *Chapter Two*

### *December 1990*

Carver was half dozing at the cash register, as afternoon was falling to night. No one had been in for about an hour, and the radio was insistent with news of the next snowstorm. The heater he shared with the owner's dog was buzzing on and off like a slow heartbeat that lit up the darkness under the counter.

He was in the woods, the old man behind him. This is how I can run away, and he pushed through the brush with his hands, darted between the trees like a fox. He was clever to keep running, to escape another beating, to live long enough to become a man. Because this time, he thought, the old man'll kill me, grab the breath right out of me with the words, "I have given you life and I can take it away, you ingrate. You complainer. You girl."

He saw his own body fallen to the leaves and beginning to decompose into the richness of the soil run through by roots of trees and wild, sweet grasses. And there on the ground his mouth was open and blood ribboned its way out from the darkness of his silence, as the man raised his hand to him again, with a bottle or was it a tool from out of the barn? And the ribbon of blood was the road of insects, who buzzed and crawled into his skull as country travelers, hungry for what was there, streamed into the city to make another life away from the green lands fenced off and stolen. He woke and put his hands up to the sockets of his eyes to feel the full round orbs under their worn lids.

He stumbled into the restroom and spat into the sink to cut the red road that was how life left when his father blamed him, when he wrapped his stone arms around Carver and squeezed him in a vise of rage as if he would slaughter him, while his mother was asleep, his brother away in the war, and only the spindly legs of the kitchen table stood to witness.

"Your brother's not coming back, I can tell it. I want to know what God had in mind to take Elias and leave me with you."

In his mind, Carver struck the old man then, pounded away at him like a jackhammer, until his soft hand somehow broke the unbreakable, the stone skull of the man. Out spilled his thoughts, out spilled his curses, out spilled his ways, and all of it could be swept up from the floor and tossed into the compost pile for his mother's garden. But then he said, "No," and laughed out loud over the sink, opened his eyes to his worn face and said again, into the mirror, "no." Nothing would flower from what spilled out. Better to burn it.

That was the evening he first saw William in the passenger seat of the old orange truck, when he leaned over the side door to clean the window, though he didn't want to, but the woman said, "Please, could you wash that side so my nephew can look out? He loves to see the buildings passing, and the streetlights come on."

"Sure, why not," he told her, though he didn't want to. Didn't matter whether the boy could see out or not. The city wasn't a show. Boy should just sit in the truck and keep his mouth shut. He pushed the cloth over the stains of the weather, the miracle cells of frost which he had to destroy, stars into glass, and revealed in the slash of his work the very dark, very large eyes of a boy staring out at him. The woman had gone to the rest room, so he bent over and stuck his face almost against the clean window, right in the boy's sight, figuring the kid would jump out of his skin, but he didn't move a muscle. He just stared back at Carver, then blew on the beaded headdress hanging from the rear view mirror so it swung up and back.

"Why you little—" Carver muttered and his right arm tensed in the cold air, and then heat flowed into his fist, still holding the wet cloth, but again the boy did not move. Just kept looking at him, and nothing came into the man's mind that could close those eyes, that could move that gaze away from his face.

"Mister," he heard the woman call him, and he sneered into the window at the child and raised himself up from the truck.

"What do you need?" he asked her, as he always would, though he could see himself chop off each long braid that snaked down over her shoulders and her large breasts, her build visible even through the heavy jacket.

She walked up to him. "I brought you a cup of coffee from inside," she said. "It's pretty cold out here." She shoved the steaming cup into his ungloved hand and it did warm him, and then she went rummaging through some packages in the back of the truck. She lifted up both arms and looked like a kid for a moment, he thought, happy at discovering something.

"I was worried I might have left these back at the cabin," she said, walking toward him with a plate covered over with tin foil. "Have some cookies," she urged, and lifted the foil to reveal them. "Nuts and chocolate," she pointed, "and better than store-bought."

"Just one," he mumbled, "thanks," and stood holding the steaming coffee and the cookie, still warm though he knew it was impossible, as they drove off.

"Damn woman," he said after they had disappeared down the street, and threw the cookie into the trash, but drank, with both hands around the cup, the dark liquid. The way I like it, at least, he thought. Black, one sugar. He stamped on the hard ground for warmth, and heard the ring of his boots repeating until the soles of his feet burned with the impact. He wondered about her, too stupid to know who she was dealing with, and drank the coffee down to the half visible brand name raised in the bottom of the cup. "Chippewa," he made out, and laughed then, crushed the cup, and went inside to wait for customers.

# *Chapter Three*

Carver was years gone from her life now, but with each disappointment, Mary thought about him.

So many days he'd walked with her along the river, and she could smell life and death in the falling leaves. He could name each kind, and she would remember, the number of points, the shape, and the colors the leaves would turn. She would remember the sound as he let a maple leaf fall, which should have made no sound, but it did. A flame falling through the crisp air.

She remembered how his steps bounced on the pavement, on the good days. And how, when he was moving away, everything she asked, he found a way to answer, No.

Now she took her walks alone, even into the hard cold. She knew the trees by their leaves, but in winter, she was lost in the naming of the forest. She had no names for their bare arms, their scored trunks, their hidden roots. She moved by them, her hands in her pockets. But when she stopped, she stripped off her gloves and ran her palms and fingers over the bark. Almost as unyielding, she thought, as his skin had become.

She sat on her knees on the couch cushion and leaned over the high back of it, cloth and spray in hand. She braced herself. She sprayed the window with ammonia and circled the cloth, slick and fast, into the new shine of the glass. She was no fanatic, she thought, glancing down at the dust on the side table, at the dingy carpet, but she had to have clean windows. It was there, at the glass, she would see what families did on their walks together, or who might pass by. She might even see what she had never seen before.

It was through the invisible hard film over the world she would go, to where her legs would grow strong and kick at the world like a pony. She would circle the glass like a lake she ran along, or like the rink where the boys used to take her, and where she flew on her back, nothing grabbing her, nothing stopping her, but where she pinwheeled across the whole rink, and not a skater could see her, harm her, slice her, spin her like a girl in a short skirt. She was more. She was a star. Whether she flew on her back or her long sturdy legs, she would reach the other side if she polished the window, but did not break it and fall through into the freezing water.

She kept the cloth and the blue spray under the couch near the windowsill. And when it was late, and she wanted to sleep but couldn't, she let the streetlights shine in her eyes and pull her to clean there. When the window was not frozen shut, she would open it and lean out, pretend that an invisible arm kept her from rolling out into the cold air above the street, and hang on to her protector with one hand, while with the other she polished up the outside of the glass.

But it wasn't often she cleaned the mirror in the bathroom. Toothpaste stuck in streaks, and in dots of spray that caught the light from the ceiling. No one else ever looked there now. But the last time Carver came over, she pulled out the blue spray from under the couch and circled her arm down to the clear image of a woman biting her lip in front of the dim bathroom wall.

Carver once asked her why she cleaned that picture window so often.
"I need the view," she said, "because I can't hear myself."
"Think?" he asked. "You can't hear yourself think?"
"I can't hear with my left ear, at any rate."
Those were the good days. He came close and whispered in her right ear. She heard him just fine.

There was no one to blame, but the boys did it. She was eleven, that July.
They gathered around the leader, and it was Billy, like it always was. Everybody crouched low, clutching the parachutes and fountains, the aerial repeaters, and waiting for the flame to propel the biggest beauty up into the air, and its streamers to lick the tops of their heads with light, if they were lucky. Not heat, not noise, but the purest sweetest light that would make them dreamers all that summer.

She wanted to be a dreamer too. She was the only girl they let in, and she knew that once the glow of it touched them all together, she would be in with them, all the time. In the club. And they wouldn't throw her down, except the way they threw each other down and rolled over the grass playfighting.

So she crouched, watching with the rest of them, as Billy lit the tail of the repeater and they all looked up toward where it would rocket itself beyond the trees and start the show. But it stuck there at the height of a child, and like a clot burst in the close air, leaving her on the ground curved onto her right side, all of them looking down at her while blood snaked out of her left ear, and the things they were saying floated above her like the chatter of monkeys on the TV screen with the sound turned off.

She knew they were saying she was out of the club. She knew she'd have to be a girl. She saw Billy saying, Can you hear me, and nodded her head, but everyone must have known she was a liar, as they carried her off home, no star now. Just like a dead thing, limp between them.

## *Chapter Four*

### *January 1991*

Carver had pulled another sixty hour week, but he'd been used to long hours. After the night of the tornado, for a while time seemed to pass like a knife cutting through the hours. He remembered what it meant to have family, and he knew that what was split apart could be made whole again, the way a river could be crossed. But then his feet started hurting. The concrete was hard, without yield. He smelled of oil, but at least he had money in his pocket and that made the land feel closer. He could hear its song. He could smell his little girl's hair.

Most nights after his boss had left, he stayed on into the frozen silence cut by laughter and sudden screams from the folks heading in and out of the bar down the street. Sometimes Carver was stiff and distant with his boss, but something in his straight back made him seem trustworthy, and trustworthy he was. He treated each customer with good manners, as he had vowed he would, though sometimes he swore in his head that it was better than they deserved. Maybe the car would smell of beer, or the phony perfume of a woman in the passenger seat. Maybe there were kids in back, with dirty faces and disrespectful looks out the window at him, their eyes wide as he leaned over the car and in hard straight lines worked the dirt of their travels into vanishing before their eyes. But each time he filled a tank he made sure not a drop of gasoline was wasted. Each time a customer asked for the washroom key he had it ready. Each time there was a problem under the hood he located it, and after blowing away the dust and wiping down the engine, he slammed the hood down with just the right force, and told the driver what he'd done, and what to expect.

Every night he ran a clean cloth over the counters and polished the register, rearranged the magazines and candy, and swept and mopped the floors before he went to his rented room and gazed out past the school and the market, into the distance and the hard frozen road.

His boss knew he had a lucky pick with this guy. Worth more than he paid out for once.

One Friday, as the afternoon began to lift the cold, Hansen told Carver to do himself a favor, go home early. He wasted time and lingered, hoping Mopstick would come in and grab a treat for Angie before he went to pick her up at the afterschool. Carver was about to give up, but then they almost knocked heads at the door.

"Can we have that drink tonight?" Carver prodded.

"No, Carver, I don't think so. Barb'll be all alone. She's been working her old job again part-time, and she's pretty tired when she gets home."

"Well, this is a good night for it then. Your Angie's being taken care of, right? So what're you going to do? Sit and watch your old lady dreaming?"

"No, I better not."

"You better. You look half dead. No color in you, no sparkle in your eye. Come on, mister, a few drinks and a few laughs. I'll get you home before eleven."

"Well, maybe. Ok. Sure. My girl's staying at the neighbor's, and if I can get Barb comfortable, she'll sleep through." Mopstick had been thinking about the offer all week. Just for once, a few hours out, like a man does. A few drinks, some talk, some noise and smoke, a real Friday night.

"Should I come get you?" Carver asked.

"No, I'd best drive my own, case I got to go and you want to stay. How's eight-thirty?"

"At the Howard Johnson's. They've got a good band there tonight."

And so Mopstick went home and put on a clean shirt. He slicked down the darkness of his hair with the hair oil the child had given him for his birthday. He changed out of his work shoes, and, if not fancy, looked sociable and clean.

Barb's heart leaped to see him. The new diagnosis was a bad blow, after she had been clean from the cancer for almost two years. No telling how it would go. Non-Hodgkin's Lymphoma. They were in for the long haul; treatments, maybe surgery. This thing could go anywhere in her body, she knew that. Her liver, her spleen, the marrow of her bones. She prayed not.

She needed August now, but she knew that a man could break, that one man couldn't do everything for three people. Even the eyes of his angel could be a burden. Even Barb's own call to love each other, and he did love her, all her flesh, as if it filled out his own skeleton, would not draw him if he were broken, and so when she saw him dressed for going out, she was relieved. She planned on letting the light of the television bring her into dreams after Anita stopped by to look in on her. It would be a rest for her, too, not to have to be hopeful or brave, not to have to ignore what was sitting behind his eyes and the work it took to push it back there. She'd pray for some good music for him, a bit of warming whiskey, and a safe ride home.

She would tell him tomorrow. He should have this night.

Carver grabbed his arm. "Hey, old man, I got a couple of peaches I want you to meet." Mopstick said, "I don't think that's such a good idea," but Carver was already rushing toward the other side of the bar. Mopstick was figuring on a few drinks and a man-to-man, or at least some talk about fishing and cars, and maybe some reminiscing about women, but no actual women. Not somebody's daughters. He surely didn't know what to say to a woman, except for the neighbors, but not someone at a bar smelling like Friday night. The dark-haired one stood next to him, her eyelids all glittery and teeth flashing, alcohol like sweet fire on her breath. And those shoes, high and wobbly like she'd fall right over onto you, without any invite, and there you'd be, feeling like an idiot or a fool kid, like someone caught doing something you don't do in public.

He noticed her sweater was fuzzy. He had to say something. "I like your sweater," he mumbled. "It looks soft."

"It should," she breathed out at him. "There's a naked bunny running around so it could look this way."

"It's nice," he said. "I'd like to get something like that for my little girl."

"I'll be your little girl for a while." She took his arm and scooted against him into the booth. She looked too large for her clothing, but still so small in the noisy bar.

The waitress knocked her hip against the table and startled him, and the music got loud, so he shouted, "I had a farm, but that was a long time ago. Then I worked at the Honeywell, and now I keep looking for something better." He waited for her to say something. "Where you from?" he asked after a while.

She pouted and swayed her head to the music as if he weren't there.

He tried again. "You're not a Cities girl, I can tell."

She looked down.

"And that's good, you know."

"Me?" she looked up then. "I came from a farm down by Owatonna, south you know. But I had to get out of there," she said. "It was all church and chores; no boys, no make-up. No money to spend, either. No jobs but at the Tasty Freeze, and I've got ambition. I've got plans, you know? They treated me like I was stupid or ugly, just because I didn't fit in."

"Now, I can't believe that. You're pretty as a picture, and smart as a whip, I'm sure."

"You mean that?"

"Of course I do." And Carver, who had been whispering something to the other girl, gave him a big wink, and raised his glass as if toasting him.

When Carver disappeared and came back with a room key, Mopstick figured they'd go up and visit where they could hear each other better, and then he'd get on home, though maybe Carver would be staying. He was, after all, a single man. Much time had passed since his wife had walked out on him, and Mary was out of the picture, though Mopstick couldn't think why. Upstairs, the two girls disappeared together into the bathroom, giggling, and Carver was pouring more than a taste into four paper cups he'd gotten from the bartender. Mopstick was sitting on the very edge of the bed, thinking about how musty everything smelled, and how the flowered drapes had the same pattern of daisies as the bedspreads, but in different colors and sizes, when Carver snickered and poked him in the ribs, and Mopstick realized what they were supposed to do next.

"Carver, they're barely more than kids."

"Well, I'm not going to be bothered with some old hag, am I? Someone all beat up? I deserve some beauty, you know?"

"No, Carver, I'm not free to do this kind of thing," and he rose to go.

But the girl he'd been talking to came in wearing next to nothing, pushed him back onto the bed, and with hands like birds, trailed the soft sweater across his cheek and then lower, to where she'd loosened his belt. And the weight of her was like breath, and she rode free, she flew above him and everything was rising, and she was his love but free of illness, free of pain, and free of the name of ugliness.

She smelled of fruit, not sickness. She glowed in the light of the neon sign. She rubbed his thin chest and bent, curled to suck there as if he were food and drink, and he was a new instrument she climbed and fell down, and she let go a low sound in her throat, until he raised his head and yelled into the ceiling, and before his cry could reach the corners of the room and begin its fall, subside like footsteps in the night, Carver smacked him on the back and his eyes popped open.

"Watch it, old man, I got to live in this town, you know." And the girl slid off him and he was bare to Carver's eyes, who dropped his gaze for an instant and then walked back to the other bed where the fair-haired girl sat, hugging her knees. She rose now, as out of water, with the sheet around her breasts, and trailed the white tail of it into the bathroom, and slammed the door hard.

But the girl touching him stood over Mopstick still, her small breasts bare and hanging toward him, and then her tongue was in his mouth. He pulled away. "Get out," he said, though she tasted like raspberries and he wanted to keep tasting more than anything in his life.

"I got to get out of here, Carver. This isn't right. I got a family."

"And I don't, hey Mop?"

"Well, sure you do. But they aren't with you. I know you got to live, best as you can. I mean, until they come back."

"Go ahead, get out of here, but remember, we're bound now. Bound together." Carver watched the door slam hard, and sat down on the bed behind him. The girl Mop had been with, dressed and left.

"Come on out of there now," said Carver, knocking on the bathroom door. He'd heard a muffled sound, but then it was quiet, and he needed to touch the girl again, so he pushed at the door and it swung open. She jumped back and dropped her comb, her hair still wild.

"What the hell do you think you're doing," she yelled, but in a small voice, and he grabbed her and put his arms around her. He pulled her from the bathroom, her small feet sliding on the worn carpet. They fell to the bed and he brushed her hair away from her face.

She stared at him as he put himself inside her. When he asked her afterward how good she felt, she said nothing. In the silence he knew he was right about many things, and got up and threw a sheet over her trembling, not sure he wanted to look at her anymore.

Mopstick, his heart pounding, drove home fast over the new ice, leaning over the steering wheel, and almost hit someone standing in the middle of the road.

When he kissed Barb's forehead, she woke, or stirred, and took his hand and pressed it to her heart, warming it there. He lay down next to her in his jacket and his good winter pants, his scarf tangled between them. They slept, and he dreamt of no one else.

## *Chapter Five*

Early that morning, Mary dreamt that Carver came back to her. He had been so cruel when he'd pushed her away, that even asleep she sensed she was entering an upside down world where all the rules had changed, and Carver was becoming his opposite, a tender boy. He was gentle again, full of need for her. In the dreaming, it was her need as well as his that sat her upon him, where he was lonely. It was her dream to be beautiful, to be whole, to have a man who knew she was his own soft aching come to ease. She wanted to be medicine and she wanted to be healed. Her hair fell over her eyes and it was black, then, that she saw him through. She burst into him and he touched her beauty and burst into her, into the quiet, and stayed.

They walked together under the trees in the fields, and it was night. Her mother had come back, and must have seen them there, their clothing slipping down, but she was calm, and said nothing. Mary realized that she was blind now, and reached out her hands to the woman to hold her face in front of her. "Mary," she said, "go in to your father now. He cannot move."

And there, at his bedside, she leaned over and touched his chest, but his whole body was wooden, a tree felled and dying, except for his eyes, which did not close and saw her every move.

"Get to work, girl," he said with a caught sound in his throat, and she ran out to drive too fast over the county road to town, where she operated the custard machine. She stood in the dim fluorescence and waited for a customer, then mixed the two sides, chocolate and vanilla, the most popular way, in a perfect pattern up to the curled tip, claw of brown sweetness hooked to claw of white fragrance, and mirroring the honeycomb beneath that held the mix.

Then someone's hands held the cone like a bowl of soup, and the ice cream began to melt, and it was Carver who licked the stickiness there and offered her some, and it began again as when they were first together, her eyes glittering and their bodies moving to the rich black voice in her head that was the music she most loved. Her body was strong and struggled against him for pleasure until her father rose from the bed and was not wood but steel, and lashed her. She could not run, and now the boy, the first one she loved, was on the ground where her father kicked him, and kicked him again many times, left him on the stained tiles while he beat her for a long time, for the last time.

42

Her sleep calmed. She walked up to the ashes of the farmhouse that she did not burn, though she'd dreamt of the blaze and her parents calling out for her as the flames lashed them. So long she had listened in her sleep for the true tongue, the straight words, "I did this to you," her father would say, and, behind the bedroom wall, "I let him," whispered her mother.

She kept listening, but it was black crow she heard, singing horse, rustling corn, it was bleating frog calling to mate. It was coming thunder, cackling chicken, endless creek. She heard it all in the wind. She turned and was at the barn door, and high and urgent the mare whinnied for Mary's hand on her nose and over her flank. She was there with the horse then, who shuddered with the crash of the barn door, her mane electric, her legs nervous in the dense air after the close strike that almost took the house. They told Mary when they called that the barn was untouched, the animals crazy and crying but whole, even the row of hooks still firm in their anchors. And this she knew, still there by the door, close at hand, no fumbling for him even on a moonless night, hung the whip, full fed on humans and animals both, by the hand hardened by labor, and by the heart hardened by tales told in the southern Indiana night where he grew from a boy. Hardened too by those nights he raised hell with the boys, who loved him, always ready for a good time was Martin, as he wanted to be called, even by the other boys, and they did. Never Marty.

He grew taller than the rest, straight and hard, and when he left, they made sacrifice, as they called it, and passed on the gift, the old well-fed whip, and he lay it over his thigh as he drove the piled-up pickup from outside Richmond to his new land, flat and fertile, in the southwestern corner of Minnesota. Met the girl he loved there, and took her to the house he was building, and with every straight nail he laid in, the walls rose up to stand without bend or sway around the woman, and then around the daughter she bore. Father, the girl called him; then, Martin, when she grew up.

"Oh, Journey," Mary whispered in her sleep above the feathery mane of the horse. Journey was hers, the one thing she still cared for up there, and cared for from the evening the foal was birthed. And that last day she returned, with lightning strikes in the distance, she flung herself up to ride around the edge of the fields. With each step of horse and rider, the boundaries disappeared, and she did not know where she rode, only that she needed Journey, and that the wind blew completely through her. She slept then, naked on a blanket in the muggy hayloft. She slept a whole sleep and dreamt within her dream that she was smooth as cream, an unbroken sea of wheat stopped by no jagged fence, no coil of wire. No one came to break her, the plow sat locked, and when she walked away from the land as the sun rose, she left her good horse, and the girl Mary dancing where the old barn stood, until strangers came in shouting, and broke the dream.

Then she heard his voice, Carver's, but soft, saying, "Would you dance with me?" and underneath his words the music started low. She strained to hear it and it was the old tune that said, "Isn't she lovely, isn't she wonderful," and she moved like a silken doll as she bent toward her partner, and away, as she spun into the dark honey of the sounds on the dance floor, but the light jabbed at her again. It was harsh and awakened her this time, and there was more shouting as a group of men worked to start a stalled car in the cold. She felt a chill and realized she had kicked off the covers. She reached for the sheet and saw the scars on her legs. A bird cry entered, and then the car engine kicked in. She pulled the sheet over her body up to her neck, and then, a moment later, over her head.

With the full break of dawn over the glittering snow that had covered the Cities, Mary dressed for work. Today for some reason she looked hard at everything she touched: the egg and the fry pan, the coffee and the milk container. Bread. An orange. Water and a multivitamin. Her boots, lined with phony fur. She grabbed her work shoes; her job had meant years of crawling through dusty files in the back room of the insurance company as they converted inch by inch to computers for their recordkeeping. "Find any cases of arsenic poisoning, from 1966 to 1971." "Find all cancer cases from 1968 and arrange them in boxes by the kind of cancer." "All falls from scaffolding of construction workers."

With each pile of folders she would see a solid story. She never knew what they did with the stories she brought them: beginning, middle, end; symptoms, illness, death, with impoverishment for the family usually thrown in. She understood from the way one thing became another, like love became hate, that work could become disease; that a job could take the legs out from under a person, suffocate them, leech their bones. She could not gather the facts without reading them into some kind of sense.

"Look at this," Mary would say to the woman at the next desk, who wore high heels around the office every day, and left them in a silver shopping bag by the door of the file room when she too crawled around from box to box in storage, or leaned on her knees running her fingers over file after file. She was an expert. Mary thought she could read with her fingers, she worked so fast to locate what she needed; then grabbed up the files in her arms, slid into her high heels, and walked to her desk, her back a perfect arrow.

"Are you from the Cities?" Mary asked her when she first began working there.

"Of course," she'd said, and swiveled her chair around to show that straight back to Mary.

Mary got up and came to face her, stood over her as she stared at her nails with her hands spread out on top of the stack of manila folders. "I'm not," she said, leaning over the desk. "I'm from where most of the people in those files come from. The farms." She walked away, her heart pounding.

44

If fifty men were up on scaffolding on the side of a building at various times of the day in June, a day threatening storms, and 8 fell from the scaffolding, most between 3 and 4 o'clock, this was enough proof that either weather conditions were responsible (an Act of God), or, if they all worked for the same company, perhaps a weakness in the equipment was suggested, a pattern that meant someone was liable for more than simple workman's compensation. It was Mary's job to prove it was an Act of God, nothing the company did.

If ten people who got water from the same well developed the same kind of cancer and were not connected by genetics, there was perhaps something in the earth that led to this illness. If a company upriver was dumping some kind of toxic materials in the river but no one talked about it, it had to be the fault of those who became ill, who had not tested the water coming up from the caverns of the earth. The earth contained natural carcinogens, and, while a sad story, there was no compensation due.

Story after story was what she held in her hands. And, often, no one believed her, even though the story she gave them was clear, photo after photo, testimony gathered from one person after another: worker, spouse, son and daughter, neighbor, even the gas station attendant who helped the man, with his hands weak and shaking, put gas in his car, and who noticed when he stopped driving alone, and when he stopped driving.

"Just do your job," Mary's supervisor told her.

"That's exactly what I'm doing," she said.

"Then remember who you're working for."

"I work for you but I listen to my conscience."

"That's the trouble then."

"What are you asking me to do?"

"I shouldn't have to explain these things to you. You're a big girl. Contrary as hell, though."

*Mary, Mary, quite contrary,*
*how does your garden grow?*
*With silver bells and cockle shells*
*and pretty maids all in a row.*

She'd heard this everywhere she went, six ways to Sunday, from the boys flirting with her, from her mother when she wouldn't listen, from girls at school who hated her dark hair and feared her rebellion. Now she expected the boss to break out into a song and dance, screaming that she was contrary. What could such a contrary woman expect?

"Get out the silver bells and cockle shells," she told him, thinking of what she'd read, of the thumb screws and worse that Mary Tudor used on the Protestants in England when she became Queen.

"You are a nut job," he said, "and don't bother to tell anyone I said that. I will deny it completely. Try to prove it."

"Then put me in another department."

"Doing what, Mary?"

"Anything. I don't care anymore."

"Anything. You want a pay cut? You want to forget about using your education?"

"Back to data entry. I don't care."

"That's exactly where I'll put you if this attitude doesn't turn around. And I'm sure you'll enjoy yourself there."

She spat out a thank you, and went downstairs. At lunch break, she leafed through the community newspapers stacked up in the entryway to the building. With her sandwich in one hand and her notebook in her lap, she began writing. She might be going back to data entry, but she could still tell a story.

# *Chapter Six*

Carver stood up in the middle of the room and listened. It was nearing dawn, but he could not break the habit of getting up before the sun pushed through, even on his days off, even when he'd had too much to drink. The traffic bothered him, the buses lurching down Lake Street, and where was the damn lake, anyway. Nowhere nearby. As if a name were blue water.

The motel sign outside was squealing on its hinges in the wind. A spritz of oil, for God's sake, he kept thinking. Nobody fixed a goddamned thing here in the city. What was wrong with these people? Why didn't they get up off their corn-fed behinds and fix what needed fixing? That's what good farm people did. They didn't let things go; they couldn't. You don't fix a fence, and the chickens are dinner for a fox. You don't fix a barn door and the horses are free to ride the plains like Indian ponies. You don't replace a broken window and you sure as hell could freeze to death. You just did the fixing you had to do, no complaints, and if you did it wrong, you did it again until you did it right. No excuses.

He paced the floor. He hated the stained carpet. He hated the view from the window, the phony lights from the street, the sign that threatened his room each time it swung. But this was it, the cheapest room he could find, and he should be used to it by now.

He put on the television. Why not, it was there, though he'd never put it on in the morning when he lived out on the farm. What would he need to do that for? Commercials, trying to get frowsy old housewives to buy stuff they didn't need, or promising them beauty in a jar, miracle creams, pills to lose weight. All they had to do was get up from their chairs and do some real work, and stop eating so much. He sat down and kept switching the stations. Home shopping, news shows with no real news, cartoons.

Breaking news, now. Of what? A car crash? A gas station robbery? As long as it wasn't the place he worked at, what difference did it make to him?

But it wasn't about a robbery. Or it was, but a great robbery, a robbery of a way of life that God had meant to go on forever. He stood up again and watched as a line of tractors drove down Pennsylvania Avenue, right past the White House, and he hooted, "My good Lord!" and slapped his thigh, closed his eyes and spun around, then opened them again to make sure it was not some fantasy movie. He'd heard about this, they talked this stuff at meetings, at least when he was still going, a repeat of '79, but as the bankers closed in on him his heart gave up, and he stopped going to meetings with men who still had a prayer of keeping their farms.

Now they were driving their tractors down Pennsylvania Avenue through the heart of Washington, D.C. A brigade of farmers, and what could stop them? A bomb? A damn nuclear bomb, sure, but how could they drop one right near the President's dining table, two doors down from his *pissoir*, a shoe's throw from his wife's damn walk-in closet? They kept going. Those boys kept going like they were going on home, or going to market. Or maybe going to vote.

That's it, Carver pointed at the TV. These are the tanks of the farmers, the weapons of the people. These are the people's troops—in a tractor stroll down Pennsylvania Avenue. The suits inside those government buildings probably never even saw a John Deere, just ate what good farm folk grew, and the animals they raised, and bought and sold it all on the Stock Exchange, let it rot in warehouses when it made them more money that way, and buried or burnt up the surplus when their bankbooks got hot in their pockets. As if there could ever be surplus when anyone went hungry.

"Got the message, Prez?" Carver asked the screen. "Hear those farmers rumbling down your street? Got the message, you fat, two-faced Senators? Got it, banker trash?" He laughed and sat on the edge of the bed, jiggling his legs, a palm on each knee, and watched it like he watched a sunrise with his mouth open.

And when they spoke, gathered between the monuments, a genuine crowd, he knew that for each one standing, there were farmers who had already lost the fight. Evicted, or out of the game by suicide, or pumping gas. Selling cars, if they were lucky. Alone.

The man on the screen wasn't talking soft. He was pounding that podium, and he was speaking plain and he was speaking smart, and he was one of those like Carver's father who had lived his Sundays in church, and sat his evenings with the Bible. He was laying it out for everyone to hear, and Carver knew he spoke the truth. The farmer was the blessing of the community, the bearer of life, the giver of sustenance. The worn hand that took from the earth and fed her children.

"Speak on," he whispered, and he remembered the way the whole church would stand up when his father came in, because they knew he would speak with that voice of thunder and tell them the way it was, and what they had to do, and why they were out there on the vast freezing plain. Why they got up early every morning when a man's fingers could break off like they were pure ice. He'd tell it, how a woman had to be strong out there, and not give in to the silliness that was okay for city women, the make-up and the shopping for clothes. "What for, women," he'd bend toward someone's wife or point at two sisters in the same row, "what for, when your duty to God is your duty to the land and to your husbands. Your duty is to work and to comfort."

And the women would shift around in their seats, but he was going, and he wouldn't stop until he'd said it, and they had to listen, sitting between the men who were motionless, men who listened to every word like it was a sign in the sky of when to plant.

"You know where you came from," Carver's father said. "The rib of Adam, the afterthought of God. You have a purpose, don't get me wrong, you have a duty. A duty to serve what you came from." He paused, and lowered his voice. "Let me tell you a story." And Carver watched, that day in church, and saw the men's faces like they were awake in a dream, their eyes wide with looking, and the women looking down at their hands. He remembered that, the women looking down.

"In the last century, that's right, before my time"—and his father gave a chuckle, and the congregation chuckled with him, knowing that it was okay to laugh a bit here—"the men came to this land from all over God's world. From Norway and Sweden and Denmark and Germany, from Czechoslovakia, and, no, I'm not forgetting you, Pete, from Finland, and they came from Russia, some Italians even, crazy with the cold but they came, am I right? They came, and they worked like dogs, worse than dogs. They worked in the mines. They worked in the fields. They helped build the railroads. They ferried the steamships up and down the greatest river in the world, our Mississippi, and all because God knew that this was a wild land, a great land, yes, but a wild one, and it needed the people to put it in order and get it producing what the people needed. But the people who journeyed here were almost all men, at least at first, until enough was set down to make it right enough for women, like with the First Creation, you see what I mean? God created Adam and when the Garden was in order, with food falling from the trees, God brought out Eve from Adam's side.

"But what about these lonely men who knew—you see, Adam didn't know there would be something like a woman—these men knew there was this creature, Woman, the one made to give them comfort, and they longed for her. So here's what the American mind did, and it's a business mind, we know that, and we know it works in wise ways, this mind of the businessman. They brought out some women, women alone, women with no one to feed them, widowed women and abandoned women and young women with no future ahead in the poverty they were living, and furnished them to these hungry, yearning men. You could go down to the stockade, and there was a tribe of women, there behind a wire fence, waiting for their men. One dollar—and don't doubt me, I've read this in a reputable source—one dollar, for comfort and love and being able to talk to a tender creature, so that these men could go back to the serious business of building a country from a wild land. You know what I mean. You see what we've built out of the wilderness. Those men needed those women, am I right?

"But you have got to remember now"—and Carver knew he would remember this for all his life, because of the way his mother was grasping his hand, like she was

49

in great pain, and she didn't look at him for days, and was silent there in the house, in the barn, in the truck on the way into town—"you have got to remember," said his father, preaching loud and leaning over the podium, "that the beginning of the lives of women here on the prairie, down in the Cities, there by the riverfront, in the mining camps and logging camps, was in sin. Necessary sin, you understand, but sin, at any rate. The businessmen knew that the women had to follow their natures, and come to this New Garden in sin, and so they put them in stockades, behind wire fences, and there, for the price of one dollar, the men made them to enter the New World, where they were given food and hope, and later on a husband and a home, and they knew that to begin in sin means a lot of labor to work it off.

"That's why our women are so industrious here on the prairie. There's no place for them to hide the truth of their origins, of how the women they're descended from let themselves be bought, a dollar a head, by our working men who had to have some comfort.

"A woman is a creature whose very essence is labor, labor and sin. She must work hard the land. Know her place in it. Walk the rows of growing things and stoop there, seed and harvest. And stick to her own tribe to bring forth the generations that will step up, as well, to labor. So be a true woman, large and generous, I advise that half of us. Bear life, tend life, nurture and mend. Work the fields with your wisdom of earth. Give your body, its mounds and valleys, its muscle, to labor beyond the delicate fantasy of woman's arms. And stand with your good man as he rises for his life of toil.

"The birds will sing for you then, woman. The cows will give milk; the hens, eggs; the beans, their fleshy coats; and the corn, their jewels. The flax will yield its quivering seed, and the wheat, its gritty spring truth. Its profit. So, work, and in that work, forget yourself, forget your sinful body, whether awkward or graceful. Think not of your flesh, whether silk of the river, or the stony soil. Forget your own rough hands and splayed fingers, bitten and mashed by the machinery's cold bite, but let them fly in the freedom of labor. This is your beauty, woman, this is your destiny as a child of the farm."

He looked out at the congregation then, moving his gaze from bench to bench, stopping for moments at one woman or another, and God only knew what he had in his mind, and said, "In this hard work, and in being a proper comfort to your man, there is redemption, redemption from your sinful past. Now, let us pray."

Carver remembered dropping his head to pray, but the voice that filled him was his mother's, telling stories of her mother and all her aunts leaving to sew sacks and work clothes for two dollars a week in the sweatshops of Minneapolis. "They joined the Striking Maidens," she used to brag. "They were glad to have gotten off the farms."

Well, redemption in numbers today, Carver thought, as he watched the men riding their tractors, sitting high up off the ground, and he couldn't even see to the end of the line. He turned up the TV, and listened to the last of the speeches. Brave men, he thought, strong and dedicated. A good thing to let the people of this country see us, see the farmers that put food on their tables.

Maybe it was too late for him. The farm was gone and God only knew what they were doing to it. He was pushing the tractor up hills by the time he was eight years old, with some help to work the pedals, but it was gone now too. And the comfort that was due him? The only way he could think to get it these days was to buy it. Who else would want him, a grease monkey living in a motel room, driving a beat-up old car?

They were yelling about how to keep their farms, but he'd already lost his, and they weren't saying anything about how to get back the farms of the casualties that had been mowed down. He'd have to figure that out himself.

Still, those yells were glorious, and they stayed with him for a long time. That brigade, he thought, rumbling down Pennsylvania Avenue like an invading army, but they are us, the farmers! They're me.

He showered and put on his coveralls, went down to the lobby and stepped out into the bitter sunlight of January.

## *Chapter Seven*

### *February 1991*

"I never expected much in the way of looks in a woman, though, you know, my mother was a very beautiful woman." Mopstick paused. "I got her coloring, but my father's the one I favor, with his too long bones." He looked up. "Tess," he called. The owner wore a blue and white shirt that matched the chrome walls of the diner with the sky reflected there. "Could I get that refill now, please?" he asked, and lifted his cup.

She was looking at him a bit fascinated, the coffeepot in her left hand starting to tip. She came back to the moment and walked over.

"Thanks," Mopstick said as Tess poured, and she smiled and walked down to the other end of the counter to serve a couple of teenagers.

"You should," Carver said, "expect your woman to be beautiful."

"But it was never just the look of a woman that had me trembling for her, even when I was a kid. It was the feel of her, and the smell, and then maybe one special thing, like the back of her neck and how it came up from her shoulders deep into the place where she thought of me. Or her knees and how the bones pushed through her jeans or stockings, these soft thighs and then this hard face of bone. Or maybe her shoulders, too sweet and delicate for all I saw women have to carry. Not that I been with so many women. I haven't. But I know women. Was women who raised me."

"You sell yourself short," Carver said. "You don't know your rightful place as a man in this world. There are some things you're entitled to. You hear me?"

"No complaints with what I got."

"Come on, Mop. You got rights. A woman ought to clean herself up for you. Fit into your arms, so you can feel your own strength. She's got to have beauty that's like heaven and earth, both. Her eyes should be doves, her lips a 'scarlet thread,' the Bible says it. Her breasts 'like two fawns' you can rest between. Imagine that."

"Carver, you can't go on and make a list of what women should be, even if the list comes straight from the Bible."

"That's the point. It's not women. It's the right woman, the one God picked out for a good workingman like you. She should look at you with God in her eyes, see Him reflected in you. You get it, Mop?"

"I hear you, Carver, but it's just talk. When you love a woman, you love her, no matter."

"Maybe, but I'm saying, face it, some women have more heaven in them than others, and some have got too much earth. Like some hard, dry field you break your back over. Look at Tess down there. She's no angel, no fruit tree reaching up."

"Carver, that's not fair."

"She's a cow, and she'd chew on a man like a cow on cud, all day every day, without a moment of pleasure in it for him."

"You don't know her. She's a decent woman, with a good sense of humor, and kind. Gives coffee and pie to the guys who come in without a job."

"Nothing good about that. Just stupid. Got herself a free ride since Ernie died and left her this place, and so she gives out in kind, freebies to the bums that know their own."

"Sometimes I don't get you, Carver. Let's change the subject."

"All's I'm saying is, you need a woman who can really give herself to you. You deserve that, same as any man. And you want it, I know you do."

"I got what I got to have. And I love my woman."

"That's what the Dakota side told you?"

"You're treading on thin ice, my friend. And I better get on home."

"You're entitled, you hear?"

Mopstick shook his head, put a dollar and some change on the counter, and left. Carver looked after him for a moment, then picked up the paper and stared at the front page, his hands shaking. Tess came back with the coffeepot, but he waved her away without glancing up at her.

He tried to read the newspaper, and made himself look at the prices corn and soybeans were pulling in. He drank some cold water from the pitcher Tess had left, and watched the slice of lemon float to the bottom and bob back up. There was a glossy leaflet from the community college, like a big playing card, inserted in the papers, inviting new students to come and change their lives. He scanned the list of degrees they offered. A course in forgetting, he thought, that would be great. I should get a degree in that.

"You—in college, boy?" he heard his father say. "You've got to be kidding me. Your brother was a good student, but you? You'd always be on the prowl for girls. Not that I could blame you. That's pretty normal."

The right side of Carver's head throbbed with it, his father's voice, the pictures that went along with it.

"Tess," he yelled out, trying to quiet it, "I'll have that refill now."

"Now, I am a preacher, albeit unofficial," his father told him in the kitchen one Sunday night, pointing his finger at his young son, "but a fine preacher. A true and holy speaker. A voice that grew up from this land. A preacher with power, like the thunder. Right, boy? You know I can preach to the farmer, and he asks me for comfort, and I am there for him with the knowledge of Our Lord and the blessings sent to me from Heaven to cast onto those who labor on earth, who labor in sorrow, as the wicked make confused the true nature of man and earth."

The boy looked away.

"You hear me, Carver?"

"Yes, I hear you."

"But I am a man, too, and in a few years you'll be a man and you'll feel what I'm feeling in my body today. I am a man and I have to confess before your mother walks into this room, talking some nonsense or other, that the new woman working down at the exchange makes my blood boil with it, you know what I mean, kid of mine? I can't sleep at night if I start thinking about her, her full thighs, the rounded bowl of her belly that offers up its wine to a good man like me. I could get lost in her hair, lost in her flesh. She's a hot one, you can tell it, can't you, son?"

"Sure, sure, I can tell it," and he looked past his father through the kitchen window.

The old man pounded his fist on the table. "A man needs some beauty in his life. Your mother's an old beast by now, a hard worker, sure enough, but I need to look at a face that's a flower, not an old sack of grain."

Carver stood up and opened his mouth to say something, but the man grabbed his arm and pulled him back down to the table. "Did I tell you to get up? Did I?" His son didn't answer, feeling the wounds of his mother, who cared for him each time he was hurt or beaten.

The farmer put his face close to the boy's and stared at him, but then Carver looked him in the eye and said, "Why do you talk that way about my mother?" The man snickered, and shook his head. "Beauty is beauty," he said, "and goddamned ugly is nothing but God-blasted ugly. There's no virtue in it."

Carver looked down at his hands, which were hurting as if he had been milking all day. "Got it, boy?" his father said, and pointed hard in his son's face. "Ugly over here, at the edge of things, and beauty here," he circled his finger around and around and stopped at the center of the table. "The Garden. The blessed and holy place. The place of good food and abundant drink, and, at the edge, the barren places. God don't waste," he pounded the table with each word, "on those that don't deserve, and He marks them, you hear me, boy? He marks them so we all can tell, don't waste a minute on this one. God ain't stupid. He made the world for those He likes to look upon." The man's words were coming slower. "'No flaw' in the beloved, the Good Book says it."

"Can I go now?" his son asked.

"No, you can't go now! I was telling you about this woman down at the store, the one God wants me to have, the beautiful Helen. Like in the Greek story. You read that story in school yet? I'll tell you. She was so beautiful, they fought a war for her." And Carver saw the great horse filled with soldiers who leaped out with swords and shouts to take her home.

54

"This woman was perfect. Full breasts, long legs, none of this stumpy stuff, like a draught horse. Golden hair, nothing dark in her except the shadows a man goes into. And that face! Sweet lips." He puckered his own and kissed at the air. "A flower face. You know what that means yet? A flower face? Do you?"

"No," said Carver, watching through the window as the ocean of grain moved to the caress of the wind.

"I didn't think so. A flower face is one that opens to the sunlight, and the sun is you, the man! Get it? A flower face opens up to you, and is soft, and smells good." He inhaled, but the boy felt like he was choking.

"Like honeysuckle," the man said after the exhale, "you can drink there. The scent of her breath like spring blossoms. Her tongue tasting of milk and honey. To lay with her in the fields brings peace to a man, the Lord says it. Right there in the Bible."

He was calm then, and leaned closer to the boy. "You can't drink from a cursed ugly face, from the leather skin of a woman out in the sun, dried up from chores. You have to be able to suck. A man is like a baby, see? A man has to be able to suck in his woman and it has to be sweet. Like a flower. A flower face. That's a woman not for work. That's a woman for love. That's the way a man survives—first, he gets a woman who works hard, and then he gets what he deserves, a woman for loving. One to dwell with him in the Garden. Don't you read the Good Book, boy?"

"Can I go now?" Carver asked again, working to ease his hand out of his father's grip. As it slid away, the man looked down at his empty hand, confused, as if something had been cut away.

"Who do you think you are? I'm telling you something, you thirteen-year old brat, something you need to know if you're going to grow to be a man," and then he backhanded the boy hard across the face, so that his chair fell onto the kitchen floor.

"Get up," his father said, and Carver did. "Now you can go."

But the boy stood there this time, ready for what was to come.

"Did you hear me? I said, get out of my sight."

The boy did not move, dreaming as he was, upright, of a victory over the lined and ugly face of the man still in his suit jacket from church. "I'm not moving," he dared say, "until I want to."

"What did you say?" the man said, as he struck out at his son as hard as he could, and felled him.

The boy stood up again and shook his head in the light of the moon, and his father saw it, something wild and hard, something he could not put back, and heard it without knowing where it came from, a sound bellowing and rare that ran with the boy out into the fields, where he paced the straight path of the rows, then bent to the furrows to smell the earth he couldn't imagine opening to his father. He lay there, breathing the night.

From his room Carver heard his father walking again. Up and down the stairs, through the hallway, shuffling his feet, passing his door like a slow sad wind, and then the creaking of the staircase again. The refrigerator door swung open and then shut, and Carver's father kept walking. When the boy heard no more, he went downstairs to make sure the man hadn't fallen asleep at the kitchen table again, and there he was, but he was awake in the dim light and weeping. Carver's mother was there with him, cradling him in her soft arms, stroking his head as he sobbed, but Carver couldn't hear a thing, and looked hard for a few more moments to make sure they were really there. "Oh, love," she whispered then to her husband in the dark, "lay down the past."

Carver looked up, just as the fluorescent light buzzed and flickered in his eyes.

"Tess," he shouted toward the other end of the long, curved, counter, "this should settle up," and he slapped a twenty on the paper placemat, right in the center of the big green map of Minnesota.

## *Chapter Eight*

### *Easter 1991*

New Year's Day for Carver was only a shift in the numbers he entered into the gas station ledger, but his little girl's birthday—this he watched for, and each year hoped would bring him a glimpse of her. Kate sent back most of his letters to Rosie, with "Return to Sender" in a handwriting as official as she could make it. As cold. She never mailed back the birthday cards he sent, but he never got any thank you's or hellos from his daughter. He imagined a hatbox under Kate and George's bed in Mankato, filling up with pastel envelopes, his and Rosie's. What sweetness he must have stolen from Katie to become her enemy, and nothing more.

Sometimes Carver dreamt of his daughter sitting in the closet, between shoeboxes and hatboxes, hugging her knees to her chest and rocking, the darkness moving up and back like a great blanket against the wind of her body as it traveled through the night. She used to sit that way in the fields, in the humming of the plains. He used to sit with her.

This year his daughter's birthday fell on the last day of classes before Easter vacation began, and it was to mark her growing that Carver got cleaned up and walked over to the school before three o'clock, and stood there with his cap in his pocket. He held out his arms and went down on one knee as the line of young girls came through the open gate and half-skipped into the sunlight, all dressed up for the Easter party, skirts flouncing and shiny shoes scraping the city pavement with the taps their fathers had hammered on to save the heels and preserve the toes. The girls would grow out of these shoes and pass them down with soles in perfect condition to younger sisters and cousins who had stared into the shine of the leather and imagined many things.

The first few girls in line giggled when they saw him, but Angie, too big now for the peach-colored dress, did not know what to do. Just as the boys came through the gate in their dark pants and white shirts, she ran away from the others to hide in the bushes from Carver, who kept calling her name and shaking the branches, which made a hard, scraping sound as she trembled and looked down at her white socks and the gleaming toes of her shoes.

She heard her teacher's voice, and then others calling to her. She picked out Carver's call, and tried to hear the way it told her things, and then didn't hear it anymore. But she knew he was still there waiting for her, and she wasn't sure why she was hiding. She did know that if no one could see her she would be all right. She would come back to school after the holidays and tell them she'd had to go home because her mother was sick, and she had to take care of her. She would tell them that. It was the truth.

She crouched in a hollow place at the heart of the bush, its limbs spreading over her. The teachers were calling her name. She heard them again and again, but she knew they couldn't find her. They didn't know the place she had gone, and she became smaller, small as a pebble, and waited for them to go. It was quiet for a time but then she heard it again, louder. They were yelling her name now. She was shaking, and waited for something in her to say yes, go now, run fast. She cared nothing for her pretty clothes but listened hard for the yes, for the moment that would open and hold her, and hide her as she ran from the man they would try to make her go with, just because he had no little girl, just because he gave her a dress, just because she promised not to tell where she got it.

And when that moment came, it opened to her like her mother's arms, and she jumped into them and ran with her, praying that Mama would not be mad, but would get better and hold her in this bubble of time away from Carver and his low voice.

It came without a sound and she ran in the silence. She ran hard on her special shoes, imagining she was still there curled into the hollow of the bush, but then the wind blew her skirts around, and her hair reached into every part of the sky, and she was happy and free.

She flew into the road at the moment an orange pickup was rolling, with no shocks, down toward the turnoff to the Sears. She was almost hit, but the truck swerved out of the way, ran over the green fragments of a broken beer bottle, and, somehow, the tires still intact, left a skid mark like a large clumsy zipper up to the neck of a photo of a woman, bare and folded at the waist, who stared out from the dark ground. Angie began to run again, no sense in her yet, but a large woman picked her up and held her, and felt the heart racing away from the girl, and whispered to her, and lay her hand there. The girl's breath calmed, her heart remembered its usual drumbeat, and then she sobbed once and fell into sleep.

No one from school had seen where Angie had gone. The city bus labored up the hill between the school, and the comforting arms of this woman Madeleine and her tall-drink-of-water nephew, William, who stood by as his aunt swayed with the girl in her arms. They got her into the truck's cabin and seatbelted her between them. William held her up by her shoulder so she would not fall and be jarred. She was still asleep and talking wild things, as people do when they are running and sleeping at the same time.

"Hey, William," said his auntie, "let's take her to the river, so when she wakes, the new waters will be singing, and leaving the ice behind, and she will remember what she was running to."

"We should take her to the police, Auntie, shouldn't we?"

"There'd be times I would say yes, but this girl is asleep with fear, and that would be a bad place to wake up to, don't you think?"

"I see what you mean, Auntie," said William, and held the girl a little tighter, and stared out of the windshield at the trees' branches in great arcs above them.

During the ride, the girl slept. She was the only talker, but there was no answer to be made while her eyes were still closed.

William wasn't sure this was such a good idea. It would be pretty clear to anyone they came across that the girl wasn't one of them. He peeked at her now and then, to make sure she was not in trouble while she was on her journey, in her dreams, as Auntie had taught him. The sun was beginning to set when they got to the cabin, so it was under a brilliant sky that they brought her to the riverbank, after they got some good warm blankets to wrap her in, and left some hot tea on a low flame for her to drink when she came back. Her shoes were muddy and he hoped the leather would shine up clean before they returned her home.

Right at the bend in the river was where they sat and held her, and spoke to her. His auntie used some Dakota words, but William was pretty sure the girl didn't understand them.

"Listen to the water," the woman said, "listen to it singing," and William heard it like he never had before, and understood that its song was a blessing. In the middle of that song, his auntie said to the girl, "Your mother is calling for you to come home. Listen to her, child, and open your eyes." She stroked the girl's cheek, and the girl jerked her head away once, then calmed and sighed under the warm, gentle hand.

"What name is she calling you?" asked William, and she answered, dreaming still, "Angie," but then she opened her eyes and forgot to be afraid when she saw that it was not Carver who held her, and not the teacher who thought her a strange girl.

"Angie," she said again, "that's my name."

"Ah, Angie," said the woman, "we have been waiting for our introduction. I'm Madeleine, and this is my nephew William. Handsome, isn't he?"

And Angie giggled while William looked away as if he noticed something moving in the bushes.

"We want to take you back home. Do you remember running away?"

She nodded and said, yes, she wanted to go home, but she knew she also wanted to stay for a while and see where she was, and what William looked like in the light. They went to the cabin where she drank some tea, but she thought she must still be dreaming, and smiled at the way some dreaming was safe while other dreaming was nightmare and sadness.

"Cheese sandwich?" Madeleine asked her. "The bread's good homemade, the cheese is American. It'll fill you up till we get you home."

59

The three sat chewing, and were content. Angie would tell her next time about her mother being sick. The woman didn't even ask why she was running away, or what had so scared her that she ran into the street near the Sears. It didn't matter at the table, and it didn't matter on the ride home.

On the way back to the city, Angie recited her phone number and Madeleine called at the first gas station they passed. Barb and Mopstick were on the porch waiting for them. Before Angie went to change, Madeleine hugged her, and William gave her a feather. When she came back, they were gone, and Barb was asleep on the sofa next to Mopstick, who put out his hand to her. She snuggled close to him, but then he asked her why she'd run away from school. Again she couldn't find the words to say, again her old promise stopped her, though she wanted him to help her. She wanted him to protect her from the man and his low voice, though she couldn't think of anything he'd done to hurt her, not one thing.

"Something frightened me, Daddy."

"What, Angie?"

"I don't know. I just don't know. But I had to run away from the line. All those girls and then a man came and just looked at us." She prayed he wouldn't ask her more about the man. "He didn't do anything," she began to cry. "He just looked at us, maybe because we're girls. Could that be it?"

"Shh, let's whisper," Mopstick told her, "let's not wake up your mother right now. But maybe, yes, maybe because you are girls," and he didn't say but thought it with a shudder, and you are beginning to grow up.

"He didn't do anything, but I was afraid," she said close to his ear, and he patted her shoulder, and whispered, "Yes, baby-girl, I understand," and rocked her.

# *Book Three*

## *How Far From the Garden*
### *Fall 1994 - Winter 1996*

"O you who dwell in the gardens, my companions are listening for your voice; let me hear it."

—"The Song of Solomon" from *The Old Testament*

"We're still traveling the road from Beirut. Still remembering how blossoms trembled in gold clouds on the trees the morning of evacuation."

—"Seasons of Fire, Seasons of Light" from *These Words*
Lisa Suhair Majaj

## *Chapter One*

### *Fall 1994*

And in that rocking, in her father's arms and her mother's arms, Angie lived and she grew, and Carver could see it. He couldn't accept it, that all a girl needed to grow up right was somebody loving and listening. He didn't know it then, but she had him tied up forever. Nature put a few pounds on her in the right places, but her hair stayed golden and her skin stayed velvet. He heard nothing from his own in Mankato. Nothing. But he still sent a money order every week for the girl through her grandparents. Never missed. He tried to see Rosie's face but the only one that popped up was Angie's, and she was leaving girlhood too, so it was hard, then, trying to remember these girls as children.

It was Angie who became his timeline. Without his farm, with only the bare tree boxed into concrete at the curb across the street, Angie was his signal that time was passing. He did love the turning of the seasons, and when he'd said that to the old man once toward the end, he saw a flicker of light in his hard eyes. His father knew time and the seasons by the work to be done, and maybe by the clothes the women wore to church. Maybe he remembered seeing his own sons growing up, and maybe he fought it in his way. As for Carver, each time he saw his angel, she was a bit taller, it seemed, a bit less like a little girl, a bit more distant. Smart mouthed, too, sometimes. He didn't like that, but then he looked at her and saw that she was only a kid trying to seem grown. Barb's illness, he thought, that's what toughens her up.

It was one of those days in fall that hit like a rock, after weeks of almost cold, with everyone saying, Yes, I can feel it coming, the bite in the air. After the expanse of blue skies, of bright light, seemed endless, this day was a thud of gray and damp, of hard chill. Mary was ready for this, counting the days till she would cover up and pull in.

It was a long time since she had looked on her afternoon walk home for Carver's back, or his gesture to a friend.

But this was just when he began to look for her, scraping over the bubbles of concrete in his new work shoes after he'd promised he would get a pair, after Hansen had pushed the twenties into his hand.

"I can't spend the money," Carver had said. "Any day now, I may get to go see my little girl. I want to have lots of nice things for her. I've bought so many things over the years, but she's too old for them, you know? She wouldn't like them. They wouldn't fit."

"You didn't send them to her when she was younger?"

"Everything came back, Hansen. That same slash with the laundry marker across Katie's address. 'Return to Sender', like it was the post office doing it, but it was Katie. I tried going out there every week for a long while, but the house was always dark and silent. Closed itself up every time I came near it."

"Get the shoes, Carver, you need them for work," and he punched the button on the register to open the cash drawer.

"I can't."

"It's an allotment for equipment. Look at it like that."

So he went to Robert's Shoes and came bouncing out, his thin frame buoyed up by the thick soles of his new work boots. He went into Sonny's to have a beer, and sat alone by the gray light at the window. The rain hit the trees pretty hard, and he watched the golden and red leaves wash through the air and hit the sidewalk. When Mary came over and touched his shoulder, he looked up, the tears running down his face. When he saw her there, he smiled, and when he realized why his face was wet, he covered his eyes with his worn hand.

It was hard to talk there but no one noticed them, no one bothered them. The night came as they spoke, and the cold burst through and was digging in for the long season.

"I almost walked away when I saw your back."

"I'm glad you didn't," Carver said, and took her hand, stared down at it, and held it to his heart. She had to lean over a bit when he did that. He couldn't say anything then, but when he tried to kiss her, something broke through, and she remembered that a man could be two men, and feared the arrival of his double.

She pulled her hand back. "I just wanted to say hello," she said, and turned from him and walked out.

When Mary looked at a man, he saw stone or cat, or gold or honey, there in her eyes. So, she didn't look, unless she wanted him, or might. When she looked at a man, she saw stone in his eyes too often, or she saw the coiled wire over the fence. She saw razor. When she looked at Carver the first time, when he bought her a drink at Sonny's, she couldn't see him at all. She heard his voice at her shoulder, that's all.

"You shouldn't be alone tonight."

"And why is that?"

"Because you're dreaming as you stand. Or maybe you are a dream," he said.

When Mary looked into his eyes in the fluorescent-lit hallway, she did not know what to think. She did not see stone or metal. She did not see wood or fire. She did not see cat or horse. She saw the land, pure and simple. She raised herself to the furrow in his cheek, and kissed him without a sound, kissed him like water at the edge of the river, and he moved that way, the way of the reeds in the water, a slight bow away, and then he came back toward her, wanting more to drink, wanting that soft kiss of water. And she gave it.

There was nothing else that first night, and for many nights, but kissing, and this kissing was like all the dreams of earth and sky meeting at the brilliant edge. Carver said, "I don't believe you're real." He held her as if she were truly water. "Impossible," he said, "I should stay away." And she thought, No, I want to build here. Water this. Dream it back into being: the tender insides of his arms, his stooped shoulders, the hard bone where his back ended and he became round enough to trace the beginning of earth.

What did they talk about that night? She couldn't much remember now; only that they smiled, that they each spoke for a moment and waited to hear the other's voice, that they seesawed up and back in this song. The weather, the land, her job and his; the usual, the facts, the way another gets by. But this kissing, he swam in it, he came to her, and she touched him and felt the earth in her fingers.

## *Chapter Two*
### *Spring 1995*

Angie had begun weaving feathers into her hair, and they hung down and spun as she talked, like nothing was unusual at all. She'd go off into telling stories about her friends, though they sounded all made up to Carver. But she was easier now with him, like someone else was there watching over her. When they sat on the porch, she seemed so comfortable, her legs stretched out and her feet crossed, resting on the railing. Carver ate over there each week, a function of being a bachelor, or a divorced man, he guessed, that was more accurate, and a skinny one at that. He supposed he always looked hungry these days, though he could do a mean barbecue himself when he was so moved and had the space to offer it.

This night at Mopstick's it would be nothing special, but he was grateful not to eat alone. He was trying to listen to Angie's prattle, that kind of teenage stuff he figured his own girl would be spouting to him at the drop of a hat, if they were able to be together. So he was attending to Angie's stories with half a mind, when she told him she had a special feather.

"Sure," Carver said, watching the sunset move through her words as they came to him.

"I'll show you," and she tossed all that shining hair to one side, let it flow like calm bright water down her right shoulder, and pulled out a feather she said she kept woven there, close to her scalp, under her hair on the left side.

She held it up at the end of its strand of gold, and blew it toward him. "I'm letting it fly a bit," she said in a serious tone.

"What's so special about this one?" Carver asked. "Duck probably, like those flocks quacking through my sleep when they fly to warmer weather. Or goose, like those making deposits of the greenest birdshit a fella can slide in when he's walking his date around the lake, hoping for a smooch in the moonlight." He looked at her then, and she looked right back like she didn't have a clue what he was saying.

"This feather has all the colors of this land and its peoples," she said.

"Do tell."

"No, Carver, look. Black night, white cloud. Brown earth, golden sun, red fire. Blue sky, green fields, blue water, red blood. And all the races on the earth. Black. White. Brown. Yellow. Red. See? In this feather, all peoples fly together, and all the earth, all the heavens, give them a home for their flying through space."

"Who told you this garbage, girl?"

"It's not garbage. And nobody told me. The feather told me. It flew to me and there it was, all the colors bright in the sunlight, flying on the breath of god."

"It's a pretty feather, nothing more, and God created it pretty because He can. Makes the girl ducks sit up and take notice, and paves the way to make more ducks to put on our table. It's a good system. Straightforward."

"No, Carver, it's flight. Black night, white cloud."

"All right, all right."

"Brown earth, golden sun—"

"Enough of this, Angie."

"—and red fire, Carver, red fire!"

"What are you talking about, girl? Do your parents hear you talk like this?"

"Red fire!" Angie yelled. Not the empty, sick heart of the tornado, she was thinking.

"Stop it, angel, stop it."

But she wouldn't. There in that moment, that quiet evening time on the porch before dinner was cooked and she would lay out once again those cheap dull plates, the ones that matched, at least, for company, she looked into the man's eyes and he saw hers were on fire, and in that moment she told Carver she would be free of him, without another word she said it. He was angry, and threw down his beer can, but he saw blazing in her eyes, red fire, and blazing in her cheeks, red blood.

She ran her fingers down the length of the feather and pushed it back over her shoulder, letting it fly in the wind, glinting red this side of the moon.

The next day Angie announced, "Mama, I'm going to the lake with William. We can bring something home for dinner on the way back." She stood framed by the doorway.

"Great. Go to Mario's. I feel like having some of that authentic-style pizza they keep bragging about."

"You look good today, Mama. You look sparkly."

"Star shower last night, you know."

"Star shower every night, then." She came in and bent down to where her mother was sitting, wrapped her arms around her and kissed her cheek, once, then many times, a stream of little explosions till Barb giggled, and the girl was happy.

"We won't be late," she whispered.

"I'm okay. Have a good time, honey," and Barb released the girl's grip and waved her away into the mid-afternoon sunshine and the clean smell of the day.

Angie jumped down all three steps and landed light. Her neighbor's blinds were closed but she noticed two slats rise up, probably Mrs. Gruber again. Always nosy. Just then the orange pickup rolled to the curb and William jumped out, lifted Angie up and spun around with her in the air until their laughter rang in the quiet streets.

Barb could hear it and was glad. Next door the two slats fell and knocked against the one below, and the blind swung toward the window and tapped there as the truck pulled away.

Barb pushed open the curtains to let in the day. She had been born in full sunlight, welcomed for the usual reasons. And as she grew, there was a certain pride her mother and father took in her, a pride they could not much let on to. Maybe it was because she knew things right off that other girls didn't understand.

As she grew up, it came to be that when she saw herself in the stream's mirror, or in the glare of the new silo, she turned away. She had once played there with the girl looking back at her, made faces and laughed to see them returned, through that transformation wrought by the haze of heat, the shine of metal, the shimmer of the waters. Then she grew taller than her rounded twin on the wall of the silo that was the path into the sky; up the beanstalk, she thought, and began to paint one on the side of the tower, the beginning of the dream of city she had read about.

She stared into the street as Angie and William drove off, and remembered then the first diagnosis, the first doctor saying, "This cancer may have been developing for decades, Barbara. We have to watch you carefully. New ones will come on more quickly." She remembered how his voice droned on, full of predictions, full of directions. "You too," he told her, "you must be on the lookout. You've got to watch for signs of recurrence on your skin. All over your body," she heard him say, then something like, "we'll hope to cut out any tumor as soon as we see it starting to develop."

And she imagined her body like Swiss cheese, everywhere there was pain a scalpel slicing away in its even circle, leaving emptiness there, darkness and silence, as at the center of her eyes, which watched the doctor pull out his prescription pad with each new diagnosis, and write out his call for surgery and three months more of radiation. He signed it at the bottom, in clear script, that first time. Each time he ripped a page from his pad, she knew he had nothing more to say to her, and she would rise to go.

She had heard the doctor's dry instructions, and tried to memorize them, like she would on an airplane in case of an emergency landing:

"Look over every bit of your skin, every blemish, every mole, every raised place. Any mark, jagged, asymmetrical. Black, brown, white, red. Especially black. Itchy. Bloody. Changing in size or shape. Whether it bothers you or not. This could save your life."

She heard him, but she couldn't do it.

Yet somehow, for a while anyway, she had won. The cancer in her skin had vanished, leaving only its scars, its battlefields. She would become a great story, cancer in remission. For that year, she was full of light, believing in longevity. Then she would learn that a new attack had begun elsewhere in her body, deep below the thin map of her skin.

But what if she had been able to look? What if she had watched for every change, probed her own body, front and back, even in the folds of her skin? Instead, she gave that half glance and told herself, I am too large and not pretty, I can't look. But I must go on, and go on she did, living outside that skin whenever she could. And now, when she understood what was at stake, it was too late. Lymphoma, they said. Non-Hodgkin's Lymphoma. Deep in her body. Rare, they said, to be attacked by a second kind of cancer, after battling the first. Rare, but perfectly, terribly, possible. She was proof.

It was this she blamed herself for. Because she could not look, she did not see. Lesion after lesion had weakened her, and she had turned her back. The treatments had broken her down, as well as the illness. Oh, but she remembered how her skin drank in the sun, how those days were some of the rare days she could look at herself, when her skin was brown and something of winter was burned off her face. Her eyes were bright back then, and she was able to dance, able to move through the crowds at the fair without feeling the lens on her of all who wandered there, when she was not so white and large, so visible. Instead, she was more like the night, her eyes piercing the darkness, and it was at that last fair she knew she could leave the farm, after the sun had kissed her and left her somehow smaller and lovelier, almost, she wanted to say, pretty, at least as long as she did not look.

What a day that was. That was when the sun had loved her.

At Lake of the Isles, Angie and William threw a blanket down on top of the earth slanting toward the lake. They faced a small island darkened by shadow but sitting in the midst of bright waters, with lines of ducks—mama ducks and babies behind them—ferrying to and fro in noisy voyage. Now that the couple was there at last, under a great tree in the afternoon, when he took her hand, she felt shy and pulled it back, and fumbled in her knapsack.

She said nothing, but could feel him waiting for a word. Then, "She was good today, William."

"Yes?"

"Yes. She was good, and just for today, I want to think of my mother as a normal mother. A healthy person, you know? Without feeling like she has a death sentence hanging over her."

"We all do, Angie, not a sentence, I mean, but we're all going to die."

"But it's close for her, it's always sitting at the table or something."

"I know. Drinking a beer. Eating a burger."

She gave his shoulder a smack. "I'm not kidding, William. Don't exasperate me."

"Not my plan."

"All right, then."

'I know what you mean, death is present. Part of life. The leaves falling, the trees budding. Even when it's not with us in a way we can see, it's down the street, in the next house."

"I know, but it's been with us for so long. So many scares. I wish it would go visit someone else."

"You don't mean that."

"Not that I wish someone else would get sick or die, I don't."

"Your mother's one of the most beautiful people I know. Maybe it's because of how close death has been to her."

"Okay, Counselor William, I hear what you're saying, but I'm tired of it."

"And I hear what you're saying, but I am so happy to be sitting at this lake with you, under the sun, with a great big basket of Auntie's fried chicken." He reached for the basket, but Angie put her hand on his, and they fell into a different world, palm to palm, exploring each finger, each line.

Angie pressed her mouth to his, and he was warm, very warm, and soft, and he kissed her, and whispered, "Sweet, oh, you are sweet," and came to kiss her again, and it was then that she closed her eyes, and a tall shadow standing to one side of their blanket was crushed into a thin dark line.

"Off to the damn lake all the time, off to the lake. What the hell does that mean? And do her folks even know if that's where they really go?" Carver smacked his hand on the night table. "They could be in a motel room for all anyone knows. It's one thing to trust your own kid but how are you going to trust someone else's? And does this boy even have a father? We all know what happens to a boy who grows up without a father."

"Leave it alone," Mary said, already regretting that she'd been pulled back to him.

"And he's an Indian. The boy's an Indian."

"Well, what difference does that make?"

"Look, Mary, when you don't know what you're talking about, you should just shut up."

"Fine, Carver, fine, but isn't Angie part Indian herself? Remember, Mop's grandmother is Indian, so then he is part, so then his daughter is part. Biology, Carver. Genetics."

"That's hooey. Look at Angie, just look at her. She's pure white."

"Sorry, Carver, a person's heritage doesn't disappear. It stays inside you, and passes down through the generations, and shows up one way or another, sooner or later."

"Look, did you come here to give me a biology lesson? I don't want to hear your dumb theories."

"It's not a dumb theory, Carver. It's science."

He took the last few sips of his beer, then exchanged the empty for a fresh one out of the styrofoam cooler at the side of the bed. He popped open the full one and drank long sips.

"Why'd you come here, Mary? I've got to be getting over to Mopstick's for dinner." He put down his beer and brushed something off the palms of his hands. "They keep me fed pretty well," he added, "and they'll be expecting me as usual. Every Thursday, you know, it's a bet."

"I was worried about you."

"Oh, you were worried about me."

"That's what I said. Wasn't I clear?"

"Don't push it, Mary."

"Fine."

"Besides, I know why you came here. Your real reason."

"And what would that be?"

"Well, come over here and I'll tell you."

She got up from the stiff wooden chair and stood in front of Carver.

"You came for your biology lesson, and you know I'm the one who can give it to you," the man said. He looked up and put his arms around her hips, then threw her down onto the bed.

"Get ready for some learning," he whispered low, and she closed her eyes, thinking that she should leave, but it was too late.

They slept for a while, the blanket pulled up around their necks although the heat was on full blast. Mary woke and sat up, the rough cloth slipping down. Carver opened his eyes and reached for her, cupping a hand over each breast. He straddled her and leaned in close. "Milk and moonlight," he said, "so many good things are white," and her face went pale as what he did then hurt her.

When they woke again, he looked at her and was silent. He grabbed the sheet fallen to the floor and threw it over her. "Here, cover yourself," he said. He rose from the bed and stood by her for a moment as she arranged the sheet around her breasts. In a flat voice he said, "I got to get out of here," and headed for the shower as she sat very still, with her eyes closed.

"You better get dressed," came his voice from the thick steam in the bathroom. "Come back when you have that thirst for knowledge again."

She swore she wouldn't, and was gone before he walked out dripping onto the stained carpet. He looked around the room as if someone were hiding from him, and caught a glimpse of his naked, wet body in the dresser mirror. Still strong, he thought, still on the young side.

Mary began to play games with them all. She waited for them to see her scars. Then she tried out stories. They seemed to like the ones where she had fallen under a tractor as a kid. They pointed to the teeth of the gears. "I can see it," said one, a dark-haired man from Mexico. He didn't care, she supposed. He made tender love to her. He even caressed the scars, traced them with the edge of his palm like a game

70

that brought him closer to the finish line. But then he left. Disappeared. She got a postcard saying he had gone home, where he belonged. He sent her a kiss, he said. She kept it.

In general, the men she dated preferred machinery as the cause of her scars. Car accidents were second. One man she told the truth. He recoiled. "Your father did that? He beat you like that?"

"Didn't yours ever beat you?"

"Well, sure, but not like that. What else did he do to you?"

She couldn't help but make up a story, the one he wanted to hear, she thought. He got out of bed. He left and didn't call her again. She hadn't liked him much, but his arms were smooth, and he tasted sweet. She knew she had to stop, but she wasn't sure why. They never seemed ashamed of anything. She wanted to learn how to be that way. She never knew a woman who could tell her how.

The next time, when she drank, she didn't care what happened. The man kept buying her drinks and she knew why. It wasn't until she was in his car, pinned beneath him in the back seat, that she wanted out. She didn't know where she was. He felt good at first. But then she understood how he touched her, like a machine. She tried to use her mouth, but he turned her over and then it was too late.

He got back into the driver's seat and drove her to her car.

She hoped no one saw her fumbling with her keys at the car door. She used to hope for more.

She missed the earth of Carver; she missed the swim toward him. She thought he had buried his heart. She thought hers was drowning.

## *Chapter Three*

*Summer 1995*

The sound of the falls got louder. Angie stepped toward it. She heard Barb's voice in it, she heard her calling like the wind above the water. A deer watched her. His doe was dead, shot by hunters. But she was only a girl stepping over the rocks, carrying nothing in her hands. Her hair held the light but night was falling, and the deer caught the darkness and ran, spreading it out behind his step and disappearing into it.

She came here with the boy, with William. She let his hands touch her deeply for the first time, and she touched him. It was lovely, full of stars, the falls never stopping, the green earth breathing with them, the old storm sleeping through the late afternoon hours. The way the falls never stopped, that's how she would be with him. She would fall into him, and rise at the same time, become liquid and then breath and then night.

She would not let him go further; he would not try. As the first people found each other by the water, as first girl, first boy, they moved their hungry hands everywhere. They gave each other visions. They were all breath. They were the ocean neither had ever seen. They were the waves. They became water falling into water from a great height, and the cries of their passion drifted into the sky. They became deep stillness, below bird cries, far off.

They had already told each other of their love. There was nothing else to be said right then.

Barb stirred at some sound far away and awoke, though she kept her eyes shut as the darkness kept spinning. She reached for the water glass on the night table, and tried to raise it to her lips, but her hand shook and she spilled most of it down the front of her nightgown. It was cold as dawn but it stilled her dizziness, and she sat up and ran her hands over the wet flannel that covered her breasts, and smiled a bit at the moment of excitement in her sick body.

She got up slow and heavy to start the cooking. Mopstick said he'd do it since he was bringing his friend Carver along, but she knew it would please him to see her up and about.

They sat at the table. Angie was out with William and so it was just the three of them in the cramped dining room, with a sprig of fresh flowers in the center of the table, and the plates still empty. The beer mugs Barb had set out were glowing in the amber wash of sunset, until the blood bolt of the sun fell below the horizon.

Mopstick went out to the kitchen to fuss with the pots. They were heavy and Barb was weak from the chemo. He knew it from her trembling hands. She looked at her guest, who shifted his weight back in his chair and moved his eyes away from her to study his beer. She could not be silent as she thought he wished. It was easier when other friends stopped by; there was always something to talk about. There was nothing this man had ever said or done that made Barb feel like he wanted to know her, but this was the man who was able, somehow, to pull her husband from his vigil by her side when he needed to be away from her sickbed. She wanted to thank him, though it made her blood cold to look at him and to sense the walls he had raised, there in her dining room, all around himself.

She blurted out his name, "Carver," and then, "who are you, Carver?" He looked stunned and put the mug down. She thought, somehow, although Mopstick was a few steps away in the kitchen, that his friend was going to strike her. But he gazed at her, for the first time dead in the face, and turned away as if he couldn't even look at her, and then back, as if he needed to prove he could.

"I'm a damn farmer," he said, "and I'm the victim of a robbery. They stole my land from me, but I'm still a farmer. What else do you want to know?"

She could feel the pain eating at her and struggled to disconnect from it, so that she could answer him before Mopstick came back in. "I want to know who you are, not what you used to be, or what you used to own. You're a friend to my husband and I thank you for that, but I wonder who you are in your heart, and how you brought comfort to my August."

After a moment, his voice spilled into the air all around her, first low and full of breath, then slicing at her, saying, "How would you expect to understand who I am? I'm a man. And I owned my land. I am a man who was surrounded by beauty, grew up with it and ate from it. Drew a living from it. How would you understand?"

It was then Mopstick came through the doorway, the light from the kitchen swinging into the room even as the darkness settled in from the window. He looked at Carver, who mumbled a low, "Sorry, Barb," and got up to take some of the burden from Mopstick's hands and place the large bowls on the trivets waiting with their straw daisies to hold the heaviness of the meal.

"I just wanted to know a little something about you," the woman said, "that's all," and she looked at her husband, who patted her hand and began to pass the food around.

"Carver's got a rough situation," Mopstick said with a nod at his friend, "but he's making a good life here in the Cities until he can work it out and go home to his land. You didn't mean to get so upset, did you, Carver?"

"No, I didn't," Carver said. His heart gave an extra beat then, and he coughed, and picked up the bowl of rice to serve himself.

There was silence through much of the meal, along with the ring of utensils, the pouring of juice and water and beer. Carver stared through the window, then down into his food. "Autumn Wheat," he was sure it said on back of the cheap plates, from the Family Value Center on Lake Street, he bet, the wheat that farmers call spring by its planting time. Never a good piece of china on this table. Nothing from generations past, nothing handed down that must be kept, valued and honored. All of it gone and this is what you get, he thought, a cartoon of the wheat that comes to harvest late summer, that raises a soft ocean to flow its sacrifice into the claws of the thresher without a cry. Just that ghost of a wind, that hushed severing, that silent clatter as the straw falls to mounds along the curve of the earth.

He saw that hard slice between dark earth and bright sky, and Kate walking up the hill in her white dress with her shoulders bare, like she was flowing through the grass—stark against the last green of summer before the cold burnt it to brown embers in their bare dance. He kept watching her move up the hill like a root of light pulled up from earth until she stood silhouetted against the sky, pale above her and flushed red at her feet.

He rose from the seat of the combine and jumped into the ocean of wheat. She was there above him, her white dress flowing about her in the rising winds, her arms lifting up to pull the pins from her hair, and then she shook her head and all the flaxen fall of it under the last rays of the sun began to glow. She bent over from her waist and shook her hair again, and he could sense its wind and its teasing touch across his chest as he lay there looking up at her. Even now, he held himself in that moment and knew it to be the blessing of beauty he deserved and had been waiting for, always, waiting to lie there at its feet, this beauty that was his, this dance of flesh and hair and light.

This was the moment to live in, to never leave. He wanted always to lie beneath the flow of the white garment, but it was not to be so this night in the city. His yearning for the past made him look up at the very moment Angie could be seen on the porch through the window, as she came up on her toes to kiss the boy, a long-haired Indian boy, who bent down to her and put his arms around her. There they stood, for the whole world to see, and her own parents with their backs to the window, blind to the dangers, Mopstick holding out a platter and offering, "More corn? More meatloaf or potatoes, Carver?"

"No," he said, "I'm done. I'm done with it."

The supper dishes had to be cleared. Barb was doing what she could, Carver supposed, and Mopstick, qualifying once again for the title of Good Samaritan, was doing most of the work. Carver knew the woman was sick but he couldn't help thinking, What a shame, again this man finds himself doing the work of the woman, who is big-handed and wide-hipped, and somehow must have strength enough in all that body of hers to clear away a few dishes from the table.

They left Carver alone for a few minutes, and he settled his eyes on that old photo of them, taken before she'd gotten so fat. Before her illness, and before years of labor had pared her husband down to a stick to be burned with sorrow. He was dark, then. Darker than Carver had realized. He was so pale now with not sleeping, so wasted with worry.

Since she'd stopped working again, Mopstick made it a habit to sit at her bedside in the blazing afternoon as soon as he came home from his early shift. The sounds of children playing outside were muffled by the heavy curtains made gray by the sun, and by the lack of a woman's care to launder and brighten them, to bring back the blue of wildflower. Carver hated those old curtains that blocked out the movement of the day. He saw Mopstick bury himself in that damn sickroom even though he'd brought him a girl, one of many who would sit with him in the moonlight and stroke him until he came into her like God would have it. But it didn't seem to have made a difference. Mopstick kept sitting on the hard chair by Barb's side of the bed, smoothing back the tufts of hair and holding her hand like it was a live bird struggling to breathe, or to fly away.

The girl did the same, each afternoon, he figured. Imagine it, this girl of light burying herself in that dark room, and singing to that old buffalo. My angel, thought Carver, having to lean over her old lady's foul breath and sing her back to life. I should have thought of some excuse the last time I saw it and grabbed her out of there, given her a break. But the song had stopped him, and the curve of her body, that perfect back and her arms like a dancer's enclosing the woman in beauty, had made him stop in his tracks outside the room.

Tonight it was Mopstick who went upstairs with Barb to sit with her, and he was matchstick-broken without a voice to sing to her.

"Let her rest, old man," Carver told Mopstick, and tried to pull him out of there where Barb had fallen asleep and was breathing hard and anguished. "There's not a damn thing you can do about it now."

The man looked at Carver, for the first time with a kind of hatred, a kind of knowledge in his eyes, and got up and walked him out without a word.

"Where's the girl?" his friend asked him then. "She should come downstairs and say goodnight."

Mopstick looked at Carver again and shrugged his answer.

What's chewing on his ass? Carver thought, and turned to leave. Let him have the darkness of that woman, he kept thinking all the way to the bar.

And August lay down beside Barb and ran his hands over her back and her shoulders and dreamt there in the heaviness of her breath. "Oh how the body eats itself," the husband heard a voice say. How the days consume her and the nights rebuild her as young and strong, the dream whispered as it ran through him. He could see it, how sickness feasted on her. But he had eaten from her, and Angie had; they had used every part of her to grow strong, to make family: her arms, wrapped around them like armor; her song, drink; her breast, food for both of their hungers;

her body, blanket. Her fierce heart, a weapon, and oh lord they needed it when the lines shut down and the strikes emptied even the broken cup in the cupboard of stray change; or when Angie was sick, in desperate fever and nightmare flight, and the doctor would not come through the blizzard, not for the promises of the poor.

And Barb's warm kiss? That was the fire, keeping them through seasons of ice.

Now the lymphocytes were devouring her, pale and formless themselves, hungry for the warmth of her flesh, for the brilliance of red ribbons she tied in her angel's hair, and green crayons she left with a pad of drawing paper for the girl to make the land fertile and rich as the old farms they used to visit. Now, each night, the wild and willful multiplication of cells in the body that lay next to him gave birth to unnatural generations that set up their colonies all along the flow of lymph.

In his sleep, he could hear the skin consumed layer by layer, the gnawing at organ and bone, and saw in the darkness how tumors were all that flourished, how they raised themselves upon the buzz of devouring, and left the emptiness growing in her eyes as she moved away from him.

"Oh demon," he called out, startled to see the doctor lay Barb down in a deep furrow of earth, and, before he covered her, raise a hasty fence around her with crooked saplings tied together, beheaded of their foliage and their reach into the bluest air. On each post was stabbed the head, or even the whole body, of a creature Mopstick hadn't seen since childhood, or hadn't ever seen: wild pigeon, lark and plover, beaver, otter, marten, lynx. He tried to go to her but it was Carver then who said, "No, Mop, this is not your land," and all the strength in his body could not push past this voice, and this fence of animal head and bird impaled, to kneel at the furrow that seemed to sink deeper into the earth, with Barb disappearing into it.

"Go off from there, Barb," he urged low, "rise from the fields," and his voice rose with his plea, and he pounded his chest with the agony of her lying there in the earth and stillness. And Carver beckoned to him, smoke and music rising toward Mopstick, but there was rage in his fists, and he struck at the air as the earth began to fly into its own mouth and cover Barb where she might lie and flower forever.

Then he dropped his fists, and "Oh," he begged, "let me go there with her," and she woke and shook him, but he knew that dream would be where he would lie with her for a long time, and her strength crumpled as he held her and stroked her face, glistening with tears in the moonlight.

"August," she called him then, and the heat of late summer came into them both and they found their way.

## *Chapter Four*
### *Fall 1995*

A month of Thursdays later, Carver had dinner with Mopstick and Barb again. William dropped Angie off in time for the meal, and she brought some cookies in with her. Had to be ones that boy's aunt made herself, Carver thought. "These are pretty good," he admitted at the table, while Angie poured some coffee into the cup set before him.

This week he made sure he had some time alone with the girl. He had plenty to say to her, and he figured it was time she listened. He needed to talk with her about their secret, and make sure she kept it. He was about finished when Mopstick came out on the porch to remind her the next day was a school day.

"It's getting late," Mopstick said after Angie had nodded her goodnight to Carver and the screen door had flown shut.

Carver rose from the porch swing and picked up his beer. "Good night, old man. I'm leaving you with the women."

"Go easy, Carver," his host said, and patted his shoulder.

Carver wasn't sure where he was going. He just drove up and down the wide one-way streets past their darkening houses, listening to the arms of the wipers fly across the sudden raindrops. Maybe that whole bunch has taken up way too much of my time, he considered. The old man doesn't get it. He's got to face it. Barb was a mistake. Even God, forgive me, makes mistakes, or maybe experiments. Experiments to see which creatures will survive and which ones won't. Maybe He was trying out his infinite gifts in the art of creation. To see how far from the perfection of Adam and Eve, how far from the Garden and the beauty of all things, He could go before He created something that just shouldn't be.

"Ha!" Carver yelled out, and slapped the steering wheel, "that's it!" Maybe we need this kind of ugliness, he thought, to make us appreciate what we've got. Or to work out the jealousies in this life that such women without comeliness are sure to have. Maybe we've got to grow strong enough to keep this ugliness out of our lives. A test of our strength, of our will power, since sometimes we've got to work hard to push away what's not healthy, especially when we feel sorry for it, sorry in our soft hearts.

Such ugliness she possesses, enough to make any man turn away from her. He stopped at the light. And such weakness, now, he thought.

"Here it seems clear—" he said out loud, and looked up to see a woman in a red car staring in at him. She floored it when the green popped back up, while he sat, no one behind him, and formulated his ideas as he would declare them to his boss at the station. Hansen would always listen to Carver.

"She got sick not as a punishment," Carver would tell the man that next afternoon, "—she is, after all, one of God's creatures—but so He could take her home. With His great mercy, take her from this plane of existence where she could never be anything more than a deformation of what God in His best moments has created. She's got to know that, and take the death that's coming as a comfort.

"It's a bad thing for Angie to be around. It warps her. It brings her to darkness." Carver pointed at Hansen. "I can see that with this boy she's been running around with, this William kid. Indian, maybe mixed, God only knows. Not a thing in it for her. Can't imagine him touching her. This girl is my angel, like my own daughter," he said, "and this isn't right."

Hansen grabbed his jacket. "I got to get on home," he said. "Family business, you know," and he left Carver still thinking about the night before.

She was his angel from the moment he saw her, he knew that. His girl, the one he had grabbed out of the ferocity of wind that God had sent down to test him. His girl, and he would watch over her. Like the man he was, nothing to gain from it. Just him and his little girl, holding secrets between them.

They had talked on the porch last night, Barb asleep inside, sick as all get out, and this dog-tired husband up there watching over her. Carver had called to Angie to bring him a beer, and when she did, he sat her down to talk. Long overdue. Whispering in the night.

"Angie," he said to her, "not a good thing in this world could come out of telling the truth of that afternoon, that fury of storm that sent you to me. That brought you to my room and to that dress I put on you." He remembered how, like the breath of heaven, it floated around her, pure and unworn even by his own stolen girl.

"Shh," he told her then, when she began to speak, but she kept right on.

"I have to tell," she said, like a little girl still, though she was already fifteen. "My mother asks me, over and over, as if my answer could make her well again, 'Where'd the dress come from, Angie?' She says, 'I'm not going to live forever, Angie. It's been eating at me since that night, when your father ran through the streets calling your name. Since that night you came back to us from out of the tornado.'"

The girl was silent for a while, and Carver let it be.

"I never said no to my mama about anything else," Angie said. "You've got to realize that."

"You're God's creature, Angie, not your mama's," he whispered. "God's bigger than that, and you can see you don't bear any resemblance to her at all, but to sunlight and lake water and the silver moon." He touched her cheek.

She started to cry then. Like truth slapped her.

"I got to tell my mama," again she said.

But he'd shown her why she couldn't, laying it all out like a map.

As Carver explained things to Angie, he glanced up from time to time at the bedroom window beneath which Barb was asleep, blind to what was going on in her own house. Angie stopped crying when she saw it, when she understood what he meant, and the moon lit up his words like something blessed traveling through the air that she must inhale.

She'll never tell, he thought on his ride home. "Why would she?" he whispered above the steering wheel, as the light turned red again.

# *Chapter Five*

The wedding photograph at her bedside was to stand among the cluster of photos that were guardian and reminder, door to her past and link to those still alive. It was part of the movie of a life Barb floated in and out of, with pain driving her sometimes to the edge of her flesh. It was in the tender rocking of her August, her light, who climbed up to the sick bed and lay there with her, holding her, remembering her, that the cloth of her future unraveled. Then arm in arm they stood within the thrift store frame, golden to the eye. His smile awkward but true. Her eyes heavy lidded with the rare plum shadow and blackest mascara. A light all around them, as if they posed in some Hollywood pavilion. His body was thin as ever, dark cloth limp around the hard skeleton he was; eyes unused to the world without his thick glasses; his hand open, palm up, with Barb's ringed hand resting there, unused to anything much but work.

This photo took much looking. Barb watched it every day, as if to discover signs of the changes growing within her. She remembered slipping into the pale suit that day, how the zipper slid up and the buttons fit snug, but just so. Even her breasts pleased her in that suit, pushing against the top of the white fabric, the pendant August had given her falling into the cleavage the new bra would offer to his hands that night, to his mouth, to his tongue.

She remembered, and lived some days in no other place, but in this frame of light, in this white suit with its magical shiny buttons, in this dream of the shedding of cloth; in his hands. She lived in all the precious moments of her wedding day that led up to her nakedness in the kindest room she had ever known. She went over the ceremony, with all their friends in attendance as if she were a princess; wild roses and violets everywhere, the dancing, the flash of the cameras, the bite of champagne and the reasons for being intoxicated. She had imagined herself at the altar in her housedress, or in her factory clothes, or her stockgirl smock, but no, Frannie wouldn't have it, and would work day and night on the old white suit, making sure it fit, and sewing into the fabric countless tiny mirrors. On that day, when Barb did a fast dance with August, shooting stars blazed from one side of the room to the other, and Frannie knew she was no stockgirl, but an artist.

Today Barb lay flat on her back and looked about the room, watching the shadows play their dreams of life on the wall. She looked down at her hands propped limp and rubbery on her chest. Here was her fate, the thread that tied her to the world: her hands. Hands that fed. Hands that had killed, for nourishment, for a living.

When she arrived in the Cities, child of the farms, she knew that her hands would provide. When she entered the hub of coming and going, at the place where the wheat sat in stillness before it traveled its shimmering dust throughout the expanse of the nation, she knew there would be others who would take her on to work. Always. She had no fear about that. Her big hands were golden; her modesty was practical. Her flight from the farm would be money in the bank for her bosses. She would become girl-on-the-assembly line, selling her strength, graceless in her factory smock, to make the only offerings she could: labor and obedience.

The gods of labor watched over Barb and her like, put them to task, each in their place according to some divine scheme.

Lesser gods oversaw each change of shift: seven a.m.; three p.m.; eleven in the dark. And overtime. Double shifts, as necessary.

Till the holy layoff. The blessed unemployment insurance. The purgatory before the hire back.

All as decreed by the headman, or the two-headed God of Work and War, and overseen by the God of the Assembly Line, many-armed, bent to the moving prayer, and like all that is divine, split and multiplied, and taking possession in the bodies of the workers watching the road move away from them.

And so Barb entered the world of manufacturing, and stood by yet another row of that which would feed the world, but this line was moving while she stood still. She fit her large and awkward body into its new place, as the economy hummed its way down the line to be born and reborn into the world beyond the factory. For all the hours of her shift, the line sped toward her and fled from her, and she moved her big hands, her rough loving hands, and placed pins and turned screws and inserted parts and gave each new being a gentle tap and sent it on its way. But what was Barb creating at her spot on the line?

Barb, gentle with her big hands, giving from her body and letting the power of it flow away from her to the farthest reaches of the planet, adjusted and tapped, and fine tuned, perhaps the foreman would say, fine tuned death.

And death rolled down the line and was born to its journey as a new thing to be sold, a cluster of death.

Barb was making cluster bombs, or as those on more intimate terms called them—bombies, but no matter how hard she and the others worked, no matter with what precision, there was a bit of a quality control problem. The errant bombies, these fussed over duds, would remain sleeping in their furrows of earth, until struck by a hoe to prepare the soil for planting, and plant it did, all manner of parts of farmer, irrigated by blood.

Work is war. Barb learned that all over again on the line, under the sting of the boss's comments each time she slowed down, as what entered her were the afterwards, the stories she was helping to spin in the very faraway.

Perhaps it was good for her to learn the world, to see beyond the eternal cycle of seed and water and harvest and farewells to the tonnage of crops. She had already shoved her hands into the work of making the good bread. How lovely for her, but she was the one who'd left the land, turned her broad back on it, and run away dreaming.

Then the Cities taught her this: a girl without land, a girl with strong body and clumsy step, a girl with love in her heart and the unformed clay of her face, is a girl for the line, a working heart, a stander. Stand over your children, the foreman urged, their shiny clustered faces that reflect back your own. Keep the line going, and send them out into the world.

Boom! they will celebrate.

Learn this now, Barbara, something told her, you are growing death, and it is good, it is the work of a great nation, and the children who pick up these toys may not perish after all—don't worry so much—but will live with you in their awkwardness, hands without grace as they claw for balance, one-legged, scarred, blind. They will live with you forever, just as what you deserted, the fragrant land and your place there, will stay with you too.

And the clusters of death, looking at Barb with each shiny eye, winked and thanked her for their birth, as she thanked them when she realized that her labor was freed from the land, and could exult in this: now freed, she could come and go and make her money any way she could find. She was not bound to her acreage, but to the whole damn story, the story of a continent, sea to sea, with its great reach of water and light and metal suspended like a caul over the face of the earth.

To birth death was honorable, her bosses tried to tell her, and she was the one to do it, graceless and alone, they said behind her back. And poor, mind you, poor, without the skill to do anything else but coax life out of a seed till it reached into the shining air.

Barb gasped now in her sleep, and woke and swore she could not breathe, and would never breathe easy again, and went back to watching the shadows, her companions, that stood by her and watched over her. And she remembered, as her eyes swept over her wedding photograph, that out of the dancing line of death, where hands with earth in their furrows became the same large hands with blood in the furrows, came life: a tale of love and family and perseverance, and the little decisions of courage.

There, over the line, or was it in the break room, or the parking lot as Barb climbed into her old beater, appeared her counterpart, and then, like a dream of rivers, they flowed to each other, caught perhaps by the eyes, each of the other, the very large eyes that took in the land around them and opened the house of the skull for it all to spin there: the earth and its harvest, the forest and its timber lost to rows of cabins and weekend woodshops, the multiplication of cow paths into highways, the beating of hooves into the rolling of tires, the gape of open pit mines speckled by great trees that appear as blades of grass to the naked eye above, and, of course, the northern lights. Maybe that was it, what they each saw, there in the eyes of their counterpart, beneath the magnification of thick crooked eyeglasses—the northern lights, the heavenly nod, the trace of the fleeing cosmos, the expanse above that mirrored the expanse below, the light (she came to believe), the light! They each saw the light of heaven in the eyes of the other, and moved to its source and found their twin, their poor, pitted mound of clay, their very own.

"Hello," they said to the milky light, "hello there."

But even this romance could not bury the clusters of eyes sent to watch over the business of maiming and death in the foreign lands of Laos, Lebanon, Somalia, and someday, Iraq and Gaza and Afghanistan. Well, the list is quite long, but so is the lifespan of a bombie, as Barb came to understand. Her own good Finnish roots said, "Hard worker you may be, but out of this work must come your new name, if you claim it—girl from the farm who seeds the earth with death."

"Claim it, Barb," said the rent paid and the fridge full and the new car a-coming, but there she was, too plain to say no to knowledge, and when each week they came with flyers and shouts on their vigils, with candles and pictures, a woman with new eyes was Barb. She saw, then, the world in black and white newsprint and the exploding children in color; and the ugliness the cluster bombs sowed, after tumbling off the assembly line, sat on her heart and clawed at her throat.

So she picked up her small paper bag of things: an extra sweater, salted crackers and a jar of peanut butter, packets of Cup O' Soup, and the thick pads she would bleed into each month whether she worked at war or at peace. Then she punched out and tore up her card. "Remove me from the book," she shouted over her left shoulder and the tatters of her timecard, "I'm going to stand on the line outside, confess my sins in my own heart, and begin my penance in the good winter air."

She put on her old coat and her gloves—wool with patches of phony suede that let her big hands rest in the darkness inside the cloth—and went to stand in the cold of the January demonstration, as the group outside the Honeywell plant parted to make a space for her, and handed her a makeshift sign on a splintered wooden pole. She thrust it high into the world, and breathed there, air in and chanting out, and stood proud to abandon these crops, the shiny-eyed cluster bombs that kept rolling down the line past her replacement, who turned and tapped, but lazy-eyed as she listened to the chanting, missed a few.

Barb was arrested that day, and this would go into her permanent record, they told her, and she would spend some weeks dazed by her own rash action, a disappointment to those who knew her by her place on the assembly line. But when she stepped out, away from the shadow world of TV and snow-covered silence, she found, like the good worker she was, a dozen places ready to use her hard, pay her less, and keep her in the back of the store, away from the gaze of customers, where she could fold, do inventory, and push the great cart of sweaters and pants and shoes and gloves, that lay in piles without hands and feet, without faces, and without eyes.

And so Barb kept working, giving shoppers an occasional glimpse as she passed by the open eye at the end of each row, pushing the heaped high cart with the clothing tried and rejected and ready to be put back in place, and once a week or so holding up a dress and checking the color against her skin in the long glare of mirror set into the wall between lamps and extension cords.

*Bride*, the magazine was called, and Barb laughed when Frannie handed it to her. She saw the white gush of fabric, the flow of headdress over the white shoulders of the soon-to-be-married, and the sparkle of something in the cloth, something radiant beyond stars, like water in crystal, like moonrock.

She would have the brassy clank of the 'Just Married' cans tied in streamers to the back of August's old car, and she was happy to go off with him, happy with his gentleness and his deep brown eyes, and the way his glasses slid down his nose in the heat, or when he was leaning to fix something, or to kiss her. She was happy, and let the pages of the magazine blow one by one, a slow film of poses amid flowers and mountainous cascades of white chiffon accenting the perfect delicate frames of the models and their clear blue eyes and etched red lips. Their something blue was not the sky. Their something borrowed was not beauty; that was their own, a kind of birthright, an eternal posture. What was new for them was not the love of a man, but the things their fathers and mothers had bought for their wedding.

Hidden on these brides were the perfect garters, lacy or velvet, under the armfuls of fabric, encircling each strong sculpted left leg. What was hidden of Barb would have to be revealed that first night, though she prayed for dim light in the honeymoon room; she prayed for that darkness, that complete blackness where she could exist as pure love, as openness, as jagged soul meeting its heart in the flesh. She prayed for the kindness of black night, and for August's brilliant vision to see her in truth, to take her in all her ugliness, the word she hated, the word that was her name, but oh, how she yearned for the beauty she suspected in her soul to rise up and be made flesh.

"Barb! You still in town?" Frannie joked, waving an arsenal of lipsticks at her. "I guess that's the way it is with you brides. Dreaming most of the time. Fluttering down the aisle with your train held up by a hundred hummingbirds, or one good friend. Living the fantasy before diapers and housework brings you back to us. Come on, woman! Speak to me!"

"Okay, Frannie, okay. Just thinking about the practical stuff."

"Sure."

"Like what the heck to wear." She shut the magazine and looked at her friend. "The white suit will have to do. Money's short." At least, the jacket fit around her waist and showed her curves; the skirt lay a bit above the heaviness of her calves, the solid scarred knees, but hinted at the warmth of her thighs she knew August desired. She fanned herself with the slick pages in the June humidity, in the flush of light sweat and beginning raw sun jabbing at her skin through the treetops. Frannie grabbed the magazine, impatient with her, and went to the pictures in the centerfold of brides around the world. Full page, it was, a bride from India, and Barb gasped.

"Have you ever seen anyone so beautiful," her friend prodded, and Barb too was stunned. The jewel in the woman's sculpted flaring nose was a ruby, blood red, connected to her left ear by a dangling swing of silver that streamed down from the proud nostril and up to the heavy, fragrant (Barb was sure of it) earlobe, pulsing river of light from one sense to the other. The chain from piercing to piercing grazed the sensual lips and flowed past the tongue hidden there, the bold instrument that would follow countless and even unknown pathways of sensation over the lips and body of the betrothed. The woman's eyes were lined with kohl, lined with knowledge, and the caption talked about the centuries old use of this charcoal, its deep blackness swirling around the woman's vision. One hand was raised, to show how it was decorated with henna, and Barb tried to follow the intricate patterns into the bride's beauty, into the way she was seen and loved, but got lost in the creases of her palm, not sure what was paint and what was her lifeline, her heartline. Her other hand lay palm down on the table in front of her, fingers spread into a fan, with great rings chaining one finger to the other, touch chained to touch, by silver, by light, by unbreakable passion. Barb saw the long red nails, the dark, unblinking eyes. She longed for the indisputable beauty of the woman caught there.

"Frannie," she turned to her friend, "you going to help me fix the hem on my suit or not?"

"Sure, Barb, sure," and pulled herself away from the kohl-lined eyes of the East Indian bride, and grabbed the fat apple of pin cushion, pulled a pin out and brandished it at her friend, the bride-to-be, who laughed and went to the closet to get the suit from the dry cleaner's plastic bag.

"And anyway," Barb called out over her shoulder, "why should a dress be the center of the wedding day?" Under the eyes of the moon, she knew, it would be tossed to the ground, forgotten by passion. She unfurled the suit in its see-through cover onto the bed, lifted the plastic and stroked the cloth.

Now she lay in bed, the four walls repeating the stories of each day past, and studied the stains and cracks snaking down from the corners of the room, the lingering news of storms. The walls, her familiars, were at last coming forth after years of hiding their true solidity, and saying, Yes, we are here. We surround you. We cannot be broken. Only by the great lightning strike, the whirlpool of wind, the crash of meteor, will the groan of collapse take us down. Only by the whisper of time.

Or the chant of illness.

She heard everything, and saw the walls begin to fall toward each other, a moment at a time, until all directions met above her, and something like a tent hovered there and warmed her, and whispered a language she did not yet understand, and there in the house made of wall and of shadow, she remembered the flash of light she was at her wedding, and danced into it.

# *Chapter Six*

Angie looked into the mirror at the vanity table in the corner of her room. When her folks had bought it for her, she'd wondered at it, thought it a plaything, and sat there from time to time with Barb's eyeliner to paint a merry pirate's moustache over her small pink mouth, or with blush for great circles of clown red at her cheeks, to make her mama laugh, but never had she thought of the mirror as something that could tell her stories of herself.

But now she came to it, an awkward girl with questions. She looked into it, as into a murky lake, wanting to discover what was at the bottom. She saw herself, the same face, the same searching eyes she used to scan the night sky for stars, and check her mother's face to see if she was hiding her pain. The same eyes that would divine her father's mood, and help her decide if he needed cheering up, or simple quiet. They were the same eyes she'd always had, she thought, so why did everything look different?

She stood, and for the first time watched herself as she did, walked away from the mirror and walked back to it, noticed how her small hips moved, a definite dance she had not noticed before. This is stupid, she thought, her face flushed, and threw herself down on the bed to stare at the ceiling and its familiar rivers of cracks, its stains where the leaks let in small threads of storm.

But then the mirror called her back. Her new body pushed her. Go, see yourself, you are different now, you are not a child, and she sighed and put her legs over the side of the bed and looked down at her toes, the traces of iridescent polish shining like opals. Ninety-nine cents, she smiled, for ten jewels at my feet. She looked up, and the mirror, unfolding its three panels to embrace her reflection, made her rise with its emptiness, as it waited for her, as it had done every day since they had brought it home and pulled it with care out of the heavy paper tied over it. She undid her shirt, an old one of her dad's, and stepped out of her jeans. For the first time, she undid the fastener on her bra and tossed it on the floor, slipped her panties down to her feet and kicked them away, and looked up into the mirror. She stood there for some time, and studied what was before her. She saw a stranger, and wanted to know her. She touched her breasts and was frightened at what she felt then. She didn't remember when she had stopped being a child, she was always so loved as one, always given arms to run to and a lap to sit on, and told stories of a magical little girl, a lot like Angie herself.

87

She took a deep breath, and looked at her hands, her fingers. She ran them down her body, over her thighs and then between them, and the pleasure in her made her tremble. This was where she came from, and she blushed, thinking of her father and her mother in their love, but understood it was from this pleasure, her body against his, that she was born, and she wept, afraid that there was little of this left for them. "Oh, Mama," she prayed, "know this again, don't die in pain, but remember always this," and she explored her body with her own soft hands and her long fingers, and was amazed at what a blessing it was.

"You're beautiful," William had said to her many times, but she hadn't understood what he meant. Maybe it was this, to live in this body that is full of pleasure that can be found with love.

She turned around, and laughed then, peering over her shoulder to see all of herself. Was this what men desired, she wondered, and touched herself there, too. She felt silly then, and sat down right there on the floor in one movement, her feet tucked beneath her.

Beautiful, she wondered, and saw her mother and thought, but so was she, and nothing, she swore, would ever make her think otherwise. Her mother's eyes and her father's, how they looked at her for her whole life, this was what was making her beautiful. And now William's eyes, as he looked at her with love, did this for her too. Otherwise, she was just another creature, she thought, and the world is populated with creatures of all kinds, the flying kinds, the crawling ones, the racing four-footeds, the swimming ones. She could have been a fish, her fish mouth opening and closing and catching smaller fish for dinner, but she was a girl. A woman. And she'd become beautiful because of all the eyes that held her in their sight, not as a beautiful creature, but as a beloved one.

She swore she would give this to her mother. She got up straight as an arrow from where her legs were folded under her, and looked once more into the mirror. An okay-looking creature, she thought, and dressed in haste.

Barb was lying on the couch, a flush of fever about her, and so Angie brought a basin of cool water and a washcloth, and sat at the edge of the cushion to bathe her mother's neck and face, and to gaze at her, leaning forward from time to time with a light kiss. As the afternoon faded, Barb took her daughter's hand and held it over her heart, and Angie bent forward and kissed the hand that held her own. "My beautiful mother," she whispered, "my own beautiful mother."

## *Chapter Seven*

### *Spring 1996*

Once again, Barb waved them on their way. "Go," she said, "it's a perfect day. Go howl!"

Mopstick wagged his finger and said, "Come on, now, these are nice kids. What do you mean, howl?"

"Maybe they need to look up into the sun and let loose a howl. They just finished midterms, right?"

By this time Angie and William were both giggling, and Barb began a low song that her daughter knew from experience was going to turn into a full wolf cry. Mop made a stern face and looked out over his glasses from his very large brown eyes. Barb's song grew to a howl, and the kids collapsed in laughter.

"I'd better feed this creature," Mop said. "You'd better get out of here while you still can. It's dangerous business."

"I never devour teenagers," Barb said. "They're too cranky."

"All the same, I guess we'd better get out of here," said William.

Angie said her goodbyes. Mopstick called from the window as William opened the passenger door for Angie, "The truck looks great! That's a serious paint job."

"Been working on it. She's humming these days." William waved to the window.

Angie watched William drive. "Where are we going?" she asked.

"There's a place I want to show you."

She leaned over to kiss his cheek and brush his hair back.

"I'm keeping my eyes on the road. There's a whole page in the manual about girls like you."

"What do you mean, girls like me?"

"You're right. There is no one like you."

"I like that," she said.

"One of a kind. Beyond any doubt."

The breeze came in through the open windows of the truck, and they were quiet. William rested his hand on her thigh, and she shivered and leaned closer to him.

"Oh, William, to be here, on this one-of-a-kind afternoon."

"Bouncing down the road in my ramshackle truck."

"I've never seen a more beautiful truck."

"It serves. Opens up the journey," and Angie felt the rushing of the road, the wind calling them, the trees whispering messages as they followed the ribbon of highway into the beginning of a true spring. She was glad the sun was warm today, and that Barb could joke with them.

They came upon a dead tree, cracked at the neck, its trunk rent, its head of leaves still green. Insects poured in and out of the marrow to be nourished there, or to sleep in the heart of it.

Then further into the woods, a clearing opened up on an elm bigger than any other. "The largest tree in the county," William said.

Around its trunk was a path of earth strewn with rocks. Its limbs sang with populations. The new leaves whistled with racing squirrels and the breath of birds that turned their heads east and then west like the sun's slow arc. The bark buzzed with insects, and the roots disappeared and burst out of the rich earth many feet away.

She had heard nothing of this tree. She did not know how long it had sat here in this clearing, how long it had made this corner of earth its domain. Beneath its limbs was deep shadow where the power of the midday sun could not penetrate. The tree lay darkness over a radius big as a house, a circle of birdsong and cool air.

Under this elm, they knew, even the shadows were alive, and they listened until the sun went down, and, later, when their breath became one and the shadow had cloaked them in its dense mantle, they exhaled the sweetness of the leaves and the rising wind of early evening into each other's hearts. When the wind was still for a moment, they rose and dressed, and climbed the path away from the water as their limbs stretched into moonlight, and were seen as silver by the traffic passing above.

The water, this was what he had heard when he'd gone deepest inside her, knowing they were still so young, too young to know about the places their bodies could take them. He could not say he had always loved her. He had tried not to. He didn't need the crossing, and at first he fought it, as he thought he should. But when the waters fell and the sound entered him, that sound of power and surrender, that wash of blessing that makes the green world thrive, he thought, with all this water even what we have can grow here.

The cold of this past winter had laughed at them, keeping them lost in great jackets of goose down and fake down, in colors they would never have chosen to wear, as they fought the wind down the avenues. He began to forget the bitter work of the counting of fingers, the work of inhalation against the wall of cold air, the gray heaviness above them swelling and blotting out the land. Yet here and now the water ran and defied the cold whose season was passing, and the river's sound was like the very flow of the earth through time, unceasing, as he touched her, as she touched him, as they found out what made desire an act that called for its own echo.

They found a place to wade, and he saw her legs bare and went to her again. She was so new, he thought, and she thought the same about him, and touched him everywhere, and everywhere he was smooth to her fingers. Again they strained through their skins to touch, to be next to each other as had never happened for the whole history of the waters that fell close to them and always in their hearing. How they entered each other through their skins, how they became water, he prayed to always know, and he held her there with him, and did not move as they hushed their breath and lived in that ache, until she closed around him and he flew into her, and they became fire and the beginning of memory.

No one had seen them, no one had heard. They had dreamt all this themselves. It was a great fall they took, and when they gathered each other, and this is what they did, gathered each other into a circle of arms and knowledge, and understood that they could not go back and be children with each other, they moved up the path to the truck and yet were surprised to see it there, a faithful being from the last world waiting to carry them back. They climbed in, and William started the truck. They heard the waters over the sound of the engine, they heard their voices in the fall and rush of it, and they sat and wondered what they had done.

"So alive," she whispered, "even the tree that was dead was full of life."

William turned to her and kissed her again, and she was exhausted by his touch, full and empty at the same moment, wanting him beyond what even her body was telling her. They drove through the moonlight and stopped for pizza before he brought her home. For a moment at the counter, Angie could not stop laughing, but William put his arm around her and the cool flame of his flesh through his shirt calmed her. He counted out the money for the bill, but he was somehow swimming, as they sat and ate and watched each other.

They kissed there on her doorstep, but did not speak. Mopstick was at the window and could not turn away, though he tried.

## *Chapter Eight*

The news after Barb's chemotherapy was not good. The invasion had entered her liver and spleen. The treatment did not destroy all the cancer cells in the lymph glands in her abdomen and pelvis. The family sat and listened to the doctor, and each imagined in their way the cancer cells swimming through the thin colorless lymph, circling through the network of roads in the body, and multiplying, always multiplying. Leaving off a cluster of cells at each organ they passed. Refusing to die.

Barb was beyond the work of imagining. Each burst of power of the disease ate away another bit of her. She knew her body existed now to serve the cancer, and to mark the place she had been, the place she would leave.

She lived for the sight of her angel daughter, the touch of her August. She lived, after all, though her body refused her refuge. She hoped, though her body refused her that as well.

She was grateful the girl had another family, another place to go. When Angie could not trust herself not to break down in front of her folks, she would go over to William and Madeleine's apartment. She became familiar to their neighbors who did most of their errands along the borders of the wide gray street, and nodded when they saw her. Some called out greetings and waved when they learned she was a close friend of Madeleine's boy.

That day Madeleine was out looking for books to pile up on her nephew's desk, stories of the Dakota, so that he would be straight and strong in school as he rose to answer a question about history, or ask one. She hoped Angie would be there when she returned, so she bought a few extra things for dinner. That girl has got to catch a break, she thought, doing all the housework along with her schoolwork. And the whole house was beginning to fill up with the presence of death.

Madeleine worried about those two being alone, so beautiful they both were. So grown. But there was nothing to be done about it now. They needed each other. They were at home with each other. The neighbors said nothing but, "Pretty girl, eh?" and when they heard about Barb, asked each day if there was something new. They'd been good to Madeleine and William, and got to know that Angie was kin too.

That afternoon Angie was beyond cheering up, and William knew he'd come up empty if he tried.

"It's bad today," she said, "real bad. I have to go back in a bit."

They stepped into each other's arms and stood still, there in the middle of the kitchen. Then he led her to his bed, took off her shoes and curled her under the blanket. By the time he came back with a cup of tea, she was asleep and heard nothing, so he sat by her side and watched her.

"Oh Mama," she cried out, and the wind rose up in her dream and he could see it, see the blanket swirling about her in the wind. He knew what it was like to lose a mother, for he had lost his mother and father both, in the flash of a terrible encounter. And the drunken boy was paralyzed, and had asked William for forgiveness, but what was the use to give it? His father, his mother, both gone before he was a man. His grandmother, too. That whole last year he'd watched the old woman struggle for breath, choking and nauseous as they drove into her with evil medicine.

Now he watched the breeze blow about the wisps of light that lay on Angie's forehead. He knew that anything might grow there, even the ugliness of tumors, when the mother was taken.

But after his parents were killed, Madeleine took him to the reservation, and with each visit, William got to feel more comfortable. Everybody asked him a lot of questions about Minneapolis, and how he liked city life. Then he turned it around, and was glad. He started to ask them questions about the rez and how long it had been there, and what was the dream that woke them last night and had them out in front of the house or down by the river, wandering through the darkness. When they talked, he understood more.

It was the land that told him the most, these trees, and the birdsongs, and the river that muttered all night. And the sky, not just above but everywhere he looked, and in everything, in the eyes of his people, in their voices and their song, in the wind at their shoulders as they were drumming.

They began to teach him to drum, and his whole being took to it. They taught him well, and when he held the stick and hit the skins that would always talk, even in death, he knew he was Indian. He sang his heart out, let his voice go out into the sky with his whole howl, his grief and gratitude. He sang out, and drummed, and knew there was a circle he had entered and nothing would take him out. If anyone or anything tried to, he would fight, and if the circle were broken, he would heal it back with this earth and sky song, this human and animal chant, this man and woman sound that went into his skull, and trembled there above the beat in his belly that was drumming. He was an Indian boy, even with his parents taken from him, and he sang to them, and to everyone Indian.

Blessings, he thought, what if he were a girl and could not drum like this, but he'd seen them, the girls in the woods beating on the side of a fallen log and singing the same song that he knew was unbreakable truth. He remembered all this for a very long time, and believed that even as an old man he would sit, fallen into his own flesh, his back not so straight as it would still be for years, and he would drum, with all the hoarseness of loss and knowledge, with all the years of labor and pleasure. And he knew he would be listening to the drumming and singing even as he left this life and went to find them, Raymond and Julia, his stolen parents, his very own murdered ones.

He remembered hearing about Angie when they were both kids, the perfect child unharmed by the twister, except for the new dress she was given, the dress she floated into after traveling through the sky. Then she landed unscratched on top of five cars stacked up and smashed against the sunlit wall of the old Sears at Lake and Chicago. There she sat, washed clean by the storm, hair lit to white man's gold by the sun, and framed by a rainbow tucked behind the automotive parts wing, which the great winds chose to reorganize in a somewhat different way than the after-school part-time workers who were then all Scandinavian and German.

"Made-up nonsense," his auntie had said in a huff, but he liked to imagine it was true, because he knew what it was like to be tossed about and come up gleaming, as he had in her embrace when she came to take him home with her. There he sat at the river's edge, with his bare feet in the water and his father's fishing pole casting about in the wind as if looking for him. By the riverbank, William looked down into the silence below that drowned the ancestors, body upon body, as the sun set. "Blood red," he swore to his auntie the first time he saw it, "blood red the waters," he pointed, and she nodded. They all knew that blood.

Well, it wasn't nonsense, although some people might say it was. It was a story that he could believe. Angie had a heart of gold, and that the wind would see fit to pluck her out of the danger of the storm was just what he would have done if he were the wind. And he was, sometimes, he was the wind. Wind that he grabbed hold of and flew away down the road of air when he was chased, a gang of boys coming at him with a knife, or with scissors to cut off the long black hair that helped him know his father. Or the wind that exploded in his fists the first time he went to Sonny's. One guy tripped him, and as he stumbled, they gathered to laugh at the drunken Indian. Again the wind of flight became the road after his fists broke a man's nose. He never told Madeleine, but that was enough for him, and now he sat, every morning, and breathed in what peace he could to keep straight and gentle as he moved through the other world, the world of their eyes and their words.

So the wind had power. The wind had direction. The wind had journey. The wind had growing and sleep. And the wind had voice, and this power would be his power.

"The wind has power," he told Madeleine once when they argued about Angie, and she laughed.

"Of course it has power, but it's no Dayton's dress department!"

"It journeys to every corner of the earth. It picks up and lays down again anything it wants to. It changes the face of the earth, and you think it can't change a little girl's dress?"

"Nonsense," she'd said again, her face flushed a bit at his answer. "And watch your tongue, boy," she scolded, but was proud of him. He'd made her think.

Nonsense or no, he could see Angie at the Sears that day. At the bottom of the heap of cars was an old fat Chevy with a broad back and fins, its red eyes glowing on and off, then a Ford smashed down to its wheels, and a few more layers up at the top, still in fine form, an old pickup truck, one like Auntie had, orange with rust and paint. Then, in its hold, like a baby in its carriage, lay a sports car, sleek and tight, a convertible maybe, or maybe the roof had been wrenched off by the twister, and there in the driver's seat was a little girl in a peach-colored dress, soft as a deer, lake eyes, sun hair, cloud smile, who could only reach home by flying.

## Chapter Nine
### Summer 1996

"Damn you," Barb said to the hospital gown she struggled with. "This is more than I signed on for." When they'd first told her she had cancer, she knew she could fight it, she knew she could win. She was a woman from the farms, tough enough, and she would make this nonsense go away.

She fought it with all her power. Like a strong man, she lifted the terrible anvil of her disease high over her head and dashed it to the ground while the spectators nodded and pointed, booed her weak moments, and commented at will on her whole performance, on her costume, her statistics.

She breathed a different air at home. Much applause. "You are the bravest mother," Angie told her once, that Christmas soon after surgery when she got right to cooking and cleaning, shopping and wrapping, doing everything she could to make her girl happy and let her know that nothing could take her mother away from her. And August, he kept wanting her, and her own body did not betray her, straining to join with his except at the worst moments of treatment, and they always passed, and she woke to wanting him again.

She had good years, free of it. But with the lymphoma, it was attack after attack, good times contaminated. She knew its relentless march now, she knew its stealth, jabbing at moments of happiness.

"Well, Barbara," and she had learned to keep listening to the doctors though she wanted to flee, "we need to take a bone marrow biopsy to see whether the cancer has metastasized."

How about burying me now and leaving me in peace? That's what she wanted to say, but maybe it was disloyal to even think it. Instead, she asked, "Is that why my leg is aching?"

"We'll have to see."

"At least it's not in my ovaries," she said, and remembered the chorus of complaints from the hens as she gathered their eggs every morning of her young life.

"What did you say, Barbara?"

"Nothing, just, why me? Why did I develop lymphoma in the first place?"

"There's no way we can know. Certainly, your earlier bouts with cancer weakened your system. You may have been exposed to substances over at Honeywell. Uranium, maybe. And the chemicals you handled and inhaled on the farm may have contributed. The nitrates in the drinking water as well."

She stopped. Everything stopped. "And I got out young," she said.

"But there's no clear data on this."

"It was the farm."

"I can't give you a definitive answer."

"I need to know."

"Some people are more susceptible to the damage these substances can do."

"Pesticides."

"There's lots of research. But no clear cause and effect has been proven. Nothing for certain."

"Herbicides."

"I have some articles about it if you'd like."

"I have to know."

"Tell Rony. She'll copy them for you."

"I'll read whatever you have."

"Set up your hospital visit and I'll check on you while you're there."

"I was very young."

He patted her hand. She didn't understand why. "And rest. You know how these procedures can take it out of you."

"I left the farm," she said to the doctor, "I walked away and did not touch that stuff again." Except, she remembered, each time she went up to help. She heard again the ringing of the canister she rolled over to where she mixed the chemicals for spraying.

"Yes, Barb, I know."

He explained again the way malignant cells grew, without connection to the brain, to DNA codes. Wildly, and she thought, yes, that was what she had sensed long ago, as she started to grow large, larger than her friends, that something had gone wrong, something within her had fallen away from the normal path of things. And as she grew, as she added weight to her thighs and her belly, to the heaviness in her arms that were worker's arms, something in her body laughed at the old idea of the farmer's daughter as the charm to draw every traveling man who yearned to stop in her softness. There Barb stood, large and tough, and growing still, as travelers passed.

But not, she had prayed even then, a thing that does not deserve to live.

She saw the doctor pick up the phone, though she hadn't heard it ring, and he said, "I've got to get this."

The mask of a face she wore began to fall from her as she left the doctor's office. This skin that held her love and denied her beauty had not protected her. She had breathed full in the poison, paraquat, that ate through the jungles of Vietnam just as it digested the weeds on the farm, their scrawny struggling heads weak in the face of the farmer determined to make way for wheat and for corn. The air that had breathed ill on the vets who came back, that killed their offspring or even their chances, this mask of hers had breathed in some of the same, and brought into her body this moment, and the battles she still faced.

He refused to say it outright, what it was that was killing her. But she knew.

She went into the hallway to get some water in one of the fluted paper cups that always smelled of chlorine and wax, but she could not swallow, and spat into the cup and watched the strings of her saliva travel down into the water, to the very bottom.

Again she went home to pack, and left the green suitcase at the foot of the stairs so August and Angie would know without her saying it.

There was growing evidence, she read that night, that "exposure to herbicides containing 2,4-D increases significantly the risk of non-Hodgkin's lymphoma." But the next article said much the opposite.

Paraquat, she'd handled it often. She'd washed it out of her father's work clothes, and her mother's; out of the soiled overalls of the occasional part-timer they'd taken on. And she'd shaken it out of her own clothes, watched the dust dance in the moonlight. Mixed it with any number of other chemicals, and who knew what that would do? It was before anyone much talked about it, but she remembered the kid across the road who vomited and then fell to the ground, his whole body dancing in the power of it, after riding in the tractor with his father and taking in a great cloud of pesticides when the wind reversed and the nozzle stuck. Caught in its path, just the way a bug would be, she remembered thinking, and then had nightmares of what it was to gasp for air when every breath delivered poison.

And, ever since, that boy was forgetting everything. Teacher would ask him a question, wanting a simple history-lesson, back-of-the-page answer, and he would stand there at his desk, silent, nothing there to fish out from memory. Minnesota history, drilled into him, was gone. The other kids laughed at first, but then they saw he wasn't playing around. He had hours of chores before school, but he was more than tired. He just couldn't remember, and it must have hurt him so to look the fool.

After it happened, Barb had nightmares for weeks, and they laughed at her when she said, "Every creature has to eat. It's when they take more than their share, they have to be stopped."

"That kid likes bugs more than farmers," said a man in a green cap, sitting atop his John Deere.

"It's not that," she began, but they wouldn't listen, and it made her so mad, because she knew she did her share around the place. "I'm going to do the milking," she announced, and they quieted for a minute as she walked to the barn, but she heard the laughter break out again. She passed the immense canisters marked as poison, and kicked the hard shell of one of them, glad for the padded tip of her boot. She went to the first, her favorite, and whispered to her as she stroked her neck, "You always give, don't you? You're so good to us," but this time the animal was trembling, her legs shaking.

"What's wrong," the girl asked into the air, and rose to go to the men for help, and for some answers.

It was later that same year she went running to her father, when the rip of crimson called out to her that some small animal had been caught in the gears of war, at least, that was how she saw it. The tractor was like a tank, like the tanks that moved through villages in Europe in the black and white films her father showed her on the reel-to-reel, leaving no blood on the screen that she could see. But that day in the fields, it might have been a rabbit, it might have been her rabbit, the soft brown one that had broken free from its cage in the barn. It was then, when she saw the drops of blood fling themselves into the field of growing things struck down by the tank her father drove, that she ran to him, and he stopped spraying, just as the wind flung a cloud of it into her small face and her open cry.

The masks they needed to cover their noses and mouths, their soft and vital eyes, were not even a thought back then. She breathed in, a little girl who could do nothing else, and clung to her father tall in the tractor seat. She was sick then, sick for some days, and dreaming of a new air that would not hurt her lungs to breathe.

Whatever Barb read that night, she thought for certain it was the cloud of paraquat that planted in her the seeds of disease and the widowing of Mopstick. It was this cloud that had begun the unmasking to bone she had grown to desire, where all were equal.

In the morning, Mopstick drove Barb and the green suitcase to the hospital, and left her there, and went to work.

What a beauty, Barb thought, when she opened her eyes after resting from the biopsy and saw the woman in the next bed. She tried not to stare, but saw the woman was asleep, saw the waves of her black hair falling like ink; her pale skin, white paper; saw her red mouth, her thin arms. The woman slept as if the room were in full darkness. She slept as if she were already beneath the earth, but when she woke, the blackness in her eyes shone at Barb, and the women fell to talking.

Barb named her family. "August," she said, "would lie right down in this bed and go to the other side with me if he didn't need to feed his family. And Angie is a blessing. Gets her schoolwork done, and stays bright-eyed about it. It's more than books to her. Studying the wars, she comes back weeping."

"Mine's like that. My son."

"My husband's grandmother, you know, is Dakota, but my girl's got that fair hair, almost white when she was a baby. But I'm talking too much. How about you? Where are your people from?"

"Don't know nothing for sure. Black hair, black eyes, all through my family, and we just figure we are part native from long times back, but it's a black land, my part of West Virginia. Black with coal. My people got black on the inside from the mines, whatever color they got on the outside." She stopped talking and hunted for air, then rubbed her hand in a circle over her heart. "You from the Cities?" she asked, and sat up.

Barb told her, "Yes and no," and that led her back to talking about the farm. "I can still hear it," she said, "the sounds at the edge of the fields, owl song in my sleep. Hard to forget, the worries and the changes with the weather and each fall of luck. There's a hold the land keeps on you. There's a beauty."

"We both come from people who dig in the earth," the dark-haired woman laughed, and fought her jealousy for those who worked above ground in sunlight, rather than light from a dim lantern, or a burning disk slung to the forehead in a world so merciless, each must carry a sun with him.

She wouldn't go back. She carried the black air in her lungs, but she would beat it, she figured, since she had never worked down there, but only in the great exhalation of the mines, around the heaps of coal where rock of blackness hit rock of blackness with the sharp aim of the pool hall men who made the dust rise up.

"I washed the coal dust out of my father's work clothes everyday. He's long dead. I kissed it off the lips of boys who would be sick, soon enough. I burned the coal, in the night, for my wailing baby. I burned it straight. Sat at the pot-bellied and breathed in that poison with the warmth. It saved our lives then."

"We're both getting out of here pretty soon," said Barb, "and we'd love you to come over and have a meal. Unless you're too busy, I guess."

But she brightened when the woman said, "Oh, I'd like that." Neither of them knew it for certain but the date would be kept.

The woman leaned back against the pillows, humming a bit, and low. The melody was off somehow, and Barb heard that, even though she didn't know the song, but it was filled with something lost, something taken, and the moments after. Her fingers went cold then, and she breathed into her hands as she did when the heat went off before she could climb into bed and curl up under the blankets.

"Oh," said the dark-haired woman, "I'm Jamie," and coughed a bit as if that were part of her name.

"I'm Barb," she returned, thinking how this woman had a different name in her eyes than the one she'd just spoken. In a while Barb fell to sleep wondering if she did also. She walked up a trail lined with birds, and listened for her true name. The waterfall ahead of her was descending into its own language, the arc of light breaking apart as it crashed, roaring as it hit the rocks, and drowning out the names that had come to this place from far away with too much pride to learn the song around them.

The next day Jamie told her about her town, and how she'd married an outsider and given birth to a son. The couple had split up, but she had her baby, and nothing, she'd thought, could take him away from her.

"He got the business bad," she told Barb, "from everyone around, everybody white, that is. Figured his mother to be some kind of slut, marrying a Jew from New York, then divorcing, so they tormented him. 'What are you, boy?' they egged him on every day of his life, but he was a cool one. He'd give them back answers that made their heads spin. Took to reading the encyclopedia at the library, one book at a time, and every time he came across a new people, he'd throw that into his answer. 'I'm Armenian,' he'd say, 'but not pure.' I loved that one. 'I'm Aztec, also. Bantu, too, and part Berber, Croatian, and Cree. Want to know more? Ask me again tomorrow,' he'd gloat.

"He knew he had them. He'd run off to the library to read the next entry in the encyclopedia, and the one after that. All that was fine when he was smaller, but when he started to grow to a man, things got ugly, and he got angry. Always fighting. I almost lost him. Brought him up here, hoping he'd calm down."

"Put him on ice."

"You bet. I have to get well. You can see why."

"How was it for you, leaving? It was your home your whole life," Barb said.

"I'm split like a bean. But it beats staying in a place that could kill you."

Barb nodded and was silent, and both women went off to their separate lands, just in reach of the breathing and stirring of the other.

Barb heard voices in her sleep, and awoke to meet the boy, Jamie's son, and hear him chanting the names of peoples all over the world: Dakota, then Edo, Falasha, Fon and Inuit, Maori, Hmong and Tuareg, she heard the names and the music of the names, many she'd never heard before, and thrilled to hear the river of it. The boy sat by her bed before she fell back to sleep, and he sang again his chorus of peoples, his answer to his tormentors.

When next she woke, they were gone and the bed was made, but there was a notepad on the table with their names in purple ink—Jamie and Sam—a phone number, and an address in South Minneapolis. Not far away, she thought. That's good.

The pain shot through her and crowded out their faces.

She had not always been this age, this sick body. Those days before she left the farm, she'd been strong, maybe not pretty, but healthy and tall, ready for learning, for new people. She'd been dizzy with her new life coming, dizzy with leaving.

She could see it in her mind's eye for weeks before she got on that train, how she would pass tree line after tree line between the fields, house after house pushed back into the distance as an afterthought of crops and machinery, the endless rows planted to part the earth with a subjugated sea of corn, of wheat, of soy and of oats. She would pass all the things they had planted in the dark earth, straining to catch sun and rain, to trap the power of the heavens in a snap bean or a bundle of flax. She had moved through the snow and bitter cold for all those years, taken in the blazing sun and watched her young skin weather. She was filled with the grit of the earth and the living and dying of a million silent creatures grown to feed the two-leggeds.

She knew she would leave behind, in the slow hypnosis of train ride, the many divisions in the land and their multiplication into fields. The sameness, the beauty, she would leave it. She would go forth from the farm to a place where her difference, the wildness of her features, need not be compared to the land's old order, with its straight lines and the imperceptible bending of earth. She would soon wake to mornings where the failures of crops, their withering or being devoured by whatever insects God released in the fields, and the poisons laid over the land to stop them, were no longer her air, her whole vision. Her fault. Her burden.

She would grow dizzy with leaving the farm, its sameness, its beauty, the silence of early mornings, her father and mother battling heaven, and praising the land when it did their will.

That morning it was the same.

"Get your be-hind into that chair and get some food in you, Barbara, dear."

She looked down at her mother and stood there, caught, her books in her sweatered arms. "I'm not hungry," she said in a whisper.

"Did I ask if you were hungry? You should be hungry, not a bite since lunch yesterday, I'm pretty sure. And I don't care what a magazine says, I don't care what some boy says, or some dumb high school girls, you are not fat and you need to stay nourished. How do you think the brain stays working? By starving? By looking in the mirror? Go on and eat. There's biscuits and some juice standing in the pitcher, the yellow pitcher, fresh made."

So, she ate. She sat and picked at a biscuit and drank the good cold juice, and did not look up, not once, but instead the sleeves of her sweater drew closer to the flesh of her arms, the collar pulled at her throat. The waist of her skirt pinched and bound her. Her breath became shallow, as she stared into the serving bowl where the new raspberries were gathered, where they bled dark into their delicate forms, into the hole in each center where they had been pulled away from the green caps clinging to the bushes along the perimeter of the family land. She sat and blew a bit of air in and out of her body as it swelled under command of her mother, who did not understand, but sat and ate, herself full-bodied and strong, her breasts fallen to rest there on the table, like part of the meal. Barb smiled and ate a few purple berries, and tasted in each feathered bubble of fruit the dark sweet earth. She took strength, and got ready.

"I'm leaving."

"What did you say?"

"I don't want to argue. But the day I walk off that stage with my diploma in my hand, I am packing up and leaving for the Cities."

"I was waiting for this," her mother said, "I was just waiting. But I have to tell you, I think you're crazy. You have everything here. You have the land here, food on the table. A way to live. This is your home, Barb. You think because a few stupid kids make fun of you, you have to up and leave?"

"That's not why."

"Come on. I know how upset you are about this prom."

"I said, that's not why I'm leaving. That's icing on the cake."

Her mother got up from the table, and walked to the counter. "What do you want, Barb?" she asked, and grabbed the canister of sugar, held it to her chest.

"More than I can have here. The same people watching me all the time, smirking if I put on a few pounds. I've had it with that."

"There's good people here."

"Sure, and I'll miss them, but there's good people in the Cities too."

"You know we need you, Barb. Your father can't quit his job at the hospital, and I can't do everything around here myself."

"Well, I can't stay. I have to start my own life, and it's not going to be on a farm. I can't do it anymore. I just can't."

Her mother shoved the canister down the long counter, and threw her spoon in the sink. "Well, what am I going to do here without you? Talk to myself all day? 'Want some coffee, Geneva?' 'Hey, how's Fred?'"

"Mom, listen—," Barb began.

"Forget it," the woman said and went into the bedroom, slamming the door.

Fred entered from the south corridor of the hospital, the same entrance he had used for fifteen years. He heard a wild cry, like something whirling in the air, and began to smell the grim disinfectant that held his chest hostage for the many hours a week he spent there. This was a day when he would not have a moment to sit down, except at break, and then, too tired to sit, he stood and mixed the powdered creamer into the cup that had no weight, that seemed made of air and filled with the crackle of dry, hot weather. Then, with his cup anchored by the bitter coffee of the workplace, he dug into the box of vanilla wafers and came up with a handful, which he ate by twos.

With Artie quitting, selling the farm and getting the heck out of here, he thought, I get his weekend shifts for a while till they hire someone else. So that's

103

Friday off, then Saturday and Sunday on—he swallowed two more wafers—Monday and Tuesday, Wednesday and Thursday. He chewed the next two wafers, spending the extra pay in his mind to fix up a few things around the house, those steps first, then that broken window, and the well pump. And buy the girl something for her graduation. He held a big gulp of coffee in his mouth long enough to taste the grit of the creamer, and swallowed. He knew his break was over and tossed the cup, let it sail into the trash bin, but he wasn't ready to go, and lingered in the corner of the staff lounge. Then he grabbed a few more wafers, and saw his friend down the hall.

"Hey, Artie," he called, "sorry to hear it."

"Guess I'll be needing a real job now."

"Farmwork somewhere?"

"Nah, I need a real paycheck too."

"I hear you, Artie," and the man waved back at him and disappeared down the corridor.

Barb banged on the door, "Ma, listen to me."

"No. Leave me alone."

"Look, I'm not going across the ocean."

"Well, you might as well be." She flung the door open to face her daughter. "You know, people journeyed thousands of miles to be here, right here. They faced the plains and the Indians and the cold to make a life on this land, right where we're standing."

"I'm not going to argue with you, Mom. Come back to the table. I don't want to be late for school." And the young woman led her mother by the hand back into the kitchen, where the sunlight streamed in and lit the breakfast table in a cloud of gold.

Barb sat and took another berry to please her mother. She crushed it in her mouth. It was sweeter than the others. It dripped a bit from the side of her lip, and her mother dared put a napkin up to her face and wipe the stain away. Barb let her.

"You'll be alright, Barb, whatever you do, I know it. You're a strong girl, a smart girl. I suppose I knew this was coming. And I know when I'm losing." The woman put her hands together on the table

And then it was the mother who let her child lean in with a napkin and wipe away the tears that were falling. But she couldn't stop crying, and waved the girl away, and found her stern voice to say, "You better visit."

"More than you can stand," Barb whispered. "Got to get to school now," and she rose and walked through the house, and stole a glance back to see her mother sitting at the table, looking into the bowl of berries with her chin in her hands. When the screen door was about to hit the doorframe with a hard slap, the mother looked up and turned her head to see the edge of the cloth of her daughter's skirt slip through into the blue air, a sky under which everything tried to grow beyond its boundaries.

"I'd better get to the barn," the woman announced into the air, and grabbed her boots.

And these many years later, an orphan now, Barb lay on the hospital bed across from Jamie's empty one, and tasted the sweet juice her mother had wiped off her chin, and saw the fields passing by the train window, and shook with the journey. She remembered her mother who had wept over her leaving, and her father, who had lowered his head and let her walk out.

She dreamt then of her father nodding with approval at how she'd cleaned up. She dreamt of her graduation dress, for once a new one, store bought—fitting her as a dress should fit a woman, the cloth touching her everywhere, whispering the song of its origins as she walked, the seams of it lying against her skin in a soft journey, tracing the way she was a woman.

She gazed at the old fields from her hospital bed, row upon row and the deep spaces between, and could hear the loss of the farms around her in the ringing of the auctioneer's voice, and saw the land taken, and prayed for the dark splendor that could not be harvested.

She remembered what Mopstick's grandmother had told her one night, when he was out running errands. It was the story she had been told by her elders of the people crowded into freight cars and cattle cars, bitter wind and harsh sun beating on the faces staring out from between the beams across the sky. She told how the children were silent, except for the tiniest ones wailing in the damp shaking journey beyond star and water into black night, into hollow day, into hunger and exile in the western lands. She told how each cell of the bodies jolting over the rails kept calling out for home, for the ride through the plains and the warmth by the cooking pot, for blankets washed in the riverbed, for the old songs some thought could only be sung there in Dakota lands.

"But now the sun sets in blood," said the old woman, "and all the fences are bloody, and no one can race across the plains with their hair flying behind them, with the old grace of foot and of horse." She began to sing and was singing still when her grandson came back with bags from the store, cans and boxes and white styrofoam trays heavy with beasts quartered and wrapped slick against saran.

"You alright, Grandma?" Mopstick asked then, knowing that her soul would tend to wander off and no one seemed able to stop it, such a determined soul, such a huntress, still strong and black-haired. Then she hugged him and sang in his ear. He saw Barb's head move with the song, and knew that their children would be right in the world, not all one people, but part Indian, part white. And Barb kept listening to the song in her head and running with it across the plains that night in the hospital, until she heard again, insistent, "You alright?" from Mopstick, who had just come in and was laying his jacket across the back of the chair, then leaning over to kiss her hello.

"I'm alright," she said, and the night came back to her, and some of her fever slipped off.

"They're sending you home tomorrow. You're coming home," he said, and she remembered the word, and reached for him.

So Barb came back home and unpacked the green suitcase that held a few worn nightgowns and her robe, and a couple of books with the ears flapped over each time she left off reading. She came home to the man who loved her, and the girl who also did, with all her heart. And the girl became the mother, and worked hard at it.

"Appointment with the doctor on Friday, Mama," Angie called out as she put the phone down. "Dad'll drop you off, and me and William will pick you up."

Barb didn't see the point of it. The tests had told her all she needed to know, unless the doctor was dispensing miracles. But she whispered, "Fine, Angie, fine," just as the girl appeared in the doorway and slowed down to a tiptoe when she saw her mother's head drooping with sleep, or with medication. She went to her room, and with the back of her heel, swung the door shut.

I might want to travel, thought Angie, and put both palms flat on her bedroom window to gaze down between them to the street. I might want to leave Minnesota, get out of all the cold and snow, and then she thought for a moment how the immense sky could shudder her out, drop her thousands of feet to the earth, just because she dared think about flying away. She set her forehead against the cold of the glass.

For now, she was going to wait for William's orange truck to come around Thirty-second Street onto Pillsbury. She was going to watch for his left leg in his soft, faded jeans to swing over the running board, and plant itself on the ground to wait for the long arc of his right leg. But she might want to leave, take William with her and see the world.

Carnival in Trinidad. The Great Wall of China. Crazy St. Basil's in Moscow, with dizzying spirals painted inside its onion domes. She would visit the great shining fields of the world and meet the farmers, and go to the workers on the assembly lines, people like her folks, and learn their languages, and sit and talk with them. Like a storyteller. Like a friend.

But now that same faint whisper of nausea rose in her throat, though she willed it to be her imagination, and failed, and threw down the beaded necklace she was fingering. She stood very still and took a deep breath. "Angie," her mama called then, and the wave at the bottom of her throat rose higher and she began to sweat, to feel yes this is real, unalterable, nothing she could take back.

"Mama," she whispered her answer, "my poor sick mama," and wanted to go to her but that moment was like a finger teasing the back of her throat. She grabbed the wastepaper basket and let go.

She wiped her mouth and heard Barb calling again through the blood pounding in her ears. "There in a minute," she called out. She breathed hard and thought, But I want to, I want to travel, and thought of Greece. She remembered the Greek restaurant down by Lyndale, at that same corner since she was a very little girl. There the ceiling fans hummed steady circles above her, and she breathed in the cool air and the music that made her want to sway. She looked into the strong lined face of the waiter, and asked for the chicken, as Barb had coached her to do.

"Angie," Mopstick had said then, "watch this!" and the flames from the *saganaki* —that's what the waiter called it—blazed in her good blue eyes until the special *kaseri* cheese cooled down and could be eaten, but a spark was left there, always in the center of her seeing.

"Can we go, Daddy? Can we go to Greece?"

"Sure, Angel," he'd told her, but now she saw the wings of her flight lose the wind that carried them, and rushed to wash the basket, and see what her mother was needing.

Each day it was the same for Angie, racing back from school to watch over her mother, waiting for William, and dreaming of travel. She could feel herself seatbelted and soaring, and peered through the round window into craggy, snow-covered mountain ranges; into endless blue waters and sudden lush islands; deep into skies where the sun never set, where the black, red, and piercing blue layers of night and day followed each other hour upon hour of her dreamt journey. She dived in a perfect arc from the white rocks of a volcanic island into the Mediterranean, and she chanted the name of the place, "Santorini, Santorini," to make it real, while her father listened in and thought it was some prayer he did not know, and it was, the prayer for flight, for singleness, for girlhood, for oceans—the prayer for running away from home. Instead, she could feel her body begin to thicken, and knew there was a traveler inside her. She awoke grim to her prison, and ashamed of wanting to fly away when her mother was so sick.

When Angie told her that she and William were going to have a baby and were determined to keep it, Madeleine hugged them both, and put her warm hand on Angie's still flat belly. "It's going to be okay," she told them, "it's going to be fine. And I'll help you. You know that, don't you?"

Angie cried in her arms. When she and William went out to the grocery to pick up a few things for dinner, Madeleine checked on Barb, then pushed through the screen door out back and lay flat on the grass between the old apple trees to stare up into the summer sky.

Even on such a calm day, she could recall the winds coming together, first in play, wind dancing after wind, then bound together into fury. She imagined their voices, hissing curse words, insults to the ancestors, taunts to manhood. The great currents of wind, instead of gliding in their own suits of air, would rage together into one spiral to attack the innocent and drag them from home. The winds would not subside until their great hunger was satisfied, fed of the earth and its inhabitants, and the growing things wrenched by their roots out of the soil into the thin whisper of air that said only, "Die." Roots grasping nothing, she thought. They'd warned her, that's how she would be, when she left the reservation for the city.

"This boy needs to live in the place of his parents," she'd told them. "He's lost too much all at once in this car crash," and they sighed and let her go, hearing the wisdom in that. She would bring him back out to the cabin for weekends and feast days, and teach him that this land was a part of him, and the life here would shape his own forever.

But it wasn't only for William, she admitted to the clouds passing. She'd known then that something was different inside her. She'd known for a long, long time. She wanted love, like any other. But everyone joked about her. "Oh, Madeleine," they said and poked her side, "so busy taking care of other people's children, you are forgetting to have your own," and the old women looked at each other and shook their heads. And the kids all ran to her, as if they knew she had no one else, that they were all the love she had.

And so she lived, and no man came to her, and she went to no man. "You are a seer," her father told her before he died. "You don't need to be a married woman and have a family. All around you, they will make family. They will need you for your wisdom."

She looked at him then, so small in his bed, the light of summer bathing his face. "As you say, this is how I have lived," and then she wanted to tell him that she had desires too, that she needed love, that she could not always remain this way. Alone. A mother to everyone.

"I'm still young," she told him. "I want more than this."

But he patted her hand and said, "You are a good woman, a good mother to the children you teach. You can see what the people need. You can help them."

And go home alone to sleep with my own shadow, she thought, but did not say. She'd gone outside that afternoon too, and lay watching the sky in the same way for the storm that no one could stop, that took up into itself whatever it wanted, eating to fullness and power. That touched where it would and lay down where it felt the need. She turned over into the earth then, her face in the coolness, and wept, and vowed to change this loneliness.

Under the apple trees now, she thought of the man William was growing to be, and was proud of her work. But that was not all of who she was. She thought of Iris, with the crescent scar above her lip, who'd sat next to her at school in ninth grade. She saw their walk through the woods, their longcut, they called it, going down to the river and circling back through the thicket of trees instead of walking the simple path to home. And then she let herself remember what she had done.

She'd stopped and turned to her friend, smoothing her wild hair away from her face, and kissed her mouth. Iris let her, then began to kiss her back, and they dropped their books and held each other. Such tenderness, Madeleine remembered it and wanted it always. Then Iris put her hands under her shirt, and whispered, "I don't know what to do, but I want to touch you," and she did, her fingers searching for the way, until Madeleine held her and made a sound she had never made before. Iris put her mouth to her ear and kissed there, and said, "I'll take care of you." And she did, that whole year they were together, looking to the others like nothing more than the greatest of friends, until after the summer when she left for school. Madeleine was alone and fell into her way of mothering.

For long years she went on like that, but after her sister was killed and she became a mother fulltime to William, she was glad to leave. Her own mother was gone, and her father soon followed. She was not too old, she thought, for the city, for the love she might find, for all of herself to live, not just the idea others had of her. With one kiss, she had broken that idea, and it was a good thing. Power not in the violent things alone, she thought. Power in the sweet kiss, in the beautiful secret. Power, great power, in her love for a woman.

She was ready for the move, and would bring William back to Lower Sioux often. She would find love, be a mother to this boy, and stay connected to home. In this way, she became the wind, journeying where she needed to, but with love, she thought, with gentleness, and thanked the tornado for the knowledge it gave her, and for the speed of its anger. And with the same speed it lay down its murderous breath, and let the people make their way back home to pick up their living.

These are good clouds to watch, she thought.

Angie saw them, too, her arms full of bundles in the parking lot at the market. She kept watching them through the truck window, and tried to imagine how they would look from above, as a jet left them behind.

# *Chapter Ten*

"Talk to me, Barb," her husband pleaded with her. He couldn't take her silence that night, not knowing if it was out of anger or pain, and praying it was anger, praying it was something he'd done that got her miffed at him. But her eyes were unsteady. Sometimes she saw him, sometimes she saw only a deep burning, the march of cells that were invading army. She saw her memories falling into water, and rising into lake sky, and then she saw him, worn and dark, and said, "You are my home, you and Angie. I won't go back."

"Go back where?" the man said, close to her.

"To the farm. Ice mornings, milking. To church. I won't go back to those women in church, telling me from when I was a little girl to have children. Lots of children, and they didn't mean our Angie. They didn't mean a thinking girl. They meant a girl like a chicken to pop out eggs we crack open and devour."

He put a hand out to try to calm her.

"I couldn't have a flock of children to take the land and be bound to it forever. Or give them to war to burn the land out from under people whose language we can't even speak. Come home to no more freedom than what they left with. With less, I'm telling you, with less."

"Some folks think it's a blessing to have land."

"A curse," she spat out and rolled her head down to her chest.

After a moment she looked up and said, "And what of them that don't have it? Who says who's to be blessed and leave the others cursed? It's a curse not to have a place to lie down and die. Rent a plot of dirt like you rent a motel room. And that borrowed key, what does it open? Opens the darkness down into your nightmares."

He didn't know what to say because she kept changing her mind as to what was good and what bad. He had nothing to give her that wasn't rented, or at the end of a string the bank could pull, insufficient funds. As if one bounced check could break a banker, some guy who didn't even know the smell of the land he owned, the land he took from a farmer like Carver. A good man, thought Mopstick, for all his rudeness and how he upset Barb.

"Let me get you something to drink," he offered.

"I'm sorry," she said, and put her face into her pillow. "I'm not thirsty, and I don't want any damn raspberries," he thought he heard her say.

"I didn't say," he started, but then, "look, we don't have any, Barb. Been too sour, anyhow. I'll make you some tea."

She looked at him. "Don't leave me here," she begged. "This room is not ours. This bed is not ours." She sat up and threw the pillow across the room. "The feathers in that thing, they're not ours either!"

Mopstick went to retrieve the pillow. He picked it up and then didn't know what to do with it, so he held it in front of his chest like a tray.

"Don't you see?" she yelled at him, and he wished she would quiet herself before the girl heard and got upset.

"I see, Barb, I see," he said.

"This face isn't mine. These tumors aren't mine. This is a bad dream. All this flesh is not mine."

"But I love you, Barb, I love whatever you are."

"It's not mine," she said with her voice rising and her breath catching, and then he knew he had to stop her, or she would make herself sicker.

"Nothing's ours to keep in this world," he said. "Everything's given us, rented us, to make something of it. You're given me, my blessing, but I can't keep you. You can't keep me. But, Barb, we made Angie and she'll always have us both," and he tapped on his chest. He came to her and lifted her back and head, lodged the pillow beneath her. Furious wings beat there in bed. The wind and its power pushed him back, and she admitted in her heart that things keep on going, and she was glad she could make her husband raise his voice and love her like she was healthy, like she was still there.

# *Book Four*

## *Walking the River*
### *Late August 1996 - October 1996*

"Back in the days of the first people, the beginning of wind was the first breathing of one of the turbulent Gods, they say. This God's name was Oni. ...

"Oni, first and foremost, is the word for wind and air. ...It tells a story. ...

"Sometimes Oni has a woman's voice, they say, full of tender whispers and urgings, and sometimes it is the deep and bellowing rage of a storm."

—*Power*
Linda Hogan, pp.178-179

## *Chapter One*
### *Fall 1996*

By now, what Carver knew of Rosie was the thud of his heart when he tried to remember her face, or her small hand in his. He did not know that Rosie would leave Mankato and her walks by the Minnesota River, two years before her high school graduation. She had never learned that her father sent a money order every other week to her grandmother, which made its way to the girl in a hushed route her stepdad never noticed. And it was certain she never found out that the letters Carver sent to her, and each package sealed with double strips of tape to hold toys, or scarves and gloves, sweaters or dresses, were sent back to him, no matter what address he tried.

Each house where he searched for her was dark and empty. No one came to the door, no matter how long he knocked. Carver supposed he could find his daughter with a private eye, but wanted to wait until he had more for her, more to tell her.

Then he was afraid. How could she need him after all these years? She didn't even know him.

He would never have guessed how tired she was of the green blue world that filled her dreams, how tired of the storms over Mankato that brought floods until Flood Control sliced through the river with concrete. Even that could not stop the long months of the gray sky above, or the way it entered her eyes. How could he know how hard she had worked to forget him, or that she would become the kind of traveler that cannot remember home.

What Carver did know was that it was up to him to protect Angie, a girl within reach, but now she wouldn't listen to a darn thing he said, and he was only trying to help. When she took her mother's car to the lake, he followed her. He had to talk some sense into her.

He lost sight of the girl for a while among the runners and noisy children, but then there she was, staring at the small island living its mystery in the middle of the waters, sun reflecting off the glass surface surrounding its shadow, its deep green. Just as he stepped up behind her, a flock of birds flew off in a dizzying spiral, their cry etched black across the big Minnesota sky.

He called out to her, "Angie—"

"Don't come up behind me like that!"

"It's me," he said, "it's Carver."

"What do you want, Carver?" She grabbed her textbook to spread open on her lap, to cover her thighs, bare against the line of her shorts. He stared at it, and she glanced down to see color drawings of male and female anatomy bright on facing pages. "I said, What the hell do you want, Carver?" and she slammed the book shut.

"Angie, we got to talk sometime."

"What about?"

"You're getting yourself into trouble, and I'm afraid it's my fault."

"I don't know what you're talking about."

"It's not good for you to go running around with that Indian kid."

"I'm not running around. He's my friend. And it's none of your business."

"It is my business. After everything."

"After what? What are you saying?" Angie snapped at him, and tried to remember back.

"I took you out of the storm. You remember."

You took me out of my clothes, she thought, and shivered. "What do you want from me? A thank you? Thank you, Carver. Thank you very much. You plucked me out of the jaws of death. What do you want for it? What?" she said, her voice rising.

"Quiet, Angie, please be quiet," he said, and came closer to whisper things to calm her. She got quiet, and looked up at him.

"You can't keep collecting on it," she said.

"I'm not asking for a thing, except you remember who you are, and what you're worth."

"Worth? What I'm worth?" and her voice began to rise again, until he put his hands together and begged her, "Please, girl, please, don't get so upset."

"You don't know who I am. You think I'm still a little girl. You don't respect my family, my friends. You saunter into our house and sit at the table like we're your servants, and better get the dinner in front of his highness. You're my father's friend, so I'll bring your plate to you, but I don't have to like it, you hear me?"

The color rose red in Carver's face, and somewhere in him, the sound of her voice made him angrier than he had been in a long time. "Look, Angel," he told her, and he grabbed her arm hard—something he had never done—"maybe you should think about liking it. Maybe you should think about how you talk to me. I got my eye out for your little Indian boyfriend, and there's plenty of folks around who don't like to see this kind of thing going on, so you better give me some respect here. I saved your life. I give and I take, you understand? Take as easy as give, and when I have to protect someone, I can't be stopped. I do what I have to do."

"I hate you, Carver."

"Listen, Angel, you have choices here. And you better choose to leave this boy alone. Let him dream about some other little white girl."

"I'm part Dakota, Carver, don't you forget, my dad's grandma—"

"—Come on, look at you, Angel, you are a white girl, sweet as a peach. A little paleskin, so that story about the Indian in Mopstick is, I'm pretty sure, just a story, and stories don't hold water," he said, staring at the lake. "Stories," he said, "don't make blood. Stories don't go on your ID card, and I have identified you, Angel. You are a white girl," and he ran his hand from the top of her head down the line of her golden hair to her shoulder, where he dropped his hand and said, "and you're going to start thinking like one."

As he came closer to her, she smelled the alcohol, and tried to make that the reason he had turned this ugly, but she couldn't, and shifted on the blanket away from his hand, and was silent. They sat like that for a long time, the girl with her legs straight out in front of her and trembling, the man crouched alongside, staring into her as if she were the sun going down.

"Go away now, Carver," she said into the air, not looking at him.

"I'll go. I'll go now," he said, but stayed where he was. "I'm sorry if I scared you, Angie, I am. But think, would you? Think about the things I'm saying."

He raised his finger and pointed to her, but when she turned and looked at him, he lowered his hand, raised himself from the blanket, and walked back toward the line of cars parked on the hill. She watched him grow small and dark in her sight.

He doesn't scare me anymore, she thought. I feel sorry for him, and she remembered back to that afternoon, to his hands that were as gentle as her father's, and did just the same things he would have.

# *Chapter Two*

Late that Thursday night, William nudged open the door of the cabin with his back, both arms full of groceries—staples they could not grow, things that had run out on their last stay. Ring Dings for Madeleine who wanted a treat like that every once in a while. Pistachios in their red shells for him, and a square half pint of vanilla fudge. He turned into the darkness inside the cabin, and, half thinking she might be asleep, tried not to rustle the paper bags. When his eyes adjusted, he saw her outline. She was sitting with a shawl around her shoulders, facing him in silence from her willow bark chair, but before he could say anything, he heard a low growl come up. "Sit down, boy," it said. "Put the bags on the counter and sit yourself down."

And he did, he moved slow and easy around the kitchen table and then settled down in the chair to see the man like a tear in the darkness, his white face on the other end of a rifle sight.

"What do you want?" William said, searching his heart for what this danger was born from.

"Don't ask me nothing. I'm the interrogator. I'm the judge of your actions. I got the scales in my hand, boy. I got a knife, and I got a rifle right here, and that makes me the voice of God on earth, and you got nothing to do but what I say."

"What have we done to you, Mister?" he wondered into the air and the man was over him like a spirit and knocked the gun against his head, hard but not so hard that he would show the pain.

Madeleine spoke in a voice like silver, "We don't have to have done anything at all. Isn't that right, Mr. Heinz," for she knew his name from the gas station, and when she said it, William got that same feeling he had each time Carver looked at him through the truck window.

The man turned up the lantern and placed it in the center of the table. He circled it as if he owned the light. "Oh, you did something," he said, "you and all your generations back did something, signing away the land and then hating us for what you did yourselves. That's how you lost this country, but I'm not about to address all that history at this meeting we're having."

"Did you get me a treat, William?" she spoke to her nephew as if the man weren't standing over them in their own kitchen, the eye of the shotgun swinging its hard stare up and back between her and the young man.

117

"I said, shut up, both of you damned Indians."

Something told William it would be good to keep on talking to him. "Mr. Heinz," William said, hoping Madeleine would forgive him later, "you see, my Auntie isn't quite right in the head, and she's been talking about these Ring Dings for days. So, maybe—" and he was cut off by Carver's order to be quiet as he walked to the bags and fished out the small package to throw into Madeleine's hands. She ripped it open and was soon chewing with great delight.

"Where's your fry bread, woman?" Carver said.

Madeleine smacked her lips and said, "Hey, Mr. Heinz, I'm an American and I need my Hostess." After she'd gotten through the first Ring Ding, she looked up and said, "Besides, fry bread is what we ate when we couldn't get buffalo, deer, turkey. Corn, squash, wild rice. It was what we made with our rations. Tasty, though." She fished out the second Ring Ding. "Now, aren't you Carver, Carver Heinz? Aren't you that friend of Angie's dad?"

The crows outside began a chorus, and the magpies swooped and called, as if the fall of night was a sudden burgeoning song and not a slow shift of the face of the planet away from the sun. The wild burst of night distracted Carver, until William tried to rise and find his way into the man's shadow. Then Carver raised his gun like a staff of war and Madeleine clicked her tongue in a way that put her nephew to sinking back into the chair. She had no intention of losing him now.

A comfortable chair, William thought, but feared its power to bring on sleep in the middle of this strange dream, as it had when he was small and his aunt insisted on watching some old black and white movie, resting her hand on his arm to keep him there next to her. But there was thunder and lightning in the distance and one bolt seemed almost to strike the house, making his eyes jump open.

Angie got to the road near the river and followed it west. She knew this much: there was a gun; William was there with Madeleine; he would do anything to keep her safe. And she knew the man with the gun was Carver.

"I'm wanting to kill this boy," he'd said into the phone, and she heard the bullets drop into their chambers, in each perfect slide downward. "For your own damn good," he said, "get here and let's settle this."

She knew Carver was lost and angry and wanted something that no one could give him. He believed that something about her could save him, but she didn't know why. After she turned off the main road onto the overgrown path by the river, her old car raced best it could through the wrench of roots from the soil, beneath the jagged electricity of storm that threatened her way.

Angie, the old voices whispered, remember how your own father could not find you in the wind, and it was Carver who pulled you from death, as the world came crashing down. Go back to that day and remember, how he changed your wet clothes for his own daughter's dress.

Instead, she saw Carver's eyes, full of judgment. She'd seen it these last weeks, worse each time, the wild swing against her, his eyes darkening, especially when William was around. How hard she'd worked to keep the two of them apart.

Tonight she'd watched him stab the slices of meat that lay on his plate, take up the steak knife and finger it all through the rest of the meal. He said little.

When she cleared the table, the carving knife was gone. She did not know that it lay close against him as he sat at the bar and could not forgive her, nor her dark love, her Indian boy.

Carver thought about pulling that knife, sharpening it against the spinning stone of his heart, and using it to shear jagged the black hair of the girl who dared flirt with him at Sonny's. He wouldn't have it.

"Hey, old man," she said in a voice like syrup, cut by a cough that she covered with the back of her hand. "What are your plans tonight?"

"Nothing you're up to."

She looked at him and without blinking said, "Try me."

He knew she was part of the earth and he thought, Dominion, have dominion over her, and looked into his drink, knowing he was for her a great mystery she wanted to solve. She sat on the next stool and they drank without speaking. He glanced over, and saw her hand rest on her dark throat as she leaned toward one shoulder and swayed. It was then he realized there was music playing. He saw her go to perch against the railing around the wooden floor and watch the dancers there.

He walked over and with his best manners said, "Shall we?" and then she was in his arms. In slow steps they moved, in circles they moved, with the other dancers on the floor, with their heartbeats trembling, in a dream they moved where he didn't know his name.

"You are shelter," she whispered, "shelter from the winds," and he awoke to the music in her voice, but did not understand.

"I'm a farmer, a builder. I plow and seed, I work the land."

"Yes," she said, "all that may be true, but you are home. You give shelter where you settle. You protect. You allow things to grow. You are not a soldier."

And he moved away from her embrace, into the last moments he spent with his brother, who perhaps was not a soldier, either.

"Dance with me some more, Shelter From The Winds," she whispered low, and yet he heard her, right in the heart of his ear.

When Angie saw the heavy knife was missing from the table, she searched its home in the compartment in the kitchen drawer to make sure it wasn't there, lying flat against the worn wood. She said nothing to her folks. That man doesn't take what he doesn't use, she thought. Then she looked up in a quick prayer and slipped out of the house.

She kept following the river. The path cut right along the tall grasses at the shore that leaned and whispered to the dark waters. The terrain got rough. She was afraid she was going to wreck the car, but knew of no other road to the cabin. She cursed a bit, then got out of the car and left it, locked and hidden in the embrace of a heavy hanging willow. The sun disappeared below the earth's edge, and the bloody horizon tamed its colors and hushed to black.

"Oh William," her heart called out, and she was afraid then. She saw that Carver could kill them all, and not know why.

The chill by the waters reached through her boots, worn thin but still tough and stylish, and worked its way up her legs and into her bones. She could still hear Carver's low voice in her ear and fought off his predictions, the way she would lose her beauty, how the world would grow small and harsh, how she would be bound to the assembly line and her small sad paycheck. How the illness of her mother would come to her, if she did not listen to him, if she tied her fate to this Indian boy and his dead mother's sister. If she loved, even with the blessing of her folks, this Dakota fellow and his song.

"If you betray your own white neck," Carver had said that night before dinner, "all this, mark my words," and she'd found in her heart a rage to slap him, but did not. He'd grabbed her by the shoulders while her folks were still in the kitchen, and she'd jerked free from his grasp and knocked over the lamp.

But now, with lightning racing thunder toward the cabin, she fell, and it was against rock, and into the riverbed.

"So, you're a repeater," said Madeleine, between her slow chewing and careful swallows.

"What the hell are you talking about? A repeater?"

"You know, Mr. Heinz, a person who lives out what's already been done in another time. It's not like following a tradition, something that connects you to your ancestors, to the Great Spirit we're all part of—you know that, don't you?—but someone who repeats, without thinking, without his heart in it. Repeats a bit of the past. Some moment in history."

"So, now you're a historian in a rocking chair."

"Someone who lives out a pattern, like wearing a uniform and killing because the uniform tells you, you have to kill. Like those Russian dogs, Pavlov's, no food but their mouths turn liquid with hunger because someone rings a bell."

"Well, who rang your bell for eating cupcakes?"

"I'm talking about someone who has no need to kill. There's no threat, no danger, but something in a man makes him start to shake, rings the bell that says, 'Now you must want to destroy.' He repeats like some guns repeat, bullet after bullet. No thought needed between firing. A repeater's not a warrior. Not a thinker. His weapon isn't fashioned from things of the earth by warm hands, for the hunt or for a battle that must be fought, but it's a dead thing. Made in a dead way."

"Enough yapping."

"A repeater, Mr. Heinz."

"A repeater. You ever been tied up in your kitchen before with a gun to your head and your boy's here?"

"Not in this kitchen."

"So how's this anything else but what I got to do? This has to stop. I lost one daughter and I'm not letting go this one to be brought down by a couple of Indians."

"A repeater."

"You think the war is over because you lost it."

"You lost it, too, didn't you? At auction. Who has your land now?"

Carver slammed his fist down on the table, and said against the woman's ear, "And why should I listen to you? You sure as hell aren't one of the three wise men."

"Oh, maybe I used to be a man."

"And a buffalo, too, I suppose."

"In an old life."

"Sure."

"And in my heart still. A buffalo woman."

"And wise, are you wise?" Carver said, weary.

"Is the land wise?"

"It doesn't think, doesn't know, doesn't give advice like a wise man does. That's why it needs farmers."

"You don't believe that."

"The hell I don't."

"Whether or not the land is wise, it must be listened to, no?"

"Enough now, if you don't want me to repeat all over this boy's head."

"Ah, so you see, you are a repeater."

"Shut your trap," Carver yelled, as he fled the close kitchen and the pair held by the threat of the gun's dead eye, to stand under the moonlight, to fill himself with its glow, to study the face of the being there.

"Angel," he began to cry as he whispered to the girl, "come and get me."

## *Chapter Three*

When he found her, some moments later, she was caught, limb of the girl tangled with limb of the tree, the water rushing over her. Blessing, oh! the blessing when he saw her mouth floating above the rapids, her head thrust upward as it rested there on the tree trunk, her hair pulled and twisted about its branches. He yelled her name, clawed at the strands so as not to hurt her when he would pull her forth in a roar from the hungry waters, but he could not release her, and her face held the smoky blue of storm as he fumbled with the ropes of gold. He heard from behind him a stirring in the waters and without another sound a man half darkness and half water lit by moonlight came to them and pulled the whole trunk upwards, ripping water from water, light from light, and mouthed orders at him that awoke his hearing. And so he grabbed underneath her dear legs, girl tangled in the river and bound to the waterlogged trunk of a tree, and then both men walked out, bearing the weight of drowning on the pallet of wood and its shedding of water, though each step wanted to pull them below breath.

They laid her down—and there was singing, but Carver couldn't understand it, and didn't know what to do, only to begin again his work of pulling strand by strand the beauty of her from the tree, but in an instant the other man, and he knew then it was William, pushed him away and he fell and felt nothing. He watched his rival take out a knife, and it was quick, quicker than Carver could see the short arc of the blade fly, but he heard the sound like a low rip of thunder. There was the flash of silver against gold in the beam of moonlight cutting through the clouds, and with another harsh slice William freed Angie who'd been bound by her hair, laid her flat on the earth and knelt down to put his mouth to hers, then raised up and with palms on his beauty's chest, pumped there as if he would break her. Carver thought he must be yelling, "My God, save her, save her, William," and then it was, yes it was, the most beautiful thing he had ever seen, the motion, the youth rising up to take in as much air as his lungs could hold and then lowering himself to the ground of her, to her tomb or her birth, and Carver prayed again, he prayed for her to take William's breath into her and let it ignite her heart, spark her lungs as human, not as failed fish, as dying fish.

Carver sat still. The woman laid her hands on his shoulders and her hands were warm, he wondered how, and she whispered to him, "This breath in William is the breath of the Creator, and it flows in each of us," and she sang, "this breath in

William flows in each of us, and it is life." She repeated this many times, and then Carver let go the breath he had been holding in the dark cave of his lungs and Angie coughed, as air met water and pushed the river out of her. Carver was weeping and laughing with the hands of the woman on him and Angie rising up to William's arms. A beautiful thing.

The woman sang, and he heard her, above all the sounds he heard her song, and let her help him up. They followed the young man as he carried Angie back to the cabin, to the fire and dry clothes and many blankets wrapped around her, and the hot tea that smelled like spring meadows after rain.

Carver saw then that he could be brought back to life too, but looked with shame at his rifle standing against the table. While the others fussed over Angie, whose color was returning as Madeleine took each of her hands and warmed them between her own, and William caressed her matted hair with a towel, he slipped out and stumbled blind to his car. When William turned after some minutes to make sure the fire was still going strong, he saw the empty room, and the shadow of the gun, and called out Carver's name, saw the tail lights disappearing, and wondered for him, wondered what he was looking for in the darkness.

He didn't go far. How could he, when all life, all that was left for him, breathed in that cabin, rose and fell with the breath of that girl, who was not, after all, his daughter.

He parked behind a hill and watched the smoke rise up from the roof into the damp air, and saw his own little girl's face and knew she was gone, out of his life. Not one letter from her. He just wanted to know if she was happy and safe. Kate had written him, but didn't say much about the girl. Cold, the letter, like the letter from the army about Eli.

Katie shouldn't have left him. It was all a terrible mistake. He would have gotten back the land, made a go of it, and the girl, his Rose, would be a fine young lady with her father by her side.

Now, all he was doing was trying to protect Angie from what all young girls might face. Make sure she didn't run off and get in with all kinds of hooligans. But he needed information. He needed to be told what was going on. He was always going to be helpless if nobody gave him any information.

He checked the pack and saw that he had three more cigarettes, and he figured to smoke them all, one after another, watch the cabin, and decide what to do. He put the radio on and caught a glimpse of the dark face at Sonny's, the woman who had called him Shelter From The Winds, and he laughed, hoarse, as he raised the window to silence the howling storm. He felt her hand on his shoulder, her hand in his hand. Her close whisper. It was ridiculous. What was she doing there in the car? What did she want from him?

123

He saw the fire glow from behind Madeleine's thin curtains. He hoped the cabin door would swing open and Angie would step out alone so they could talk. He lit another cigarette and closed his eyes, smelled the good wood smoke from the house coming over the ridge and curling through the crack in his side window.

The woman in the car pushed her dark hair back from her face and it was Mary's face, but then, Shelter From The Winds, he heard her call him again, and he laughed. Shelter From The Winds couldn't even save his animals from auction, so how could he save the land itself? And how could he save these young girls?

He'd heard stories of the great droughts, land turned to dust, wind carrying off the land. He'd heard how the earth slipped through a man's fingers like water, like something once buried under the ground had let go its hold there and taken flight, left the land without a body, without muscle to hold roots, without the deep dream of feeding the people. And then when all was fertile, too fertile in the long Depression, the livestock were buried or burned, the crops the same, or the fields left fallow to raise up the crop of money. This was the shame of the land, he thought, growing dim now in his sight.

The trees, clogged and swollen, leaned toward him over the car, ready to punch through the flimsy glass. He lit the third cigarette, and fog and smoke hid the house and covered the land, the poor land left to lie there under all the elements, all the wrath of weathers, all the greed and nonsense of men. A volley of thunder rolled through his hearing, and something broke nearby.

He saw beneath the cascade of water against his dark windshield the tree trunk that had lain in the river. Angie's dear face upturned into the downpour. Water rising over the land.

He looked through cigarette smoke. He saw water turn to fire in great conflagration, as it had that long ago season when they'd needed money more than food.

"Six million pigs," his father had yelled and ran about with a gas can in one hand and a torch in the other, setting aflame the heaps of corn, of soy beans and wheat, that poured from the silo, that sat by the thresher, that spread like ocean in the barn, little heaps at the crossroads of field after field. Everywhere the flames began to rise, and the man still ran, his two hands busy, working to burn what he could not sell for more than insult.

Carver ran after him, but each time the boy caught up to his father, another blaze began. The man was unstoppable. The horses were whinnying, the cows by the fence moved together like passengers in a ship rocked by storm.

When it was over, all was smoke. When it was over, the man sat on a blackened bale of hay and dropped the empty can. Buried the torch in the earth.

"Six million pigs," he wept the words.

"Surplus," Carver's mother said to him as they stood nearby. "All those pigs burned or buried in the Depression, among so many starving people, to bring prices back up."

Carver tried to see how many pigs that was.

The old man could have just given the food away, he'd thought.

Carver slept long after the burning. He would not eat again for three days. He inhaled smoke of the corn. He heard sizzle of wheat, dull pop of the bean. He would not eat until the smoke cleared and only then because his father's hand forced him. Chores to do. Carver ate then the charcoal of waste, held it burning in his mouth.

The land must yield, it was said. And so it had. Bushel after bushel. Truckload after truckload. Drought gone. Insects losing the arsenic war, the mercury war, the great war against their nature. Hunger had pushed them to eat through leaves and cobs, devour the seeds. But dominion over the land and its creatures said, they must die. And it was good. The land yielded, and yielded.

And so smoke circled the farmhouse, filled the nostrils at milking, soaked through clothing like water. It billowed and settled above the perimeter grasses, which, useless to the human stomach, stayed upright in the morning sun, drank heartily the waters that fell. And Carver's father ate, but he did not speak.

Carver wandered away from the car then, away from Madeleine's cabin, hunting for the edge of his lost fields. He lay down in the dew of morning, soaked cold to brutal bone. He buried his nose in the fertile smell of earth. But the fires still smoldered somewhere nearby him. Smoke grew legs and circled him. Grew a dull chant. The chant gnawed at him. The chant was a belly chant. The chant was a song of hunger. He turned and lay with his eyes up to the sky. Legs of smoke buckled all about him. One small cloud of it crawled onto his chest and became warm, hissed tears, cried for milk, for bread, as the wheat became ash and the cows refused milking in the storm of burning crops.

Heavy cloud moved over his body and pawed at his clothes, was insistent, pulled them from him, but he ran, ran through the smoke, as the one small cry at his chest became many. One clung to his left leg, one clung to his right. His arms were crawling with little beings of smoke and all were biting at him, his back, his chest, all biting.

Useless, he thought, how could his body feed them all? More smoke was coming still and the hunger was harsh and ate into his skin until one column of smoke grew and became a solid man rushing at him.

Man knocked him down and he rolled through the morning dew. Man hit him, like a woman, slapping and slapping. Another column came, and the sky opened to new rain, blessed rain, and it washed him free of the hungry ones that would eat him alive. He looked at his hands then and saw he had wrenched great tufts of grass from where he lay and would not let the smoking ends go, but in the center of each fist, it was green, still green, still alive, and he understood it was this the hunger came for; the tufts of grass, as if that could feed anyone.

125

He laughed, and put the green hearts to his mouth as a joke, and chewed. Oh God, he chewed the green hearts that tasted of smoke while the good crops that could have fed them all were burning in the fields of his memory, and he did not understand but knew it was a sin and cried, he cried for his family's part in it.

Then William dowsed his burning shirt again. He laid Carver down in the back of the truck and they flew through the night. Madeleine sat beside him, her cool hands on his head, and William carried him like a baby into the emergency room, where the smoke rose again and the hungers tried to feed, until he passed out.

They would each come to see him, Mopstick and Barb, Angie and William, and Madeleine most often. They would each tell him stories, try to get him to speak.

He began to, one afternoon. But it was never about that night.

"They paid us, the farm admin guys, to not farm. They paid us, and we needed it awful. I would sit in those fields we had to hold back, and look at the whole blank earth, thinking, hungry people. Other times, we were angry, all the guys around there. And we dumped milk. Turned the trucks over. All that milk, running down the highway.'

He kept his head down when he talked, except when he spoke to Angie.

"Hey, Carver, brought you some flowers," Angie stood at the foot of the bed, waving the bouquet in the air.

"You didn't need to. That's awfully nice. After everything."

She rinsed out the empty vase and let the flowers fan out into a blaze of color in the white room. She sat for a while as the sun went down.

"Take it easy," she said. "Watch those cigarettes. I've got to go."

"I know Angie is like your own daughter," Madeleine said, as she passed him some water, "but you can't tell her who to love. She's a real girl, not some story of one."

Carver was silent.

"So, you think Buffalo Woman nudged her into life? Found the girl in the snow? Heated the air in the great furnace of her belly, and with blasts of warm breath, melted winter from the child's blue body. Or, maybe she grew from a seed dropped by an eagle onto Buffalo's back? There she sprouted good, strong legs to hold tight to the earthen smell of buffalo, and they roamed the plains together…"

He said nothing.

"How do you think such beauty arrives here on earth, Carver?"

He looked up at her from the hospital bed.

"From the whims of ideal woman and perfect man? Or from the messy love between two people who've labored all their lives and bear the marks of it. You know what I'm saying, Carver."

"What do you want from me, woman?"

"That child is Barb's daughter. Mopstick's girl. Nobody else could have made that beauty, that spirit, that big heart she has."

"That she does."

"And what she and William do will make beauty, no matter how jagged a fit you or anyone in the world seems to think they make."

The pain bit at him, blazed from his chest like a ruby on fire, in the pale light of the hospital room. He moaned, against his will, he moaned. She opened his fists with her fingers, and something fell from his hands. She took them in her own. He could not speak, first from the pain, then from the absence of it, as it fled through the scarred whorl of each hard fingertip.

# *Chapter Four*

Carver was sitting with Hansen counting the cash drawer after a busy autumn weekend; Hansen the bills, Carver the coins. Something about this was funny. Carver began to laugh, covering his mouth at first, swallowing back the sound.

"More coffee, Carver, please?" the older man asked, keeping his eyes on the pile of bills, and raised his cup in the air.

"I'll get it," Carver managed to say, and burst into laughter.

"This isn't funny," Hansen said, "I've lost count six times since the story about the rabbits," and he lost count again, and began to laugh along.

"What's so funny?" Carver asked him in the next short silence, and that was all they needed to set off another round. "Lost my farm," he sputtered, "my wife left me, and I live in a room with roses big as your head on the crummy curtains!" This didn't help, and they both shook with it then.

Carver had been back at work for almost a month when Katie called. They spoke for a moment and arranged a meeting the following week. He did small things each day to prepare for it. He spoke in a gentle voice to all the customers at the station. He listened to them all, with respect, he hoped. He called Barb and Mopstick every day, to ask how everyone was. He sent messages to William and Madeleine, but was still ashamed, and didn't know how to say anything much more than, sorry, and thanks.

That morning he checked the mirror and tried to see what it was that looked different about him now, since he'd come out of the hospital. He did have some scarring, the worst of it on his chest, but nothing he couldn't live with. And, really, he was a new man. He could feel it. Mop and Barb could see it, Angie, too, he hoped, and maybe, just maybe, Kate knew it. He didn't suppose she was coming back to him, but maybe she would let him see Rosie. After so many years, hold his girl in his arms. Whisper jokes to make her laugh. Buy her presents that wouldn't come back unopened, that marker scrawled across the address.

He put on a new shirt. It had a crisp feel, and a light in it that would go out with a few washings, as with any cheap cloth, but it was bright today, and he was a new man in it.

He got to the restaurant well before eight and picked a booth by the window where the sun was pouring through. Such power, such heat, he thought, and squinted, adjusted the curtains a bit so the glare wouldn't disturb Katie when she arrived. Tess came over with the coffeepot, and he thanked her when she poured, thanked her when she stopped, thanked her when she smiled at him. "You're sure in a good mood," she commented.

"Why not? Sun's up high today, good and warm, and I got my new shirt on."

"Well, you look great. Enjoy," she said, and walked over to the next booth to refill the coffee cups.

He poured some milk and was studying the light swimming in the dark liquid. "Carver," the voice came from above him, and he stood and moved to embrace her, but she held her hands out in front of her. He tried not to stare.

"Let's sit down," Kate said, "I have some things to tell you."

"You look good, Katie, real good. How's life been treating you?"

"Look, Carver, I'm not here to talk about me."

"Well, then, Rosie, how is she? How's she getting along with her stepbrothers? I mean, I don't mean to butt into your family business. I know it's no affair of mine."

"Listen to me."

"Sure, no problem, that's why I'm here, to listen. I'm better at it now than I used to be, I promise you that."

Her voice softened a bit. "Well, that's good to hear. But, now, please, just listen." She looked at him and he quieted, and sat forward to hear her better.

"It's about Rosie. Some things have happened. I have to tell you—"

"Well, sure you do, I'm still her father and you know—"

"Please, Carver, shut up. This is difficult enough. Just let me talk. Rosie ran away."

"Ran away? For God's sake, where'd she go?"

"Look, she ran away, went all the way to New York City. Took a bus and I didn't hear from her for months."

"Why the hell didn't you call me? I'll go tomorrow and find her and bring her back home."

"Carver," said Kate, "you can't do that—"

"—I sure as hell can—"

"No, you can't," and her tone told him to keep his mouth shut. "No one can," she said. "Nobody in this whole world can bring her back home to live, to go back to school, to grow up and get married and give us grandkids, nobody. Nobody, Carver, can bring her back to life."

His mouth worked to speak but nothing came. All was a silent wind blowing around his heart, cold in the light through the window.

"She's dead now, Carver. Rosie is dead. I'll tell you the whole story when I can, when I can bear to, but she was in New York, and she was taken from us. She got very, very sick, and by the time we found her, she was at the door to her death. It was too late to call you, and she wouldn't have recognized you anyway. No sense to it."

129

"No sense to it? No sense? I would have held her. I would have held my little girl. She was my little girl."

"You wrecked that a long time ago."

"No! Not in my heart. She was my girl, and that never changed."

"Look, I can't argue with you now." She got up to go.

"Don't," Carver said, and grabbed her hand. She pulled it away and dug into her bag for an envelope she put on the table in front of him. "There's some things here for you, some of her drawings, and letters she wrote to you early on before she knew her stepdad better. Some photos of her, school pictures, things like that. Family pictures. She had a family, you know, mother, father, brothers, and it was a good life for her. She'd get upset with us, like any kid, you can see that in the letters, but she had a good life, a good home. I want you to know that."

He took the envelope in his hands, the smooth, clean paper that held all this, and traced with his index finger the seam that cut it in two.

"I have to go, Carver. I couldn't invite you to the funeral. It was all too upsetting to the boys. And the casket had to be closed. You wouldn't want to have seen her that way."

"You took her from me, Kate, how could you do that?" He looked up at her. "You sent back my letters. My presents."

"I didn't want to confuse her. She had what she needed. And I was through with you, Carver, through with your anger, your phony apologies."

When he said nothing, she was satisfied that there was nothing more to say, and walked out.

At the bottom of the pile of letters was some of Rosie's artwork. The drawings were rolled up, and Carver tried to lay them out flat before him on the table, pushing aside his coffee. With each one he unrolled, a breath was released, as from a flute split open.

Rosie had written the date in the corner of each, below her name, and Carver arranged them in that order. He used the edges of the coffee cups, the sugar dispenser and the napkin holder, to weigh down the papers in the places they were curling up, threatening to pop back into their scrolls as if a long red cord might be freed. Then he looked down at Rosie's gallery. Simple drawings, pencil snapshots of the things around her. A pair of clogs. A vase with wildflowers, vibrant with many colored pencils scraping into the paper, leaving the heaviness of gold and red and purple. An ornate frame with carved sides echoing each other, but no picture inside. White space, framed. He wondered, thought he heard the ripping of paper.

The last ones were self-portraits, found in the room where she died, Katie would tell him later.

In the first, she was dressed and made up like a million kids out in the city streets. Transformed, the child hidden. She looked hard-edged, like a thing to be auctioned. He did not know as he ran his long fingers over her face, that, indeed, auction had become her art.

"How much?" said the man peering out of his car window.

"Depends what you want," Rosie said, easy with the words. Tonight she would be the flower that opens, and in the sunlight, closes and rocks there in the wind scouring the alleyways.

She got good at it. She was a real woman, they said, as she pushed the plunger of the syringe down to the river of her blood. There she sank and smiled and they did what they always did, while she rode the waves of her high and of their pushing, and kept her head above it, magical and strong, a real woman, then nodded out, not needing anyone from home, not needing home anymore.

Indeed, Rosie, apple blossom of her father's memory, had come to understand there in the city streets of the never-setting sun, what it was that had been passed down to her from generations back.

It was thirst.

She was always thirsty, and remembered the stories of drought, when everything, everywhere a man or a woman or even a cow could see, was thirsty, and she thought about water and the brown grass that struggled without it, and the dusty earth hard and cracked beneath the feet of journey. She thought she could hear, just like in the stories, the animals crying, and then she heard it, the shots. When a farmer had had enough, he would shoot the cattle and sometimes himself, and sometimes his family, and this her grandfather had told her; told her, too, how the sins of their origins, the sins they could not leave behind in the old country, and the sins that began their homesteading in America, would not be forgotten and would not be taken lightly.

She'd laughed at that. What had she done? She saw herself as the small child she'd been. She saw again the silent back of her father, his turning to rage if she laughed or sang, or skipped into the house to put a bracelet of daisies around his wrist. And she saw her mother standing against the kitchen sink, biting her lip till it bled and the house was a house of rage.

She understood now, as she became earth and men walked over her and took of her flesh, and became, or thought they did, her masters. She understood, as she lay quietly in a locked room that was not hers, that her past was drought, that her body was no more her home. She understood drought and the powerful winds that followed, the winds that without mercy carried off the faces of all those who were called her family. She could barely see the parade of memories living behind the dim light of the midtown day. She understood that she was dust of the earth, and that in times of drought, the winds became hungry and more powerful and consumed the earth, and with it, every bit of her as she lay there, as she tried to stop her thirst.

The winds came up, the winds went howling as she looked down at the ugly rows of marks on her arms and was glad to become nothing. And above her, over the place where she had been earth, the winds still raged, though there was nothing more to take, nothing more to carry away, and no one left to cry out for drink.

In the very last self-portrait, there was no furniture, just a window crossed by its frame, large over her left shoulder, with six black stars and a thin burst of light in one corner. And Rosie beneath, her mouth set, hair spilling over her eyes, which were smudged with dark lines above and below. Rosie staring out at him, her face too large for the small white paper or her thin neck, her eyes without color. Only after a while did he realize she had drawn this last one on notebook paper, with its thin blue lines running across her face at every half inch, slicing her eyes, her nostrils, her mouth. There was no date in the corner, no name, just three letters: R-I-P, in black ink at the edge of the paper.

When Tess came to take his breakfast order, Carver shook his head, paid her for the coffee, and left.

# *Chapter Five*

He drove away from the Cities. He drove out to the old farmland. He left the smell of gas fumes. He left off wiping the grease from his hands down his thighs. Boss had asked when he'd be back. "Couldn't say," Carver said. "Couldn't say." He couldn't say much of anything, and that was why he got in the car and drove.

He lived in that car for six days on the old place, hidden in a grove of trees. He watched the land, watched all that he had lost. The mornings came to him. The evenings were fragrant. He listened to the calls of animal life in the wind.

Fast food would do the trick. He went on a run down to the strip once a day for the first three days. The early hunger came creeping to him with the light, as when he was a farmer, but he ignored it, since he would not have to labor with his hands and his back. He pushed away that hunger and stayed in the car. Birds sat on the nose of the hood, and above him on the roof. He liked that, and rolled down the window to hear their songs.

Before he began to feel too weak to drive, and he knew that moment from farming, when his mind clouded over and whatever gnawed at him had to be attended to, he drove to the strip. Without thinking, he decided burger, pizza, or chicken, placed his order, and ran to wash up before the meal came out in styrofoam and silver paper. He missed waxed paper, the great rolls of it with their long row of teeth, sharp enough to pierce it in one straight line, with always a tail at the end of the slice to say it was human hands had made the cut.

He hadn't shaved. By the third day, people asked him questions.

"You okay, mister?"

"Can I call someone for you?" one young girl said, like his Angie, sweet, but not understanding.

He looked up. "Medium basket. Corn. Biscuits. Fries. That's all," Carver told her. "Good for what ails me. A remedy of butter. Blessed rain of salt on the fries."

"Ketchup?" She stared at him.

"Sure. Parted like the Red Sea, so I can get to the Promised Land." He stuck his head out of the car as far as he could and grinned.

"Sure, mister, I'll get your order," said the teenager, and with both hands gripped the ledge of the window above her and pulled it down.

A few minutes later a young man raised the window and put a hand through the opening with the aluminum foil bag. "Would you like a beverage with that, sir?" he said.

"Yes. Milk. Milk of human kindness."

"Right away," the voice said, still almost a boy's voice. He didn't look at the man as he poured a large plastic cup of milk, snapped down the cover, and put it in a bag with a straw, but something about the man was very familiar. It made him want to cry. He handed the bag through the raised window.

"Four dollars and seventy-six cents, please."

Carver laughed and gave him a five, stuck a fry in his mouth and drove off.

"Thanks," the young woman said behind her co-worker, adjusting her cap. "He gave me the creeps."

He was still watching the car move down the twisting road. "I hear you," he said, after a moment.

After the first three days of eating once a day when he got hungry, Carver missed a day. He saw how hunger could subside, or seem to. Maybe it was the way he had locked himself into the car. Small space. Just a trace of fresh air over the top of the window. Couldn't work the land if he wanted to, he thought, even if he had the strength. Wasn't his anymore. He had no kitchen table for sitting with a cup of coffee. No barn. No fragrant fields. Nothing but that strip mall down the road. Those fast food joints. He knew how long it took to grow corn, raise chickens, bring a cow to beef. Nothing fast about it. Nothing that would fit in a square container.

He lost his hunger.

On the sixth day he wanted nothing. Only to lay himself down in the earth, but it wasn't his.

On the seventh day, he wanted nothing more. It was a day of quiet. All the voices were gone now, silent in the earth, or the trees, or the clouds. He looked out over his farm that was not his farm, and he knew he was through.

He needed strength to pull the trigger. Otherwise, he would sit in the car for as long as it took. Till he could see his own bones and would drink foul water. Pull his hair from his scalp like dead leaves.

He laughed. He was the one who fed others. Used to be. No way to tell who had his job anymore. The farm was motionless, as if it ran itself. Vast fields. Fields repeating, the same bean, the same grain, the same colors lined up like soldiers. Couldn't hear the hens, the roosters. Couldn't see any signs of life up at the house with its view of the monotony of fields. No one lived there.

It was just as well. A motor somewhere, but silence over the land, silence like paper wrapping him up.

He fainted.

When Carver came to, his head was reeling, like a planet on a bad orbit. He could see the stars he passed, the Belt of Orion, the Seven Sisters, and there was Rosie, the missing dancer in the peach-colored dress. He grabbed the steering wheel, looked through the windshield at the spinning earth, rolled down the side window and spat the foul taste from his mouth. When a man was starving, his stomach with its own juices would digest itself from the inside out: a man eating himself. He thought that was funny, awfully funny, and began to laugh until a cough stopped him. He tried to swallow, stop the dry ache in his throat, and thought about a baby starving, a child eating itself in hunger. That wasn't funny.

He remembered punishments. No dinner. No lunch. Falling to his knees in the fields. The belt across the face that came when he was too weak to get out of its way. Not always. "Often enough," he said out loud, and laughed again, this time without collapsing into a fit of coughing.

If he was going to do this, he was going to have to be strong enough. The gas gauge read empty, and he figured that meant, just enough. He took off. Off to get the last chicken. He giggled. The chicken at the end of the road.

"Freedom," he said the word aloud. "Freedom from chicken." He almost skidded into the cornfield, but saved himself after he left tire marks in a crazy dance over the pavement.

This time he parked and went in. "Hey! I know you," he said as he leaned over the counter. The young man looked up, and saw who it was.

"Can I help you, sir?"

"I want some chicken. I want the very last chicken."

"I hear you, sir, the chicken that has no other place to go."

"That's it. The last chicken born from a hen before mother of chicken became styrofoam box. You hear me?"

"Yes, sir, I do. But maybe you don't want the last chicken. You want a real chicken."

"How would you know, boy?"

"I'd appreciate it if you didn't call me boy, sir. I could take it as an insult, as a black man."

Carver looked at him, craning his neck and swaying a bit. "Why, so you are, black, I mean. I knew that, but I was trying to give your youth its right calling. I guess you are a grown man, but just by a hair."

"Okay, I admit that. But please don't call me boy again. It's an insult, or worse."

Carver was shaken. It was the word his father used when he beat him. "I'm sorry. I didn't mean anything, honest. You look like a nice young man."

"That's all right now, sir. What was your order?" He wanted to get away from the man but was worried that he would fall onto the floor, hard. He got him seated and prepared a Big Guy's Bucket of Chicken, and dished out some mashed potatoes with gravy and hot biscuits with the order. He smelled his breath and there was no hint of alcohol. If not drunk, then, the guy must be hungry. He remembered it from back home, though he didn't see it here so much.

He brought the meal and a big cup of water with ice over to the man, and watched him. Carver drank down the water like it was saving his life.

Carver looked up at him. "What the hell are you doing here? You're not from here."

"I'm at the campus. I'm a student."

"Well, that's dandy," and he leaned in to read, "Freddy," in golden letters on the young man's shirt.

Freddy moved back from the table. "I'll get your check, sir," he said.

"Never mind," said Carver. He threw a twenty on the table. "I'm not going to quibble over the cost of the last chicken." He grabbed a biscuit from the plate and left, moving like he couldn't feel the ground under his feet.

Freddy had a great view from inside the chicken place. The sky was immense, almost as big as the one at home. He sat for a moment and watched the car labor down the road toward the vast fields, swerving a bit.

"I've got to go out," he called to his partner reading behind the counter, waiting for customers. He waved with his book and then bent back over it.

Freddy was poised for a battle, but his car started right away. He kept driving toward the new moon, already up, hoping to find the man who had just eaten three quarters of what he kept calling the last chicken. And, of course, they had to be from three different birds. That's how the slaughterhouse worked.

# *Chapter Six*

And he named her Rose, Rose of the Prairie, Rose of the Corn and Wheat and Soy Bean, Rose of the Flax Bundle, and he ran with her through the fields, played hide and seek with her at the belts of trees sheltering the land, listened for her dove cry as she bounced off the yellow bus from school to find him. And she called him Daddy, My Daddy, and inhaled the smell of the land in his arms, and it was a wonderful thing, until those days when he came to demand she call him Father.

Those were the days of worry. Those were the times of nightmare. Always on the table the ledgers, the stacks of bills, the sound of the auctioneer's voice approaching, the fight of a century gone out of him. And he ached for the fight. He ached to see his neighbors stand and bid as a mass of power, a solid block of fighting men, shouting out the numbers, the laughable numbers, as they had done in depression times.

"Fifty cents!" one would say, and then, "No, man! I'm going all the way! I bid a dollar!" and on up to three-fifty for the sport of it, and no outsider dared bid it up. No one dared. And after the auction the farmer made much of digging in his pocket for the three-fifty and buying back his land from his buddy, fair and square. And sometimes the workers from the Cities came, and one would raise the price a quarter and joke, "Maybe I won't sell back to you, old man, this'd be the first land I ever owned! But hell, I wouldn't know what to do with it. Looks like too much work for me," and the farmer, shaking now with his reprieve, slapped the dollar bills and a little change into the big scarred palm of a guy from the meat packing plant, down from St. Paul or up from Austin, and they shouted and played at brawl, and raised the farmer up on their shoulders.

But that was the past, those were the stories of the fathers and the mothers who stood, shoulder to shoulder, and dared the invaders to come into their house and take what they had built. Carver had heard the stories, and wanted to make them true again, but now the banks were all powerful, and the failures grew, rows of numbers that told a story he didn't want to hear.

"What!" he shouted at the girl when she came in from play, and grabbed her and hit her, and her shocked face saw that he was not her daddy that afternoon. "You have some respect for your father when he's working," he shouted, and twisted her arm while she wailed.

This was the thing that he grew. This was the thing that he watered, then. This was the crop that would grow past its season and keep growing, an unnatural thing, a crop that the bankers did not try to take from him, no matter how bad the figures looked, no matter they took everything else.

This was the harvest that would not end, not until he put the gun to his head, and—with her small face on the screen of the sky before him, her small shocked face—he pulled the trigger. And he saw how he would be then—a corner of his skull, the size of a child's fist, flying away from him into the wind of his journey, and he flopping and twitching, a bloody scarecrow in the fields of his old farm, among the rows straight and mechanical, there where the tractor had to lumber through a turn, and missed a row.

They used to say, "Don't skip a row in planting or surely someone close to you will die."

They were right.

And Carver looked out at the fields shifting beneath the winds of his memory, saw the great storms and twisters that picked up the things of the farm and settled them in another county, saw the big one that had brought his angel to him, and he knew that something must be buried in the fields, cloth and blood deep in the furrows of earth, buried and feeding worm and soil and burrowing thing, crows above in chorus urging, Die, you bloody scarecrow, die, and go home to your little girl.

# *Chapter Seven*

He slept in the car with his stomach full, and was awakened by its heaviness. His legs had gone numb in the cramped space. He feared it, not being able to walk, to do what he had to do.

Even in lean years, he could go out and get a deer, a bird. He had forgotten that. His family had never wanted for food. What he hadn't given them, he didn't have. Patience. Gentleness. Peace. He just didn't have it.

"Get your ass into this kitchen and tell me what this slop is you think you're feeding me for dinner," he'd once told Katie.

"Make the kid shut up, I'm trying to sleep," more than once he'd shouted, after a drunk.

And every year on the anniversary of his brother's death, or rather of his funeral, because they were never told the date he'd died, every year he was silent for days before and after, and went off with his gun up north where he and his brother used to go hunting. Eli came to him in the moonlight, trailing after the call of the loon, out of the shimmering lake. He said nothing to Carver. He didn't have to. Carver had stayed home to take care of the farm. And, soon, the farm would be lost.

"Okay, old man," he said out loud, and thumped his favorite drum roll on the dashboard.

He got the rifle out of the trunk, and walked in slow steps with it balanced across his outstretched hands. Processional, he remembered church, and laughed.

This is no laughing matter, he could hear the old man say, and his face turned grim as his father beat the laughter out of him.

"Just finishing up," he called out his report.

He had never shot a man. Ducks, yes, rabbits, geese, deer, an elk. He'd shot at a bear once. Didn't get him, and was glad not to see the collapse of the massive flank, the drop of the neck and the great head. He only meant to scare him off. And, once, he'd shot a buffalo. Like killing the past, he'd thought.

This would be his first man. And his last. It would be wonderful, he thought, like an eagle flying off. And he would never have to shoot again, never again the warm blood running down the body emptying of sound. The last twitch of muscle.

It was awkward, but he knew it would work. Others had done it before him. It was a great tradition among farmers. He started chuckling again, but caught a glimpse of his white face in the side mirror as he collapsed against the car door. "This is important," he told himself, "you've got to do this right, for Rosie," and he put his legs straight out in front of him and looked at his boots. His breath was more peaceful now. A crow cawed above him, that damn black bird, impatient for it.

He put the barrel of the gun in his mouth and moved his eyes west to east along the horizon. It was beautiful still, the land, and that bright line between earth and sky. He looked up and let the sky wash into his sight. Then he pulled the trigger.

When nothing happened, he swallowed his fear and tried to still the trembling of his legs, opened his eyes wider and pulled the trigger again. And once more. But the sky came back to him when he opened his eyes. He didn't understand. He rose to his feet and held the shotgun with the barrel to the sky, aiming at nothing.

It was this shot Freddy heard as he sped along the curving road. He'd had a bad feeling when the man had walked out, and wasn't surprised to hear gunfire. Nobody was going to buy an order of chicken from him and then go do himself in, or somebody else, not if he could help it. He'd seen enough. He leaned forward and cleared his mind, scanning the fields for a car, or a man.

Freddy came bumping down the hill at a speed his junker wasn't used to. It made Carver start laughing again. A cartoon strip car, he thought, and held his belly, waiting for the wheels to pop off one by one, the hood to yawn open, and great geysers of steam to announce the demise of the vehicle. But the car eased up toward him and stopped, the engine chugging to a last gasp.

The young man walked up to him and knelt beside him. "Mister?" he touched Carver on the shoulder. Carver shook his head.

"Sir, are you all right?" With that, Carver slapped both thighs and laughed so hard that a coughing fit came on. Freddy got some water from his trunk and Carver drank into silence. He worked to catch his breath. He looked up at his savior, and erupted back into full-blown laughter. This time he showed no sign of stopping, and began rocking back and forth, collapsing into himself, then throwing his head back and howling again.

Freddy waited. The man calmed down and managed to say, "Here I am being saved by some kid with an accent from...where the hell are you from?"

"Somalia. I am from Somalia."

Carver drew a blank.

"In east Africa, the Horn of Africa."

"Well, what did you do over there in east Africa?"

"We were farmers. On a small place."

"How the hell did you get here?"

"There was no rain. Then war drove us away from the land."

"And you came here?" asked Carver.

"First, a refugee camp. Then, a few years ago, we came here."

Carver reached for the young man's arm. He patted it and looked off into the fields.

Freddy spoke. "Sir, what was so funny?"

Carver smirked with his knowledge and leaned over toward his companion's ear, "There was only one bullet in the gun, and it wouldn't shoot me." He sat back and winked.

"That's a good thing, then."

He leaned in again and whispered, "It let me shoot God, though. I aimed straight up into Heaven, and it went"—he covered his ears—"boom! Isn't that something? I shot God!" He laughed some more, like it hurt.

"Well, I don't think you killed God or anybody else."

The laughter drained away.

"I've hurt people. Lots of people. You understand me?"

"We've all hurt people."

"No. I mean, I'm telling you the truth here. I've hurt people, good people, people I love. Or could love." He saw Freddy looking right at him. "My Rosie," he whispered, "that was my girl. And her mother." He thought of the woman he'd dragged from the bathroom back into bed. "I've made people feel like dirt." He saw Mary's face when he'd pushed her from his room. And he remembered that last time with her.

"And Barb," he said, "I had no reason to treat her like she was less."

"I see," Freddy said, though he didn't. He was silent for a while, breathing with the man like he would breathe with a child battling nightmares. "I'm glad I found you," he said.

"Carver. I'm Carver," the man offered.

"Let me take you home to your people, Carver."

"Home? My people? They're all gone."

"Where do you live, Carver?"

"Oh, my address, sure. Home, they took away. My people left me, and I am one lonely son of a bitch. Got a room in South Minneapolis. I can make it back there. Don't worry about me. Out of bullets, out of courage."

"Look, we're going to take your car. I don't think mine will do all the trip. I'm going to leave it at the bottom of the hill where nobody will bother it, and we're going to South Minneapolis, to your place. To your friends. And then I'll hop a bus and get back here in time for what I have to do."

"And I can get to what I have to do."

"You're not killing yourself, man. Not allowed. You've got a lot going for you."

"Funny. What have I got going for me?"

"Your looks, maybe? We'll think of something on the way. Please, get in the car."

They drove for a while in silence. Carver thought about what he had almost done, and didn't understand why he hadn't succeeded. "What do you think, Freddy," he asked, "how come the one bullet in the gun went up into the sky instead of down my gizzard?"

"Gizzard?"

"My throat, Freddy, my throat."

"Because you're not meant for a bullet. It's not your time." Freddy peered into the mirror and pointed back over his shoulder, "Now, that's a sunset."

Carver saw it behind him, the red road, brilliant, heading straight into the dreaming of the sun as it lowered itself to rest in the earth.

By the time the city skyline greeted them, it was late, and Freddy thought he might stay in town with friends. But the man wouldn't let him go.

"How many more payments you got on your vehicle back there?" Carver grabbed his arm and shouted over the wind and the rattle of something in his trunk.

"Funny, sir," Freddy answered, a bit offended and trying not to be ashamed of his old car. "It's a Toyota, Carver. I'm sure it needs only adjustment. They run forever, they are telling me."

"Yes, they do. Yes, they do," Carver said.

Freddy stole a glance at him. Carver had shifted back down into his seat, and stared into the lights up ahead.

"Let's go to the river, buddy. Please," he added.

They walked in silence. Laughter drifted out from under the trees along the river.

"So, that was your farm," Freddy said.

"Mine, and my family's, and my family before us, back a long time."

"A hard thing to let go, the land. Not like a shoe too worn, or a broken cup."

"We were what got broken. But we loved it. We loved the land," and he stared up into the face of the moon.

They walked for a long time along the riverbank. Then they came to sit on the rocks above the rushing water, the precious blood of earth.

Who is this man, Freddy wondered. He knew this night had tied them. He searched Carver's face for that hard hunger for death, and did not find it. He didn't know how, but it looked like he had stopped this thing. He said a prayer of thanks, above the night waters.

They moved down over the rocks until they stood in the wet, sandy soil licked by the river's journey. The sun moved up from the edge of earth, and Carver looked at Freddy as the young man turned, just at the moment the day threw down its first light. Sudden. Yellow.

Carver noticed a deep scar running from Freddy's cheekbone down to his chin. No accident, he figured.

"And what's your story, Freddy?" he blurted out, thinking then, too late, now I've gone and done it. "Looks like someone plowed up the side of your face, son," he went ahead with it.

"Everyone has a story," said Freddy. "Like the one you told me about Angie. I've heard that before. People told of this girl taken by the tornado and dressed up by the winds in a new dress, with fresh roses and wildflowers, and returned home, safe and sound. Everyone out there around my school knows the story, and we tell it again when the winds come and the children get frightened."

"Out there?" he said. "You heard about that all the way out near my farm?"

"Yes," said Freddy, "and I don't forget it, because it reminds me of the power of wind to throw seeds around, make things to grow. Reminds me of stories we used to tell at home. When we had storms back there in Somalia, those were blessing days, and we gave thanks with many prayers, because so long the sky was dead and still."

"But what's your story, friend?"

"I can't tell you all the story," said Freddy, "because I don't know it. I can say, we were from a village between two rivers. Juba and Shebelle. I can tell you, we were farmers, like you, Carver. When I was a small boy, I thought I could hear things grow. I could hear the green voices. You understand. Maybe someone told me that. I don't remember it. But the growing things knew to reach for sun, push roots deep and drink up water in the ground, and turn their mouths up to the sky to drink more the blessing as it fell. Me, too, I stood with my head up, my mouth open, drinking the rain, when I was small. Did you do that, Carver?"

"Sure I did."

"This was all my family wanted, to grow food, for ourselves and for the village. Me, I came to this world during no rains, and I screamed for three days, they told me that. I could have died, but no I did not. I had strength in my bones, I was big. I was not one of those skinny children the wind can push down. Each thing I took into my body gave me its power. They slaughtered the last goat in the village when many were ready to die, and they gave me some of its blood to drink. This saved me. I lived. I was always yelling for something good to eat, and when they gave me, my fist would close like a trap and hold that little food to my mouth."

"But drought came back many times and brought us famine," he said. Carver looked down and jabbed a stick into the earth, half expecting a geyser of water to rush forward. "It was a greedy old uncle demanding the food before any other. A withered soul wanting everything around it to be dried up, too. Like him.

"He took some of us. Two sisters, and my younger brother, dead in his bony hands. Not me, I said. Not me."

"What did you do?"

"My mother kept praying, but my father was so angry. Me, I heard water all the time, rushing like this waterfall in my head. I don't know how I saw this picture.

Maybe because of my Somali name, Geeddi. It means traveler, from when we were herders, and we brought the animals to the water. But our river was nothing like this water I saw in my head. It was hard road. Rocks and dead things. Whispers, saying, go, go someplace else."

Carver thought, river, the rush of it, the way it could take life. Bridges, to walk above the river, and flood walls, to stop its angry, wild play. He'd seen the winds spiral along the riverbank, pick up water and drop it miles away. Water had terrible power, but as great, he knew, was the power of its absence.

"Our father left us this way," said Freddy, "by the road of the river. He couldn't look at us every day, me always getting by, but the others, too weak. He went to find a better place, and when he came back, we packed our things and walked the river with him. We were like a crazy music orchestra, two pots clanging against each other, the broom tapping on the box of knives. A few peanuts they gave us for the journey, shaking like a seed gourd. And my mother, crying like wind in the night."

Something in Carver's stomach turned around. He looked down at his shoes, but the young man's voice went on like machinery that couldn't be stopped, no matter what was caught in the spinning of the gears.

"There was war everywhere along the way," Freddy said. "Not a big battle, but some shots here, there, someone grabbed, someone never going to come back. Whistles, long, low, then a grenade explodes. Sometimes Soviet grenades, sometimes American. All the leftover weapons in the hands of warlords—clan against clan—what do we care about that? We were looking for a place to grow food, grow children, grow old. We wanted to walk through fields of something that is alive.

"One night, we were sleeping under the scrub trees, against the rocks, the sky lying to us, crackling with promises of rain. The moon, that night, was full."

Carver didn't want to hear. He began to see the night, the moon, the dry riverbed, as Freddy talked.

Freddy touched his arm.

Then his voice became the wind and was a human voice no longer, except for the smallest whisper in it of the boy he had been when his father was taken, led off between two clan soldiers, and when the man kicked out at his captors, as he called to his woman and his children, his legs were grabbed and he became a sack of a man. The moonlight was falling, and the flash of dry lightning showed the boy his father flung into a pile of sacks in the bed of a lorry. Then the tail lights raced off, shining on the emptiness left behind.

"Maybe he became a real soldier, I used to think back then."

"Did you ever find him?"

"We never saw him dead. We never saw him alive. We don't know, and they tell us there is not a way to know. Maybe he fights with the warlords, or maybe they knew he wouldn't, and they killed him. Maybe he starved, like we almost did in Mogadishu. But, no, we never saw him again, not even for one day."

"How long before you came here?"

"Three years, almost."

"My sister, she is named Magol, she still draws his face," said Freddy after a while.

"Your father's?"

"My father's face. She draws it, in ink, in pencil. She paints it when she gets some tubes of paint. She paints him as he was in Somalia, and she paints him as he grows older. She keeps him for us, alive. She keeps him."

Carver saw his old man's face, how it hardened, how the light was gone from it at the end.

"I tried to stop them, you know, but my mother, like a football player or something like that, she threw herself on top of me just when I am running off, just when I open my mouth to yell and reach out my arms to grab him back."

"She tackled you."

"Yes, she tackled me, that is the word from football. She knew I was old enough to be taken into their army, too. And I had to be the man for my sisters and my brother who still lived. But maybe we will find my father. Maybe he's here, no? Maybe he is here in Minnesota. After all, he was a farmer."

The shadows settled back into the deep scar in Freddy's face. "What about that?" asked Carver, and curved his index finger along the same part of the bone in his own face.

"I had to stop something," Freddy answered.

"What?"

"It doesn't matter. I couldn't stop them taking my father, but I had to stop something else. For my sister's sake. This was in the city, in Mogadishu. We left not so much later, and we came here, and we are lucky. You know? We are very lucky."

The sunlight struck Carver's eyes, and he covered them, as he watched Freddy walk toward the trees. He did not know what to do, so he waited.

They would draw close. They would be friends, and meet and talk, and hold the pieces of their stories out to each other like bloody rags they didn't know what to do with, and like gifts they had fashioned with their own hands.

# Book Five

## Sun and Moon in the Afternoon Sky
### Winter 1996 - Early Summer 1997

"History, like geography, lives in the body and it is marrow-deep. ..."

—*The Woman Who Watches Over The World*
Linda Hogan, p. 59

"Light and darkness, life and death, right and left, are brothers of one another. They are inseparable. Because of this neither are the good good, nor the evil evil, nor is life life, nor death death. ... But those who are exalted above the world are indissoluble, eternal."

—*The Nag Hammadi Library, p 142*

## *Chapter One*

### *Winter 1996 - 1997*

This was the way it was for Angie, life and death at work all around her, as she was swept up into the strictures of biology. All female. Soon to calve. Her perfect thin girl waist? That was a sight no more, noted some of her meaner, more jealous classmates. Her wonderful breasts, not quite ripe, soon to serve God and greedy child.

She was new moon thickening; walked upon, some liked to think, by the heavy boots of exploration. The silent liquid cries, the weightlessness of float in the travel chamber, the odd dance with the other traveler—she'd done it all, the gossipers could see, and now was marked.

Others thought, why the hell not? This girl had next to no childhood, caring for the sick mother, trying to make a home for the hard-working, almost-widowed father who was dutiful to the corpse bride, man and daughter both living with the mound of death that was their kin, and loving her, too. And the girl got As in each and every class, and the man never had a vacation. Both were good. Daily, and with heart.

Can you beat that? Who can live that way, day in and day out without a whimper, without a break, without a fall? And perhaps the girl wasn't the only one in that house who had lapsed, some of the neighbors whispered, always on the lookout for news.

Regardless of the talk, somehow this angel, child-mother of the green suck, had fallen into womanhood, her perfect head shamed, her perfect body hooked up to service the next generation, her new womanliness a thing explored by a long-haired, dark-skinned boy. Handsome, it could be granted, but dark against her brilliant light.

Now, there were neighbors smug at her fall after so much goodness, while others were in a fury about it, wanting her banished from high school grounds. Yet others saw the whole affair as full of grace, a bit wrong because too early in the morning of the lives of these kids, but astonishing in the way the two found each other after their separate rough roads, and were soon to bring forth a new perfection of child, a mix of the loveliness of each; the history, the laboring and loss and magical strength, of each.

These folks, it didn't bother at all, and they wished everyone well. They prayed for the health of the grandma-to-be, sat with the great-aunt-to-be, brought cakes

148

and knit booties and never made a pot of soup without a bowl for the sick woman. Soon, they would be cooing over the baby and yearning for a little one in their own home.

Some folks heard their angry God and stayed away, lest they catch the darkness of that house. Darkness, yet others were heard to say, is one thing. Mixing it with the light, like the sun and moon floating toward each other in the same sky, that is quite another. Their ancestors didn't journey across an ocean, then jolt over the bone-strewn plains, to mix their blood. Shed it, they might, for their own, but mixing it was out of the question. The age of the parents was just a footnote, these folks sighed, and they quoted articles and newscasts and the homespun wisdom of their forebears about the doomed lives of mixed-race babies. They kept a sharp eye on that shabby house. A few even raged at the sunlight that washed its windows to brilliance and thawed the icicles that shed their pure bodies like a melody of chimes, some time ahead of those hanging on from the eaves of their own respectable houses down the block, still in shadow.

All in all, it was something to talk about, but their own hardworking lives kept most of the folks near Chicago and Lake living like the good neighbors they had always been, and wishing that misfortune blow over their houses without touching down.

And so it happens, some late afternoons, that the sun and the moon both look down upon the neighborhood, keeping their distance from each other, but shining their different lights from their faraway points in the sky.

It is the paler light, almost ghostly, one might say, that will stay the night, her pitted face appearing from between the limbs of trees, her glow dissolving in lake water, while the sun, youthful in its passionate gift, will slide under the horizon of earth and sleep through.

Under such a sky of sun and moon together, with her pregnant daughter off at school learning about the Aztecs, staring up into the great calendar wheel of life, Barb was reading her doctor's journals. She could see the laboratory mice stumbling about in their cages with breast cancer and prostate cancer, and yes, someone feeds them, and true, someone watches them, and daily, someone waits for them to live or to die, more tending to than your average mouse gets as it runs about the fields, devouring and being ignored, except when it is caught in the shanks of the plow and bleeds, and makes bloody the fields, the crops, the day in memory.

The first time young Barbara saw it, she wept, and climbed back up on the tractor with her father, who held her to him as well as he could, driving through. Late, if he didn't watch it, for his shift at the hospital.

"What a terrible death," she called out to him above the engine.

149

"There's worse for us, if we're not careful. Remember. So look what you're doing. Always pay attention."

"It's terrible, all the same."

Yes, thought the farmer, it is.


Now, as for Barb, she kept wondering why she had been chosen to bear the burden of such illness; why, each time there seemed a victory over its brutal progression and she began to feel better, the cancer came back.

A decade before, on the day she was first told it was there in her skin, she went to stand in the yard while no one was home and raise her face to the sun, which she believed had loved her, and ask why it had marked her so.

Stop wondering so much, there were those who wanted to tell her. Someone should have tapped her on the shoulder and said this: cancer has been around since the beginning of time. That's right, the very beginning, before sun was poison, before food was poison, before water was poison. Before history lay silent in the ground, though some might say that it's been buried since the first event, the first meeting of humans and earth, since long before the first word.

These greedy little cells, these parasites without loyalty to the order of the body or the superior knowledge of the brain, of its DNA codes, are developing all the time, at every moment—why, at this very moment—in the body of each of us, sun worshipper or housebound hermit. And thus it has always been. It's only lately cancer has been winning in such numbers, the hum of multiplying cells rising to a roar.

It was Barb who flung off her hat in defiance of her mother, Barb who insisted on rolling the great canisters of pesticides and herbicides to a corner of the barn and mixing them herself to prove to the men she could do the job. Ah, moon-lovely young Barb, her skin a bit blue, with a smattering of adolescent craters, what was she letting herself in for? Why not a hat? A long-sleeved shirt? Why not cover up? She left the farm, brushed off the chemicals she had worked with, hung up the gloves she wore to mix them, but only to find herself up to her elbows in uranium on the assembly line at Honeywell. And now Barb lay, heaving forth the smell of dying in the bed.

How, then, to look at cancer as anything but the way truth gnaws at us, the way the past surfaces, as the pitted face of the moon rises to watch over the fields, and breaks the sky with its stolen light?

But the innocents? Barb kept asking, for herself and for the others. Plenty of people got caught in a cloud of paraquat; she was not alone. Ask a Vietnam vet. Why, ask Vietnam. Remember Agent Orange? Some of the neighbors nodded at this.

But had she never heard of sacrifice?

"All great cultures, and which among them think themselves otherwise, practice it," said Angie's teacher that very day in class, "and think it well worth it." Some of the students, dreaming of spring break, of sunbathing in Cancun long after the fact, now imagined themselves robed and sweeping up the steps to the Aztec temple at Tenochtitlan to wait beneath the shining blade, with its blaze of jewels in the handle, and tremble for the incision, believing they would feel the uprooting of their hearts, sense still the beating when held up in the breath of copal to the god of civilization; their sacrifice like no other; each one's own bloody, pounding heart a music that could never be duplicated, even among the ten thousand who climbed the steps each year.

"They must have wanted it," said the students in the front row of desks, turning over in their minds to sun the other side. "No victims there. It's cultural."

Easy, then, Angie thought, but did not say, to make sacrifice of others.

## *Chapter Two*

### *Winter, Early 1997*

They fought, a little every day.

"Angie, what's wrong?" William prodded her to talk.

"What do you think is wrong? Look at me. Look at what I've done to my life. My family. My mother is dying, but she has to worry about me."

"Angie—"

"No! Nothing you can say is going to make it any better. It's your fault, too, not just mine. But how's your life going to change?"

"My life is going to change plenty."

"I asked, how, William."

"Look, I have to step up, ready or not, and be a man. Make a living, Angie, for three people. Quit school, at least for now. It's pretty major for both of us."

"Well, I can't do this!"

"Look, Angie, if you can't, you can't. I'll take the baby home with me, and Madeleine will help me, if that's what you want. I'd rather be with you, but—"

"Are you crazy? You're not taking this baby away from me. I just want a life. I want to see things, go places."

"We still have legs. We're just starting out. We'll have a chance to see the world. Give it time."

"Why are you always so damned philosophical, William! I can't stand it!"

"I'm not, Angie. It's just the way things are. We made a mistake and I'm sorry you have to pay for it more than me, but later we'll both do the work, equal. I promise."

"Look, my heart is breaking—"

"I know, Angie."

"—my mother is dying, and she may never see this baby."

"She will, I'm sure she will. You be sure, too. She's holding on. The baby's keeping her alive, doing for her what the doctors can't."

Angie sat down, her legs splayed for support. My mama's medicine, she thought, and ran her hand over the arc of her belly. William moved behind her, kissed the top of her head and then fell closer to her, kissing her neck, moving his hands to her swollen breasts, leaving his palms there until her body rose up in warmth. He knelt between her thighs and wouldn't stop touching her, the baby swimming inside her, the boy who would have to be a man moving everywhere over her body and then into it, and she knew she was the sea, and the waves carried her to sleep.

He lifted her from the chair to the bed, where she mumbled into the pillow as he let the blanket float over her. He went to check on Barb, who also slept, then moved from her labored breathing through the hallway and bounded on quiet feet down to the kitchen to begin cooking. He read then as he watched over the pots on the stove, and all was clear, the history of his people in this place they call Minnesota, and the way he had to tell it in school.

He would tell them about Mankato—Mahkata—Blue Earth, and the hanging, all at once, of thirty-eight of his people. How they chanted. How the chanting stopped. He would tell them why the Dakota rose up to war against the settlers, how the whites had taken millions of acres of his people's home and given them nothing for it. He'd tell them of the thunder of the buffalo over the plains, and how it ended with slaughter. He would talk about the greedy traders who kept the treaty money, about Trader Myrick and the others, who dismissed the men who came to beg for food for their families dying of starvation, men almost dead themselves on the rack of their own ribs.

"Let them eat grass," the trader had said, but it was Myrick whose eyes rolled up to his heaven as his mouth was stuffed with it, the truth of the earth, the green truth. And Angie, when she could, read with William, and wept with him, and was silent. The heart of him knew then they could bring up this child right. He closed the book for now to make plates for Barb and Angie, and carried them upstairs, the steam rising from each outstretched hand.

Angie didn't say a word when she saw him. She took the plate and sniffed at it, then dug the fork into the mound of beans and rice and shredded chicken. She smiled at him and ate, but she still wanted to run away. She still wanted wings.

That night it was time. When she thought of flying, her body remembered the night of the tornado. She saw how she could be carried aloft. She heard the ripping of her dress, wrenched off one shoulder. She felt the cold rain enter where the cloth flapped open from the waistline, how it doused her with fear that the dress would fall from her, leave her trembling and wet at the school door. That they would find her this way.

Was it this trembling that Carver wanted to cover? Maybe, yes, it was this, what he wanted to do. To cover her. To warm her. Make sure she was safe. But she shuddered to remember, so small she was, feeling the hands of the storm on her, and the shame of her dress ripped away by the splintering school door.

She understood more this night than in all the days since the tornado. It was time, then, to tell, and she went to her mother's room and found her lying on her side, reading a letter, her favorite old band playing in the background, singing "Take a load off Fannie, take a load for free."

"Mama, listen," she said, "I have to tell you a story." Barb clicked off the radio. "I have to tell you about the peach-colored dress and the tornado." She stroked her mama's head and the sick woman shifted her weight and worked to sit up.

"At last, Angie. I'm getting ready to leave town here," she said. "This has been a wonder and a doubt for all these years since that night."

Angie couldn't tell if the sound in her mother's throat was a chuckle or a gasp for air, but she sat on the side of the bed and began the story of how the great door of the school slammed shut in the rain and left her, a thin leaf against the power of the winds. Then she told how it was Carver who came out of the dark sky and swooped her up in his arms.

"He saved me, Mama, no matter what else, he saved me."

"What else?" Barb said after a moment. Her eyes seemed to float on their own tiny lakes, but they were unblinking. Angie laughed, nervous to tell it.

"His daughter's dress," Barb said after a while. "He dried you off and put on some clean dry clothes, and this was his daughter's own dress."

"She'd never worn it. They'd already left when he bought the dress, and his ex-wife never gave him a chance to give it to his little girl. She sent it back, she sent everything back."

"And he wanted you to wear it and to sit with him. Nothing else to it."

"That's all. It was strange, and I knew it then, but it was like a fairy tale. Carver was the tin soldier who came to save me from the storm, protect me from danger until it passed. I knew that without him I could be tossed up into the funnel and never get home. I was so scared of the thunder and lightning, but plenty scared of him, too.

"I think I knew something wasn't right when this man I didn't know kept whispering to me, acting like my own father, drying me off from the rain and toweling my hair. He kept saying, 'There, there, that didn't hurt a bit, did it, Angel?' He kept calling me Angel, as if that was my real name, not Angie."

"You were an angel to him. To a lost man, a man who'd lost his own daughter, you were like the angel of all little children."

"It was weird, Mama, but he got much worse after. He treated me like we were bound together."

"I guess you were."

"And I was never supposed to tell. He made me promise. All this time, I felt violated. I didn't even know the word for it."

"But you knew something was wrong."

"He pulled me into the middle of something that had already started. Like this was a play somebody else had written down, that the actors have to perform. Sure, they change it around and walk across the stage. They take off one costume and put on another one."

"That's what you did."

"But it has to happen just the way it was written a long time ago, and if something goes wrong, if an actor trips on the stage or forgets what to do, if even one character refuses to say the lines just right, the whole world will cave in. If the costumes don't fit, everyone will go nuts, throw things, go into a rage worse than the storm outside. I don't know if Carver meant it that way, but that's how it felt to me."

"It was in him that way. We've seen it."

"But it's crazy, because at the same time, I felt safe. In the middle of something terrible and dangerous, I knew I was safe. And the dress was so pretty, and he was so gentle."

"That's in him, too."

"But I was ashamed whenever I saw him after that. Ashamed and afraid, like he was watching me to see what I'd say."

"It's always hard to keep secrets. But no more, baby. You have nothing to be ashamed of, nothing to hide."

"No. No more."

She waited to see if her mother had anything else to say about what had come out.

"Finally," said Barb.

"I guess it was wrong, what Carver did."

"Wrong, maybe, because he was not your father. Wrong, because of the secret he made you keep."

"He wanted Rosie back so much. And now that will never be."

Barb was silent.

"It was a beautiful dress, though, wasn't it?" Angie said, and they both remembered the small waist encircled by the dance of tiny roses, and the smell of peach and cedar that never faded from the cloth.

# *Chapter Three*

## *May 1997*

The birth would not be sorrowful, but a race to bring forth the child so she could be held by her grandmother. Barb lay ill, cancer traveling the silver tangle of lymph, her body shrinking as she moved down the road out of it. Her agony was beyond words, and she gripped Mopstick's hand with a power that tried to equal her pain. She strained toward the baby's first cries and vowed she would be around to hear them.

Her husband could not bear to think of the moment after her leaving, and so stayed with her each moment before. He became a new man with each breath, born into the knowledge of his love and how it had sustained him for all these many years.

He got into bed to hold her body with every part of himself. Her fever turned to chills and shook him, but in his embrace, her pain became lighter. All his love flowed into her. Her body went back to its moments of pleasure. She held his hand to her breast. "Remember that night," she whispered, "we made Angie," and he moved with her then to the fields, where they fled the silence of her parents' dining table during a dutiful visit.

"She's our blessing forever, that girl," he told her. He caressed her tortured scalp, with its patches of hair left after the failed treatments, and closed his eyes to see what she was remembering, to hear the wind play its flute and the leaves chant, to gaze up at the stars, the Seven Sisters in their dance. Barb took the windsong into her and her breath steadied, and in his heart he went into the soul of her and was cradled, grew to man, and died with her.

They slept while the night birds sang and Angie was screaming in her hospital room at the passing of the plug of bloody mucus from her body. The doctor patted her arm and walked out. She turned around at the door to wag her finger at the young woman, "You'll be fine. Don't worry so much. I'll be back in a bit."

Madeleine took her place at the bedside, and washed the girl's face with a cool cloth, singing low and smiling. "Angel," she said.

"You're the angel," Angie said.

"Oh my god," Angie called out as a wave of contractions came. William heard her from the hall and rushed in. "I'm okay, I'm okay, I'm okay," she chanted at him with her breath. She gripped both his hands and looked up at him as the pain subsided.

"Did you call my house?" she asked.

"She's bad, but she's holding on. She's asleep now. Your dad can't leave her."

"I know that. Did you tell him I'm all right? Did you tell him not to worry about me? Just take care of mom? Oh god, I need to be there with her."

"You will be," said Madeleine. "She's not going anywhere until she can see you again and hold her grandchild. You can bet on it."

"I can't lose my mother." And she wept, until the next contractions came, she wept.

Do it now, thought Madeleine. You won't have much time for it later.

She was glad to feel the pain. She wanted to know something, an atom, of what her mother was going through. She clutched the sheets, and saw them all around her: Madeleine, William, the nurse, the doctor, and breathed in the air thick with the coming of life. She rocked and swayed and tried to raise her hips up from the bed, above where the child would fall into the arms of the world. She howled and learned her voice, threw it against the green cliffs guarding the river, and when it returned, took back all her breath for the sound that would open her. She swam through the river then.

She screamed for her mother, and the infant came to them all, down the red cord of road into the circle of those who waited, and then someone put her there on Angie's chest and she cried, and moved her arms and legs and blinked her blind eyes in the great winds of desire that would make her strong and carry her home.

## *Chapter Four*

Barb waited, how she waited for the child. The baby gave her back, time. Made it more than her little death sentence. More than the waiting room.

"You can come in now." "The doctor will see you now."

And how he saw her was as a woman without time, without the simple unfolding of days that would put her back in the generations, that would let her breathe between a knife in the ribs, and starlight. And now, underneath all the tests she had failed, was the surging of her blood to push her to know the transformation of her DNA, and Mopstick's, and Angie and William's, in this new spirit made flesh.

Barb knew the world was changing. Opening itself. She rubbed her cheek against the soft pillowcase. Baby's breath. First skin.

What god had finally loved her enough to keep her hanging on to the cloth of the day the baby would come home to her?

There was no rise in the earth that could hold her yet. And there was nothing in the room that smelled of death. Madeleine had made sure of that.

Then the one cry reached her ears. She pushed herself up. Her heart was racing. She wiggled her toes. She wanted to be all there. All live and in motion. All grandmother. Able to hold her arms out from the pain to make a cradle. She wanted still to be flesh.

Some neighbors said not to bring the child into the room. Angie ignored them, went, from the front door left open, with her small firm steps up to the bedroom, aching a bit but so young her body remembered the lift in her muscles that brought her always closer to the sky, more than the exhaustion of giving birth.

She placed the child in her mother's arms. It was, this room, these arms, the first place at home Angie went, the first place she lay the child down. "She's Winona," Angie said, "Winona Rose Sofia." Then she couldn't say another word. It was the most beautiful thing she had ever seen.

Barb remembered for an instant the blur of breath and light that Angie had been, the hush in the room, the hummingbird of heart, and had thought it would be the same feeling, but it was not. The dark-headed child had a different weight, a different strength to her. A little hummingbird heart, for certain, but it was not just her appearance that was different. It was that she had come from the body of her daughter. Barb's own body was one she always knew would yield. She was a laborer. She was earth, she thought at times. But her angel was different. She had understood her daughter's passion, her loss of childhood in the arms of someone who loved her as more than a child. But this? Her daughter split by birth, giving forth. It was hard to understand and she stared at the infant but then looked up at the daughter she had borne. Angie spoke then.

"Winona, that's Dakota for the first born child, for a girl. Sophia, because she is going to be wise. And Rose, you know, for Rosie. Mama, what do you think?"

This was the child of her dreams. This was the yawn of time, the shudder of passing into the world, as she would pass out of it.

This was the being to help Angie go beyond her mother's death. Barb's generation would fall off the ends of the earth, and yet it would keep turning.

She held the child, a little teacup not to be tipped. She kissed her, many times. This was the generation none could live without.

Winona was the last baby she would see.

"Mama," Angie startled her. "I have to feed Sophie now."
Barb gave the baby back to her mother.

## *Chapter Five*

Barb saw the door push open, and heard Madeleine's voice. She wanted to understand her words. She couldn't, at that moment.

There was tea and toast. There was jam—raspberry, how did Madeleine know?

Barb worked the worn muscles of her face. She wanted to smile. The plumes of steam moved into spiral. Madeleine was stirring the honey in.

"You made it, Grandma," she said.

Such a steep path to this moment. First Carver, then Madeleine and William, had brought Angie back in the night. Barb's own girl carried off by wind, by water, by her own heart. Then Barb heard the cries of the child whose life would unfold without her.

"There's so much to talk about," Madeleine said.

"How did William come to you?" Barb wanted to know. Madeleine's sister's boy.

"I'm from Lower Sioux, near Morton," Madeleine said. "The reservation."

"You left—"

"—when I got William. When his parents were killed. A car accident. Some kid from a farm town. Drank for hours with his buddies, then went off to a party to check on his girlfriend. She was dancing with another boy. He went into a rage."

"That's an old story."

"His head got crazy with jealousy and alcohol. He jumped into his car. He didn't stop for one light, didn't slow down. He drove straight into them, Raymond and Julia. Ray died right away. My sister, she hung on a few days."

"They were right in that boy's path. God knows why."

"And he lived."

"What happened to him?"

"He's in a wheelchair. He goes to their graves every year."

"And William—"

"William was seven. I could have brought him to live with me on reservation land, but I wanted to keep things the same for him as much as I could."

"Such a sad thing. But it gave you and William each other."

"It did."

At times Barb did not know if Madeleine was really there.

Madeleine watched Barb sleep, listened to her dream talk. She slept in the chair, left to tend to Angie and the baby, make space for August to sit.

In the morning, Barb remembered that Madeleine was a history teacher. "I bet you're good at it," she said.

"People love stories," said Madeleine. "Some stories are full of lies. Lots of lies are in print. Many truths you can't get in books. They're in the stories people tell."

"William has stacks of books on his desk he says you told him about."

"I use many history books to teach the students to listen for the lies, and untell them."

"Some kids get angry, I bet."

"They defend themselves. But I say, listen to the stories of people you don't know. I bring tapes, films, not only what I say in my own voice. And the students gather stories from their own people. When everyone feels like they've been heard, we go into the hard things. How power works. How crimes linger."

"How crimes linger," Barb repeated.

"At first, some non-Indian students are afraid it will only be about the Indian world. And they'll disappear, the way they think we have. Indian teacher; Indian stories. But I also bring tapes and books with the voices of miners and farmers and factory workers, men and women, kids. The voices of people from Laos and Vietnam, Somalia and Ethiopia, from Scandinavia and the rest of Europe, from the south, migrants from Mexico. Everything I can find, to bring more of the whole story."

Barb wanted to speak, but couldn't. She grabbed for the tea and drank. Sweet and thick, it quieted her cough. Still, she had a hard time saying it.

"I don't want to go. I don't want to leave." She grabbed Madeleine's hand and pulled her close.

"We'll keep you with us, Barb, I promise. You'll shine on these children, don't you worry."

"And August," she whispered.

"No one will ever touch his heart the way you do."

"I don't want him to be alone."

"You'll be with him. Inside him, you'll live together always."

Late summer, my late summer man, she thought. But the clock at her bedside whispered how good it could be, how right, if Madeleine were the one he would love after her. Something struck then against the bell of her heart. She hesitated, then said it. "He was with someone else after I'd been sick for a while. We never talked about it, but I'm sure."

Madeleine took a sip of her tea, and licked the sweet syrup from her lips. "Did he love you less afterwards?"

"No, but I think he suffered for it."

"Good!" said Madeleine. "He should suffer a little bit for that."

"But I know why he did it."

"You're smart then. He might not have known."

"They were cutting the life out of me. I wanted to give up and leave. He looked at me and saw death."

"That's it, isn't it, the reason for so many things."

"I don't want him to know I know about it."

"Then he won't. But he's a good man, that's clear."

"One mistake."

"One mistake. Pretty good."

"I didn't make any," Barb laughed.

"Bet you wish you had!" and they both laughed.

"More toast now?" Madeleine asked.

But Barb's eyelids were thick with closing, and the words in her mouth, "Yes, yes please," would stay on her tongue as she slept and watched August in embrace with a shadow.

When she woke, it seemed many days had passed. She held on to the sides of the bed, the water within her seeping to the sheets. She was sorry to be this way, like a baby but at the end of life. She pushed herself up against the pillow and called for Madeleine, who had been listening for her.

After Madeleine cleaned her up, she sat by the bed and took her hand. "I wish I could stay here and get to know you better," Barb told her.

"Not so much to know."

"Ever married?"

"No, not exactly."

It had to be said. "Could you ever have feelings for August? I don't want him to be alone."

Madeleine stayed quiet for a while, then told her the story of Iris.

"Does William know?"

"He does now. He didn't for a long time, or at least I thought he didn't, but these kids are smart."

"What you told me about Iris, it's pretty romantic."

"Romantic?"

"Yes," said Barb, "first kiss in the woods. Secret love. How you hold that memory. It's plenty romantic."

"You're goofy with painkillers," Madeleine said, but loved that Barb thought of it this way. Passion, pure and simple.

Barb kept thinking about Madeleine and Iris, and said a prayer that her friend would not be alone when the kids went off somewhere. She had so hoped that August and Madeleine would be a comfort to each other. That she could leave knowing the woman who would lie beside her man someday, and that it would be someone Angie loved, but this news made her think, and filled her dreams that night.

Later, she awoke in a panic, sweating in the darkness she knew would be her home forever. "No, no," she kept repeating, but low, hoping that no one had heard her. Then she thought of Madeleine, Madeleine with a lover, and felt a great excitement, a deep comfort in the flesh as she imagined woman enfolding woman, giving each other a place to be, the way a mirror never could.

To be in love with a woman, she'd think now from time to time, that's one thing I've missed in this life. She was thinking about it so hard one afternoon, that when August came in, she jumped.

"What's wrong, Barb?" he asked.

"Nothing. Just come here."

She held him, and licked the place of salt behind his ear.

"Barb!"

"Oh, hush," she said, and hugged him for dear life, folding him into her body the way she thought a woman might have done for her. He rested with her, and was comforted to feel the strength still in her, the warmth of her.

Madeleine came up to tell them dinner was ready. She saw them there, and stayed in the doorway for a few moments. Then she closed the door to keep out the noise as William played with the baby.

## Chapter Six
### June 1997

This was the child: a dancer, calming to sleep in the arms of her mother or father, sometimes the grandfolks. Hair the color of the inside of night, brilliant with stars. More hair on her head than the usual newborn. "Like a little buffalo calf," her auntie said. Her mouth, a tiny rosebud. All four limbs strong and well-formed, making it a battle to get the sleepers on her. Much kicking girl. "Dancing in the stars girl," Madeleine said.

"Winona Sofia." They hadn't yet told Carver her middle name was Rose, like his own girl's name. "She sure shows her spirit," Mopstick said and held her with his memories of Angie as a baby. He sat in Barb's empty chair while she lay in her sickness upstairs, and made himself a moment of joy to fall into, as he inhaled the scent of beginnings and called to her in his heart, Hey, grandma, we continue.

The child was a beauty, made more so by the mark on her cheek, a small and perfect raspberry kissed by all who loved her. A whisper of the past. This was the child that Carver came to see. He sat in the bright room with his Angie and said nothing as he watched the perfect round face, the dark eyes that fixed on the newcomer, as he shifted in his seat, full of a speech he was already making, thought Angie.

"I'm glad to see you, and the baby, too," he said. "Is Barb any better?"

Before she answered, William came in from fixing the back porch step, and Carver rose and let his long legs take him to face the young man. He put out his hand. "William," he said, and his hand was received in the warm, strong hand of the new father, who pulled the stiff sorrow of him closer and embraced him, in the way that men do when they can clear the path to each other.

Carver blurted out, "I'm happy for you guys. She's a beautiful baby."

"August told me about your daughter. I'm so sorry," the other man said, and put his hand on Carver's shoulder. "You're welcome here, you know."

Carver stepped back into himself for a moment and then remembered, "I have something for the baby." He brought out a box from inside his large jacket, wrapped in paper of bunnies and birds, and held it out in his immense, worn hand. "It's for the baby," he said again in the silence.

"Open it, William," Angie said, "I bet it's just what we need."

Carver looked down. And from the box, one by one, came seven silver cloth stars, plush and sparkling, on a curving path that led up to a cap of strings from which they danced like sisters. "It's a mobile," he said, "good for the baby to watch from her crib, good for her eyes. She'll reach up, you know. Reach for the stars."

"This is great," William said, "very beautiful," and Carver grinned, against his will, but there it was.

"Stay for dinner, Carver." Angie looked up at him.

"I'd really like to," he said, as best he could because his heart was breaking open and he didn't understand what it was that was happening. It was warm in the room, so warm that his heart was leaping in his chest, calling to him with its powerful rhythm. He didn't think he deserved anything but a hard chair pushed up to the wall, straight and rough against his back, until he could make amends to them all, but Angie rose with the baby and kissed him on the cheek.

"So, stay, Carver," she said.

"I can't, Angie, there's something I have to do, and I just today got up the courage to do it." It was then that he saw the purple stain on the baby's face and said, "Oh, the baby has a birthmark."

"Yes, a little raspberry. It's okay, Carver," said Angie.

"It's a sign of her history," William said.

"Her history?"

"Yes. It started with a hen's egg."

Carver went quiet, wanting the rest of the story.

"You know, the people were starving. Banished from their land."

"Signed it away, didn't they? For money."

"They were cheated, Carver, cheated out of what was promised them for millions of acres of Minnesota territory. They had to watch their babies, their whole families, weaken and die. Then four young men out hunting found a full nest by the fence of some settlers. Some of them were afraid to take the eggs. But they all were so angry that they killed some of the whites, five people, and a terrible war between the Dakota and the whites began."

"The country was already at war. The Civil War."

"This was a war, too, Carver, a war for survival. And the war grew. It ended with many dead. Many whites, many Indian. Hundreds of us imprisoned in Mankato. They hung thirty-eight Dakota, right on the bank of the Minnesota River. All at the same time, with one cut of the rope. But now some say the last one's rope broke, so they strung him up again. He followed the others."

Carver wanted to say something, but couldn't think what.

"A long story," William said, "an ugly story. Seventeen hundred Dakota force-marched a hundred-fifty miles from Lower Sioux to Fort Snelling. Many died on the road, or were beaten or stoned to death as we passed through the settlers' towns. And Fort Snelling was a genuine concentration camp, Carver. So many dying of disease and starvation, of the cold. Women raped by white soldiers while their men, locked up, could only pray and chant and call out to them. You see? There's testimony.

"In spring the survivors were thrown into steamboats and railroad cars and deported. Dying on the journey, or sent to barren lands. We had a great leader, Taoyateduta – Little Crow, who hadn't wanted to go to war but would die with his people. My people. After many battles he led his band away to the Dakota plains, even up to Canada, but came back to Minnesota to find horses. He was picking raspberries with his son Wowinape over by Hutchinson. A few raspberries to take away the hunger of the journey, that's all. The farmer came and shot at them. He killed Little Crow. Didn't know who he was, but they were paying twenty-five dollars for each Indian scalp, so the farmer scalped him."

Carver smelled the dark juice of the berry. But to be killed for it? "I thought it was the Indians—"

"—who did the scalping, I know. There's a lot to the story, Carver," said William, "a lot more to the story of my people than you've ever heard."

"I'm sorry."

"There's lots to read, if you want. But, you see, the baby is marked, and the mark on her skin helps tell the story of us, what was taken and how we fought. How we tried to live."

Carver sat down. He saw Barb in front of his eyes, how marked she was, how much story he'd never learned. Marked with story, he thought, and looked down at his own lined, trembling hands. He saw his hard work, and the emptiness that filled the furrows in his flesh. He saw the dark knuckles, felt the ache for the land in his deeply jointed fingers, and wept a little into the cup his hands made.

He brushed at his eyes as casually as he could manage, and rose. "Please tell Barb I stopped by, and was sorry not to see her," he said, and then stumbled to the door trying to get out before the tears came loose and his voice collapsed in a cry. When the wind hit his face, he heard, "Come back for dinner, anytime, Carver, anytime," and the rains began to fall, a real Minnesota storm.

# *Chapter Seven*

He drove less than twenty, stuck behind some farmer in a pick-up. He laughed at that. Some farmer he was, in a useless city model. But then some drunken Indian began yelling at his car, walking beside it all the way down Franklin Avenue, as long as he could keep up.

"Who are you?" he shouted at Carver, who looked through the window at his angry face, his blazing eyes.

"Who are you?" the man kept insisting, and answered his own question, "The Great White Father who blesses us with whiskey," he said, and held out his hand beside the window, pointing to his palm and smiling. "Go ahead," he yelled, "bless me!" Then the pick-up ahead of Carver turned right at the corner, and so he sped up, watching the guy in his mirror waving at him like a well wisher at a train station.

Carver shivered, remembering the fight, four boys punching and shoving and yelling. He hung back, smaller than the others, tagging along until something burst, something very old, and the boys threw each other down and rolled over the grass, red trickling from their noses, their lips; bloodstains blossoming from their clothing. That wild storm, what boys do until they are men, he thought, and then they go to war.

The Great White Father, it came to him as he drove, who stills the feet of the rabbit, and he heard his father shoot and shoot and shoot and saw him coming down the hill with a bloody batch of fur hanging from one hand. The Great White Father, who silences the cry of the bird, and again shots rang in his head and they began to fall out of the sky, the ducks and geese, still opening their wings but without a sound. The Great White Father, who makes muddy and low the waters, makes a girl almost drown in the mud of his very own hatreds, makes the crops to burn while the belly hungers of millions are raging. And makes the cells of death to grow. He saw Barb before him, tumors devouring her face, the great crop of cancer cells humming at their work within her. He punched the steering wheel, and the horn got stuck and blared its warning as he jiggled the panel of sound into quieting.

After Herman had punched him that day as Carver ran between the four large boys fighting and tumbling down the wet green hill of the afternoon, the Indian boy looked down at his own fist and shook it out to a flat palm. As Carver was falling to earth, he saw Herman run away, followed by his brother. Carver hit the ground just as the two white boys who had pushed him to come along for the fight fled in the opposite direction.

He got up and wobbled away as the last rays of the sun reached for him and sent a shaft of light over the fields to guide him to the house. He collapsed in the arms of his mother, who washed his face and hands, set a cold slab of meat over his left eye, and sang to him as he lay winking at her with his bad eye in the darkening house, while his father strode through the kitchen and vowed he'd teach him how to fight before the next season took the land.

Carver kept driving down the Avenue and then south until he got to Mary's building. He sat in the car while the sun dropped below the horizon, and entered the darkness of the street. He rang the intercom buzzer for her apartment and prayed, "Be home, Mary. Be alone."

"Speak," blurted out the electric voice.

"It's Carver, Mary," and he waited. "I just want to talk to you." Something roared in the vestibule—his own heart, the rush of his blood—but she didn't answer. He waited. He listened for her. He sat on his heels and looked up at the silent board of buttons, the dark holes in the speaker. He waited until the quaking ring of entry brought him to his feet, then pushed the door open and heard it click shut behind him as he raced up the flight to her door.

She was dressed to go out, her lips redder than he remembered, her hair darker. Lovely, he had to admit to himself, and wondered at the change in his sight.

"What are you staring at, Carver? What do you want?"

"I wanted to apologize to you, Mary."

She looked surprised, and said nothing.

"For everything, from the beginning, that wasn't right. How I treated you."

"You mean, how you threw me out, half dressed? And humiliated me again when I should have stayed away?"

"I don't forget it."

"What on earth could you say to make it right?"

"I can't make it right. I can only try to make amends."

"What are you, in some kind of twelve-step program? My name is Carver Heinz, and I'm addicted to cruelty."

"Maybe there should be one, you're right. But it's not a thing somebody told me to do. My head was ready to explode. I was living blind, running away like I could smell the slaughterhouse. I went knocking into every wall along the way, until I knocked some sense into my head."

"Why should I believe anything you say?" she said, and tried not to soften. But she could not throw him out into the darkness, like he'd done to her, even on this spring night, warm again after the storm. This blessing of nights, she had thought, as she'd dressed to go out and have a drink and find some folks to talk to.

"Every word's true. The lie's been dragged out of me. Through fire—"

"I heard about that. I asked after you."

"—through drowning and wind and fasting and shooting—"

"What are you talking about?"

"— through my own ugliness turning on me—"

"You have been ugly —"

"—but I'm looking to do right, I swear it. To know myself, and the people around me. I got to stop the voice in my head that judges and beats them down, like was done to me. I swear to you, Mary—"

"Enough, Carver. Enough."

"I just wanted to apologize. Leave you to the good things in your life. I guess I was thinking maybe you could forgive me."

She remembered when he was the good thing in her life, those moments that were true and gentle, when his heart beat against hers with nothing between them. So alive, she was in those moments. He looked different now. Tested, gentle. But he was a master of that, she thought, a face for every occasion, one for wanting and one for getting rid of.

She wanted to touch him.

"I'm not a fool, Carver," she said. "Not anymore."

"I've been the fool." He wanted to take her hand, but didn't dare.

"I've got to meet someone," she lied.

"You're busy. Thanks, for hearing me out. I'm sorry, and always will be, for everything I did wrong. There's more to tell, if you want to hear it sometime. About how I learned. How I keep learning."

"Maybe. Sometime."

He got up to go, and she saw how thin he had gotten. "You been sick?" she asked.

"No, I guess I'm not eating like I should."

Lord, how she wanted to feed him. Stew in the fridge, a big garlic bread ready to go into the oven. She smiled. "Well, you better get your strength up or some irate woman's going to kick your butt all over town."

"If it happens, I hope that irate woman is you."

She walked him to the door, and he burst out of his tough body to hug her, fumbling a bit in the attempt, but she let him, and he was gentle and smelled like the good air. They stayed for a few moments in their breathing together among the dancing shadows of leaves.

"Call me if you want to talk some more," he whispered. "I'll go about my business, hoping you do."

"We'll see," she said. "Take care, Carver," she instructed, and turned to go inside.

"And, Mary?"

She looked back at him.

"Thank you."

"Sure," she said. She closed the door and leaned against it for a moment. Go about your business, she told herself, hoping.

She walked around the living room, not daring to go into the well of shadow and dreaming that was her bedroom. She was still angry and would stay that way, she told herself. She did not want to sleep alone in a bed meant for the twining of two bodies, and instead lay on the sofa, her head against the hard pillows thrown there more for show than for comfort, and dangled one leg over the side, gliding it back and forth as if in the waters below a wooden dock.

When the church bells rang, she woke up in a rage. The unholy hell that man put me through, she thought. Something burned in her throat, rising from the pit of her stomach. She drank down a glass of milk, hoping it would calm the release of acid, and went to shower. When she saw the old marks, the deep angers against her skin, she sank down under the water, and hugged her poor legs to her chest, not remembering them when they were whole and clean, a girl's legs, and she cried into the water, cried into her own flesh, which was fragrant and soft, and not anything to be punished, not by any man. She shuddered in the cold water with the blows of memory, until she rose, her belly contracted against itself, her nipples hard and pink, and said, "Damn you, Carver. Damn you all."

She pulled on her clothes and went out with her hair wet, daring the cold, and drove her car up to the diner. But there in the window was the saddest back she had ever seen, curved down toward the counter. The forehead rested against the man's palm, and nothing about him was moving, except for the shallow rise and fall of breath within him, that mix of air and shame she understood Carver was to breathe for a long time.

# *Chapter Eight*
## *June 1997*

They had driven out together, the six of them: William, Angie and the baby, Madeleine, Mopstick, and Carver. They left Barb for the day with Jamie, much recovered since her stay in the hospital, and her son Sam. Carver had to pull Mopstick away from his wife and tuck him into the backseat of the car, where he stared out of the window in silence for the first hour of the trip.

They drove past the farmhouses nestled in their groves of trees, past the silos raised like lunar shouts on the prairie, a male posture in a female body, thought Madeleine, sloping and round. She saw the powerful mountains of clouds above them that broke for the light, for the eye of the Great Spirit. They drove on into skies that were black and red, then gray and pure water, then blue and heavy with brilliant cream-edged clouds that flew around that watchful eye, that joyful opening. They drove under the shafts of light that pierced the clouds, held them, joined Heaven and Earth, cut up the sky into angled segments, then, like a joke, erased each straight line and flooded the land with sunlight, with warmth. In this way they saw each other, in this light.

They drove out to Lower Sioux Agency, and walked around the trading post where food had been refused to the Dakota, though the millions of acres taken had not been paid for. Though the people were dying.

Dying of hunger, thought Carver, with food sitting on the shelves. This he could not forgive, but couldn't forgive himself either, nor his father, for the burning of crops, for leaving them warehoused, for growing nothing, as he was told to do. They walked up to the building and each put their hands on the great cold stones pressed into its wall. The baby fussed as they all fell silent.

Madeleine wondered where they had found Trader Myrick, and tried to see him there on the hard steps. Empty of words, after saying the worst ones, "Let them eat grass, or their own dung." Teaching him in death what he would not learn in life. Grass stuffed into his mouth.

Behind the building was a place left to the Dakota way of growing food. Mopstick walked around the circle, his eye following the bright spots of ladybugs, and remembered the things his grandmother had told him.

"Your grandfather was a miner," she said, "not one of those straight row farmers, one of those taking food out of the earth and forgetting to put back."

He thought of the open pit mines slashing the Mesabi Range, and shook his head. But her family had never bent to the white way of farming, and it was as he kept circling that he remembered her, singing in her garden.

"Corn. *Wamnaheza*," he read, in the mystery of his other tongue. "*Wamnuzizi*. Pumpkin."

"We lived in the woods," she'd told him. "We fished, we ate wild turkey, and we grew things this way," she had gestured with her new cane, "in a circle, and we picked the wild things that grew, and made our soups, our stews." He kept walking around and could feel it, the pain of bending to the ways that would make the crops straight, the tasseled heads lined up under the sun, ready for sacrifice. The corn had a different taste, free and healthy, tended by a hand that would put back into the earth the minerals taken out. It was why he loved the garden Barb had brought forth from the lot where the old house sat, with ivy crawling up and down fences, and the surprise of morning glories; no prize roses like the neighbors had, but purple wildflowers and sweet grass, like a patch of prairie, with bird feeders swinging in the breeze.

He knelt again at the circle, saw beans, saw squash, and read the Dakota names, "*Omnmia, menominee*," and saw the tepee, the good sheltering mother, put up for display.

He went inside and sat down. It came to him there why he had so desired Barb. It was the way she freed herself, the way she rolled beneath him and made him feel as if he were riding the hills of night, the weight of her breasts in his hands and his mouth. It was how he could fight with her desire. How she lifted herself to him, caught him and kept him in a circle of heat as he pushed his way to her, and found her again with his body. Oh, thought Mopstick, how could it be they thought she was ugly, and he felt her tongue at his neck, her breath in his ear, and ached at how empty his hands were becoming, at how Barb was becoming a dream.

They were waiting for him at the car. They went on to New Ulm, south and east of Lower Sioux, and here William did not know what he might do. He tracked through the town the path of the Dakota rising up, number by number encircled on the brochure, the one that counted the white settlers dead at each skirmish, sometimes adding, "and an unknown number of Dakota."

He wanted to scare someone. He wanted the whites to look up from behind a closed window in the building where the settlers' women and children were barricaded in against his people, and have their hearts leap into their throats when they saw him, with his long ponytail, with his Indian face, with his anger. He followed the map to the old Erd's Mercantile building facing the *biergarten*, still empty at this time of day. He put his palm against the stone wall, and heard a cry, and then many. He didn't want to hear the cries that place held within its walls, but he did. He swung open the door to listen better, and a man looked up from the staircase.

He wore a white mask against the fumes from the varnish he was laying on the banister and on the stairs, the path down to the restaurant. He lowered the mask to hang at his neck, and coughed a bit.

"We're renovating, son, or you'd be welcome to come in and take a look."

They were always fixing things, these people.

"No problem," William said. "Those chemicals would get to me too." He began coughing, and the other man joined in.

William pushed the door into the street. "You should get some fresh air in here. I'll use this brochure to prop open the door. I can get another one."

The other man smiled and lifted his hand in goodbye. He pulled up his mask, and William continued down the street.

The Outrage, he shook his head, as he stopped and leaned against a fence to read through the next brochure. But he could still hear them crying inside that building, its roof floating like a nightmare above the old foundation. He could see their faces, white women and children, waiting for the blows. He didn't know if he could have done it. Then he thought, yes, to see what the white man had done first. To see his family as corpses, starved and hacked. To live always without the land under his feet. To be invisible, recognized only in a flash of blood, in the blow, in the war cry.

The Outrage. Little gods they thought themselves, naming an event with no memory of what came before it, what happened next to it. Naming his people, dogs and savages. What of the outrage against the Dakota, he wondered, under the blind eye of their Christian god, and the smiles and cheers as they hung the thirty-eight in celebration, not of vengeance so much, but of their power over us. He could not smile and kill at the same time. He could not cheer at how a body swings in the air at the river's edge. He could not throw rocks at children, as they did, killing an infant as the Dakota were marched through their town to the concentration camp at Fort Snelling, many miles away, and all, all of it, whatever they named it, was Indian land.

They met back up at the car. "I never knew about that," Madeleine said. "They put a twenty-six year old woman down in the basement with her hand on a detonator to blow up the building, filled with women and children, if our people got in. A twenty-six year old woman, who would have to kill herself and all the others, rather than let them be taken by our warriors."

William listened for their cries, but it was silent in the street now. He could feel his hand on the detonator, how it might shake before he pushed down. He thought that the woman must have possessed great strength to sit there, ready not only to die, but to kill her own people.

They drove toward Mankato. Carver did not take his eyes from the window. He wanted to show them: over there is the road I took into town. See that old farmer in the pick-up? He's on the road to church. That's where the stand selling fresh corn went up, and right beyond it, is where the neighbor's boy went into a ditch. That was a hard thing. He didn't make it. Everywhere Carver looked, the years of his life yielded up pictures of what he'd lived. Of what he had tried to do out here and what he'd lost. This was the road he took to bring Rosie home from the hospital after she'd gotten her tonsils out. She lay curled into her mother's arms while he drove, slow as day. That same road the ambulance took them down, while he held his father's bloody hand. It was the road of the sun, whose light rushed over the land each time afternoon punched a hole in a storm. It was through that eye he saw his Rosie's face, always a little girl for him now.

In the car, no one spoke. After a while, William found a voice to make a joke, to get everyone laughing and exclaiming at the moody sky, but then he was plowed under, fallen to silence again in the damp dark power of what the earth held. Cell by cell the liquids of anger rose up, and his breath came short as they got into town.

"Stop the car," he thumped on the door, and Angie did, without a word, as if she were waiting for the order, for the plea. He sat for a moment, then pushed open the handle and sprang out. The next moment, it seemed, he was wandering by the river, where no one could see him.

He was going to weep, he knew that, but his heart hurt so, he feared it would stop. When he put his face in the water and stared through the moving current to the river bottom, this was what he begged for, that this pain would lessen through each generation, and that the heart of his people would remain strong. That his daughter and the children to come would know what had been taken. That everyone would know it, not pretend there had been a deal, fair and square, treaty signed. Not call the desperate response of his starving people the first blow. Not wipe out their memory like they did the forests, the buffalo.

A war cry is still a cry, he thought, as it broke from him.

He heard the hammering in his chest, as he saw each town marker go up on this earth become the New World for those in flight, this earth that could have held them all in her song, now dotted with their towns—New Ulm, New Sweden, Norseland, Saint Peter, Saint George—and oh he would have been the firebreather slain by the sanctifed sword. Morton, Franklin, Sleepy Eye—and he closed his own in the waters, to dream back the old world, to be born again out of the earth. This blue earth, this brown water.

He had his pony. He had his knife and bow. He had the old ways of growing food, of building home, of sitting. He had the pipe. He had his mother and he had his father, and the bottle that had killed them was what was shattered and empty, not his people, not his family, not their ways.

He opened his mouth into the air when he was pulled up.

"William," Carver said, "come back." It was different, what he breathed then, but there was still the pounding of hooves, still the smoke that rose above the tepees, still the pain in his chest.

"They didn't even let them stay buried."

"The thirty-eight," Carver said, having read the plaque at the execution site.

"The thirty-eight. They dug them up that same night. Before they were cold, when the hearts of their families were drowning in their pain, doctors came, the great and compassionate white doctors, and took the bodies away for anatomy studies. Cut them to pieces."

The last place they lay on earth was taken from them.

"Do you know where your family is buried, Carver?"

"I do. Except for my brother. Only parts of his body came back to us from Vietnam. My mother looked for him until she died, I think. In everything. Like he could be there, in a chair or in a cloud. In a bird or in the shot that takes it down."

They sat. They were quiet and they sat by the river for a long while.

The water was calm, as they were when they got back to the car, where Angie was nursing the baby in the back seat, and Madeleine was leaning against the trunk with Mopstick. They stood gazing at the wildflowers and grasses that took root where the scaffold had been raised in 1862, and torn down in the constant busy work of forgetting, leaving behind the silent river and the hushed hills as witness.

So much to take in, so silent as they did it, except for the sound of the baby, sucking hungrily.

William's whole body ached. What was never said rumbled through him. In the tourist center, an old railroad car, he walked by each framed bit of memorabilia hung on the walls between the windows, not seeing, until the number jumped out at him—Time Table 38 for the Chicago Great Western Railroad, with the schedule below. Nothing else. He turned to show someone but the car was empty. "Don't you see?" he cried out to no one. "Don't you see?"

Someone had picked that time table. Someone had laughed at his own joke, hammered a nail to hang the old schedule that was leaning confidentially up against its frame. And no one would notice, he thought. No one would remember, but each time he heard that number called out, in a store at the register, or from the scoreboard at a game, he swore he could hear the gloating in it. "Yeah, we hung their red behinds, and Lincoln signed the orders!"

He walked up and back through the railroad car, and stopped where the schedule hung, hoping to see a different number there, free from the tricks his eyes must be playing on him.

But there it was, 38. Time Table 38. He stumbled out into the air, and everything that was gone began singing at the edge of the river. It wasn't the true number anyway. It was never the true number. He saw his woman holding their child, but he could not go to her. He could not move.

That night was the first time William went out and did not come home. Angie was frantic.

## *Chapter Nine*

William sat under the dim lights of the coffee shop. The slight smell of disinfectant underneath the smoke from the grill sickened him. He'd been there alone for hours, after staring into the Mississippi from the St. Paul side.

Customers came and went, but no one bothered him. No one looked at him like they saw the broken thing he was. He wanted to heal into a whole man, a whole Indian. He wanted to hear his Indian name, to leave William there under the surface of the waters, the grim Minnesota River, flowing by the concrete barriers of flood control.

There would William lie, he thought, and he, Caske, first born and only son of the murdered couple Raymond and Julia, would race into the forest, the hard edges of trees disappearing to either side of his swift run as he sped over the black earth and became all that he truly was, with the sky to witness. No more would he have to feel sorry for the white boy who had killed them, doomed forever to a wheel chair, but breathing in this life, as they never would again.

A couple came in, a black man, a white woman, and their child filled with some impossible presence of both, something defiant, something healing. The other people in the booths and at the counter looked up for a moment or two, maybe to wonder at the crossing, to judge it or just note the beauty of the child, his cloud of hair, before they got their checks and went on home.

William worried then for his daughter and his children to come later, for people were not always so accepting of the mix in the blood – what had Sofia ever done, what was she guilty of? Guilty of split heart? Guilty of two winds, the way tornado comes, the cold and the warm meeting and rising into raging spiral, wrenching up the story of the land?

But whatever anyone thought about it, his joining, his forever and his everyday, was with Angie. His woman till his death was this girl who was white and Indian both, with her great-grandmother Dakota. What else could he do? Leave the child? Blame the girl? Take a path away from them? Or would he just live, Indian in everything he did, Indian in his words and dreams, Indian in how he loved?

Angie could not sleep as William wandered away from her. And the winds were coming. She saw the coffin lid slam in her mother's face. She saw her father pulling her to safety, from the winds, from Carver. She saw Carver caress her and hated him for that, for what he had never done but what he'd left in her mind. She forgave him a million times over for the things he'd done, but couldn't forgive him for what she'd imagined he wanted to do.

"Oh, Angie," she heard him that night, aching for her to be his girl, and she knew then that he just meant, Daughter. She closed her eyes. She didn't want the great emptiness to appear in the room, to push out her dying mother and her gentle father, to block the doorway when William was ready to walk back in, but in that emptiness stood Carver. Lean and stooped, with farmer's hands, but so gentle now when he brushed her shoulder, as he had been when he'd lifted her wet dress from her body, over her raised arms. It was that, she supposed, and all the secrets, all the years of secrets, that made her think of him, for a moment, as a man who might want her, though he would never hurt her that way, never break the journey they took to heal together into family.

William, come home, she thought, please come home, and went to check on the baby, who slept in the sweet and constant breath of dreams and did not see her mother standing there, clutching the railing of the crib.

She sat on the couch and put on the news, something in her always afraid of the local reporting of accidents and crime scenes, after the things William had told her about the moment that took his folks. Nothing touched her life, she thought, relieved, but she could hear whispers all around her, brushing her skin, and alone she began to touch herself, as the baby slept and William was somewhere in the dark night, and Carver was a man her father's age, repentant, dreaming of the land, in love, she thought, with Mary. It was impossible not to search herself for pleasure, to move into excitement as William appeared over her in the light of the television she could not hear above their breath, as he fell to her and in a hurry, in desperation and the fullest ache she had ever known, they came into each other and wept in their joy. But in the silence that followed her hushed call, the house was still, and she pounded the cushion with her rage.

Every time he thought about that white boy riding around with his buddies in their drunkenness, speeding through the wall built between them and the Indian neighborhood, something rose in his throat so foul tasting, that if he swallowed it coiled burning through his intestines. Gutted, he thought. Deer, fish, women. Babies ripped from the womb. It doubled him over. He could grow straight, or bent over, chewing memory.

All he knew was that they were gone, mother and father both, stolen and strewn over the road the way so many of his people had been. Dead on the road, dead on the way home. Madeleine had told him more than once about the boy, about his grief and his sad legs that would never walk down the street again, and sometimes that moved him, but he didn't want it to. Why should he care?

He stood in the street in front of the apartment building. He heard shouting, but it was only some men at the corner store joking around, challenging each other in their games of being men. He stood there for a long time waiting for Madeleine, and thought of smoking, but did not.

He stepped toward the middle of the street and trailed his eyes after each car that moved down the Avenue, as if presenting himself on a dare.

A car screeched by him and around the corner. He couldn't see the driver at all. He spat on the sidewalk, went upstairs and entered the quiet kitchen.

Madeleine had stopped at the library, and then at the grocery. William was staring at their photos when she opened the door. He did not speak, and she did not ask him to. He'd started the soup, so she added some meat to the pot for the strength it would give him.

She went out after the meal, and he did not ask where. He didn't care who she might be with, but she didn't trust that yet. He wanted someone to love her, to help her.

He slept on the couch a while, and awoke to the photos of his parents facing him from the coffee table. When Madeleine came in, closing the door with a sound he heard only because he was listening, he stepped forward from the shadows, and they sat down and talked about Raymond and Julia, how they met, how much they loved their boy, how much they were missed.

"William," his aunt said, "what would you say to them if they could hear you?"

"They can hear me."

"What would you say?"

He needed to find that tender voice, that voice of a boy they would recognize. He said, in the softest tone he could find, past the harsh cut curse and the rhythm of his fist, drumming, drumming, drumming into the truth of his loss, "I needed them. I needed them to bring me down the road. You did it, and you blessed me, but I still needed them."

"I know. It's fine for you to say that."

"And the way it happened pounds at my heart each time I hear talk about some drunken Indian somebody saw, or thought they saw." He looked away from his parents' faces and wept. He didn't want them to worry.

She covered him with a blanket as he lay there on the couch. She rubbed his back, as if he were still a little boy. After an hour or so, he slept and she sang an old song she had learned with Julia, and he turned to listen in his dreams, and did not rise till almost dawn.

William got home in the early morning hours. It had been two days since he'd been there, and he opened the door in fear that everything had been taken, that they were gone now. But Angie was standing at the window, her back to him.

He said her name, then, "I'm here."

Angie didn't turn. "I was worried," she said.

"So was I." William came to stand behind her. He put his arms around her. If anyone came to this house to harm this woman, or our child, he thought, I would fight them, I would stop them. This makes family.

She turned and stepped out of his arms. He saw the red beads he had given her, tracing a line around her neck like drops of blood, like an angry scar, and shuddered. He had meant to give her beauty with this necklace, not knowledge, but she wore it as both.

And the feather always tied into her hair hung down the side of her neck in the stillness. He blew it into dance, and kept blowing on it until she shook her head and moved toward him.

She had worn the feather through the birth. She had worn it through the illness of her mother, through each strange homecoming into emptiness from the hospital. She wore it always, drenched it under the shower thinking waterfall, let it hang in the moisture-laden air of summer, let it fly about her face in the breeze, and crackle with storms next to her ear. She wore it always, and knew that she had joined herself to the bird, and William knew it, too.

He saw her as bird, and as woman, and as girl that his aunt had carried to the river and brought back from fear. He saw her as the odd one, landless, the one pulled into the air and dressed for flight. He wrote stories about her for their daughter, and drew pictures, and bound each into a book with thick wool thread, leaving a long tail hanging down as if the book were part animal. He hoped to keep Angie by him, and believed they would still be flying when they were old people, though Sophie and her brothers and sisters would be bringing them dishes of food and extra blankets, and seeing them as slow and earthbound.

Maybe in some towns their baby was a curiosity, a shame, a dark-haired mistake come forth from the pale skin and hair of the girl the tornado loved, but in this one, there would be nothing else to do but give up your heart to her and listen as she read the little books her father had made.

Some people in the neighborhood thought that the long ago tornado had been trying to wrench the child Angie up from the land taken in millions of acres from the Indians. But there were those who thought the whole story ridiculous, and knew full well there was something of a lie in it. No possible way a girl could be lifted by the brutal power of tornado and then dressed by gentle winds and delivered to her own doorstep.

"No way," said the cynical camp of the next generation of kids when the story was told.

"Way," said the young believers in flight, while others insisted, miracle or no, that when the winds subsided, this angel was set down without a scratch in her daddy's old Ford and found wild-eyed but calm, turning the steering wheel up and back.

Some said it was in the moments before she was returned to them that her mother had agreed to give up her health in exchange for the girl's safety, but as the good Lutheran minister said, God does not make deals, willing though a mother might be.

Whatever people believed about what happened the day of the tornado when Angie was five, she would dream many dreams of what she might have seen if the winds had taken her up in their spiraling journey, if she had whirled over the land from inside the ferocious green funnel and followed its course over the Minnesota River, past Mankato and New Ulm, until it laid her down upriver near Morton to rest, and then delivered her back home, washed by starlight.

She would have seen the world, or more than that. She would have had the vision of one world next to another, like the banks of a river with liquid breath between. She would have seen the bones within the hills and lining the plains, and the thundering herds playing the earth like a vast drum, disintegrating fences and walls with the power of their hooves and the blows of their massive heads. She might have seen the early wars—even the very moment when the young Mary Schmitz Ryan, waiting in the basement as the women and children gathered on the floor above her, got ready to set off the explosives as the town had instructed if the Dakota came, to obliterate with the detonator the truth of what might happen. Angie might have seen, instead, how young Mary let go of the lever and raised her hand to hold the thunder of the buffalo to her hearing.

Angie might have seen the whole world at once, all of its peoples circling around an axis of truth. She might have heard all its languages, the ones spoken and the ones silenced, and searched in vain for the line between peoples that the winds could not cross, and come home happy not to have found it.

She knew William would fly with her for many years, and help her come home, once a little girl who flew with tornado.

We are lucky travelers, she would think in their flight over the earth, and bow her head to her teachers, and to the winds.

"Bless the storm, in which we lose our foothold," Carver heard the voice in his head that day William returned to Angie, or maybe he heard it in a dream, or in his bones, as he watched another storm let loose. Blessed old storm, he thought, picked me up and put me back down somewhere else. Aching for home, but pushed, duly pushed, to go on where I found myself.

"That's really something," he said to Hansen, who didn't come in to the station much anymore, not since his last heart attack. Carver was the one running the place, and Hansen was glad of it, even had the signmaker come in and put the man's name up next to his own, and shared the profits with him as much as he could. Sometimes Carver stood there and watched his name on that sign, swinging with the breeze. "That's really something," he repeated.

."What's that, Carver?" the older man said, wheezing a bit in the dampness that played in the air that day.

"I got it, boss. I just got it."

# *Chapter Ten*

Carver began to search for Mary every day as he walked back to his room or strolled down Lake Street on a break. He played a game with himself, noticing someone's back that might be her, and he would work to see in his mind's eye the details of her face as she turned around.

"Hello, Carver," she would say, and then he would take her hand. He knew there were some men who would never try to explain themselves, but he would do it this time. She was worth it. And he would see her there in front of him in a new way, like a faded curtain had parted.

Once, she was there ahead of him, and he raced up the street calling her name, but then, when he got close enough for her to hear him, he could not speak, and he stopped there and let the people passing by move him further away from her until she disappeared.

The next time he saw her, he swore it, he would invite her to dinner. Or maybe he'd call her, out of the blue. Ask her out on a date.

"I wasn't expecting you to call," said Mary, as Carver grabbed her coat and held it open for her to step back into. My god, he sure is trying, she thought, and let him draw the coat together as he stood in front of her.

"For a long time now, Mary," he said, "I've wanted to hold open the night and wrap it around you like velvet—"

She laughed. "Carver? Is that you?"

"That's what I want to do—wrap you up in the cloak of night. Stay with you there in the darkness." Then he said it. "You wouldn't have those scars, Mary, and I wouldn't have my ugly past."

"Carver, stop it."

"You'd look into my eyes and see how beautiful you are."

"You're a liar."

"I mean it, every word. How I treated you, it was a mistake."

"Look, Carver, I'm not playing this game."

"I want you to know I have feelings for you—"

"Then why did you throw me out?" He put his hand on her shoulder, but she pulled away. "You threw me out, Carver, out of your room! All of a sudden, you didn't want me. You couldn't even look at me. Maybe all you saw were my scars."

"I'm sorry, Mary. I was stupid."

"Is that it, then? My scars? I earned them by loving the wrong boy, the wrong color. Quite a beating I got. Probably like the beatings you got, Carver."

"What beatings?"

"Come on. I recognize a man who got beat when he was a boy. There's an army of us out here."

"Beatings was what a man did to raise a son," Carver said. He saw his brother's face, and realized he never knew what happened those nights in the barn when his father got angry and marched Eli out through the cold passageway, his haying boots still on. It all happened while Carver sat watching his mother at the sink, the water running over her red hands.

"What we don't know, we don't live by," he said.

"What are you saying?" she asked him, as much to bring him back as to get an answer.

"I know what happened to me, but I won't ever know what happened to my brother. What the old man did to him. That's what I mean. Can't go by what I don't know."

"Carver," she said, and looked so straight at him that he shifted his feet. "What we don't know, that's exactly what we're living by. We're puppets of it."

"Puppets—"

"Yes. Our arms and legs dangling around the stick of the past. It makes us run from things, makes us strike out. Makes us sick from wanting—"

I want you, Mary, he didn't dare say.

"—look down on what we've got. Makes us bury, deep, the pain."

"Bury it. Why the hell not bury the pain?"

"And bury the truth with it? I can't live like that anymore. There's no grave big enough to put the whole damn story in and cover it over. Only way to do it, is to jump in there with it."

Carver laughed.

"What's so funny?"

"You know, I tried that."

"What?"

"Didn't anybody tell you?"

"No," she shook her head. "Mopstick said there was some trouble."

So Carver took her coat back off, and lay it folded and waiting on the sofa. "Let's sit," he said. He took both her hands in his and looked down at them. Then he went back and told how he got to pulling the trigger with the gun in his mouth.

"That was what Mop meant," she said.

He nodded.

Some weeks later she would open to him like a lost spring.

"It's a miracle," he whispered, tracing her cheekbone with his long fingers, "a miracle." To feel like a man again, he did not say.

## *Chapter Eleven*

The world was spinning away from Barb. The shadows moved by her on the walls, the lingerings of the people she had loved her whole life, even before she knew their names.

The baby's cries pulled her back.

"Please, Angie, bring the baby to me," Barb said out loud, hoarse. Her eyes seemed not to focus, but she did see, the small legs kicking, just fat enough, the little arms stretching, fists punching the air.

"Ready for a fight, huh, Winona Rose," Angie said and sat next to her mother on the bed, her arms full. "I was getting lots of homework done, when Miss Baby Girl started yelling her cute head off. Sorry she woke you, Mama."

"She didn't wake me. But she made me remember we have a baby in the house, and that my own girl isn't a baby anymore."

"Oh, no, you don't," Angie said, "I'm part grown, but still part baby," and leaned closer to her mother, hearing then the terrible effort of her breath.

"It's not easy, is it, to go to school and be a mother, both."

"No, it's not easy. But William's great, and Dad and Madeleine—"

"— and then there's me, laying around all day."

"Well, you can supervise."

"Wish I could do more."

"Come on, Mama, give yourself a break."

And she did. She closed her eyes then. Angie kissed her cheek and carried the baby off to her crib. And Barb could feel it, the flesh house falling away. The prison of it. This was the fulfillment of all those days, those nights, when she told herself it didn't matter, that the body wasn't her true home, just a temporary address. Ugliness, the signpost of a moment. Being in this life, that was the dream.

But such a real dream, and she inhaled, the smell of baby powder and her own daughter with breasts full of milk like a grown woman. Such a beautiful dream, her husband climbing into bed when he could sit up and watch her no longer; August, stroking her cheek, her arms, and she, Barb, falling asleep in his embrace. Such a real dream, to be in this body and learn what it needed to teach her.

She sat up. She pushed down the blanket and pulled up, an inch at a time, her big nightgown with its dance of roses spiraling toward her. It was caught beneath her but she had to see, she had to know what was falling away, what she had dreamt all these years. The cloth scraped her flesh. But then she could see the house of the body she'd been dreaming, and she wondered who had dreamt it first. What god had lain drunk, and in the tremors of the night, formed her, a great drunken world full of caves and crevasses in the hills, and long curves scored by glaciers, by the sharp weight of ice.

The covers cast away, there she was. All dream.

Flesh dimpled and scarred. Her belly still round. Her breasts still dreaming, the nipples drooping to each side of her chest. "Cockeyed breasts," she laughed, and then grabbed at the covers in case someone would hear her, walk in and see her there, in her awful house. Her ramshackle costume. She laughed again. Still alive, there in her laugh.

Dead weight. Is that what they would say when they tried to move her? She'd read chapters of *Gulliver's Travels* with Angie. She could see the tiny men swarming over her with ropes and pulleys to try to lift her.

But then she saw how her legs had grown thin, and her arms, even her fingers, had not the same thickness, the same journey around, and she knew it was true. The awful house was falling away.

The wind entered through the screens and stirred the air around her. She remembered the dress that swirled up like white petals to show off the long firm stems of legs that stayed planted even in the wind, the view of the body obscured by the painted fingernails that tacked down the skirt at the place of desire. She knew the famous woman, the blond Marilyn, had been caught by the camera standing over an open grate, and that her legs were parted wide to give her balance on her high heeled shoes over the darkness below her. She wondered at what was hidden of the famous body, and then at the whole back of her own body, lost forever to her scrutiny. She squirmed and remembered her behind, how it moved under dresses in waves. Dismissed. Desired, too, she recalled. Men whispered at her, and she still heard the things they'd said, and burned with embarrassment. She recalled the day she decided that nothing she couldn't see could hurt her, and gave up staring at herself in the mirror and weeping there, begging God for beauty.

She saw all the pretty faces turn to look at her, the fat girl, focus on her with eyes thick lashed and heavy lidded, pure blue, deep brown, ocean green, filled with the old scorn. She'd walked out of one house, out of one town; she would walk out of this one, too, and be free of what flashed at her from magazine pages and television screens, from the thick-voiced movies that appeared from behind old velvet curtains. Free from the ever-present gaggle of teenaged girls at the mall, their tumble of perfect limb and precise pour of breast, their hair that fell like magic over the forgotten skull and its electrical sponge that was not beautiful, that was not the color of cloud or flower or rare dark wood, of berry or spice or intoxication, but a gray sponge sparked to frenzy by the deep charge and wild turnings of the feeling mind, that knew nothing of the embroidery of hair that sat above it and veiled its true ardor.

186

She'd walk out of the belly sag and the crushed breasts and the pitted garment, the ragged crown and the shriveled lips. She'd leap out of her own eye sockets. She'd storm the barricades of flesh, and she remembered that, the workers in nineteenth century Paris, the poor with their wooden shoes and their weary, soot-encrusted faces, hungry for better, storming the barricades and bursting through the prison walls, and she would, she vowed, burst through her body, burst through, and pull her heart from it, like a madman rips a phone out of the wall. Only this would not be to disconnect, but to take her heart with her and connect it to the great heart of earth, the great heart of creation.

She looked down at her dry broken feet. She'd never walk out of here, she thought. But she'd fly, fly out of herself.

"Tell them," she yelled, "this is not me. Tell them," she whispered, afraid, "to look for me in the beautiful things." I'll be there, she thought, in the lightning strikes, in the sudden reaching down from the sky. She looked at her feet, her legs, her belly, her breasts. "I'll be there in the land. Sit with me," she cried out, and August ran in and held her, and put his hands everywhere she hated and would leave, and then she wanted to stay, always, in this house that she loved like no other.

# *Chapter Twelve*

"I hated myself," said the woman on the screen. "I couldn't look at myself. I undressed in the dark so my husband wouldn't have to look at me, either. I was so ashamed." And she cried then, as pictures emerged from the shadows of a large woman still half hidden in darkness, and a man waiting in bed, his lean, toned arms crossed over the white sheet.

Angie lay on her stomach, watching. Her hair, dazzling in the light, covered her whole back to her waist, already slimming down after the birth of her daughter. She rose from the living room floor to see if her mother wanted the blinds raised in the beauty of the afternoon.

But Barb was asleep, curled into her left side, her right hand resting on her heart. With each release of breath, her belly fell closer to her bones, and she made a sound, as if from her dreaming. Angie lay her hand on her mother's forehead to see if there was fever again, and there was, but not much, better than the night before. She went to get a washcloth and a basin of cold water, and as she crossed in front of the television, noted the same woman, transformed and golden, sleek in white pants and belly skimmer top, kicking her way forward with an arched foot through the rush of ocean, which parted for her now. Angie imagined the startled fish, darting off. She watched how each step left a clear footprint in the sand behind the smiling woman, until the water rushed its fury back in, to break down the marks of her womanly kicks and carry off the small creatures scuttling by her.

Angie stood there, not understanding why the woman was on television. Then she went to sit with the trapped and shallow breathing of her mother, and lay the cool cloth over her forehead. She began to dream there, eyes open, weaving her breath into the harsh music of the woman's breath, until one steadied and deepened, and the other finally went under.

She tried to think what to do to make her mother alive again. She got up to run for her father, but he was there in the doorway, awakened from dozing in the kitchen chair over a sandwich he had not touched. He saw, and fell to his knees. His cry, raw and weak, scraped at his daughter's ears. Angie held onto him and cried into his chest, and then he knew it was true.

He had to go to her, so he pulled the girl to her feet and looked down at the bed. He saw Barb was smaller then. He had heard this and saw it was true. The dead grow smaller as their spirits rise up. She did, and he gave a bitter laugh, knowing how much it hurt her to be a big woman, a woman who saw herself without grace and without form. But he had seen her, the worlds in her eyes, and knew that she was a being formed and full of grace.

He lay down with her body and journeyed away from that day, and as he lived again, Angie went to check on the baby, who had been dreaming at the moment of her first great loss. Angie spun the wooden carousel of the lamp, and it played a tune that made Sophie coo in her sleep.

She knows more than one world, her mother thought, and went down to the porch where she sat looking for any sign of flight, any way to look down at the world and see it all at once, small and in motion. Before the shadows of approaching night came to cover the place where she sat, she saw the world in its luminous shell, and thus blessed, got up to call and make the arrangements, and let people know. She kissed her mother, and began to bathe her and dress her, once more.

Madeleine walked the path up the hill and looked down into the group of people gathered at the grave, the earth dark where it had been opened. She saw Carver, standing apart from the rest, his hands folded behind him. She saw Anita, that neighbor of theirs, flanked by her two sons; Barb's dark-haired friend from the hospital—Jamie, she thought her name was—and her son. Friends from work were there, and from those demonstrations against the bombs. She scanned the faces and recognized most of them. It was good to see how many people loved Barb, and came to say good-by to her under the threatening clouds. She saw her William there, a head taller than his Angie, and he bent to her, as if whispering his love. So this was how their families were joined, not only over life, but over death as well.

We all make our way into the earth, Madeleine thought then, whether lowered into her heart or resting in the limbs of a tree, or scattered from above. She leaned against a tree and looked up into its arms, listened to the breath of spirit in the leaves. "Good-by, Barb," she whispered, and wished her good journey and warm return to her ancestors. A graceful ride home.

She looked back down the hill. This Angie-girl is not what people might imagine by looking at her, thought Madeleine. She is stronger, without vanity. Who would think? She is devoted to her father. She was devoted to her mother. A good child.

She watched William and Angie emerge from the group and walk up the hill toward her. She reached out her arms to take the baby. William took the invitation first, gave her a bear hug and stayed for a moment. Then Angie put the baby in her arms. The new mother's eyes were red. She leaned over the baby to kiss Madeleine's cheek.

"I can't see it, the world without her. Without my mother," she said.

"It's not without her," said Madeleine. "It's a world filled with her having been here."

"Please, don't. Don't tell me these things. I need her arms around me," Angie said and walked a few steps away to gaze up at the traces of sun, so dim today.

She looked back at them, her family now. "Sorry," she whispered, and turned and ran down the hill, back to the grave, back to her father, who was caught by surprise when she flung her arms around him in such tight embrace, a deep sob came up from below his breath and hung in the still air.

"She loved you so much," the man said, bent a bit awkwardly over his daughter, but she felt his embrace as wings wrapped around her.

"She loved us," Angie said. "I want this to be a dream. I want to go home and find her there. Sit with her and see her laugh at what the baby does. I don't want her to be gone."

"I know, angel," he said, and that night, and for many nights to come, he would lie on the couch listening to the whisper of traffic and the news on television, low and repetitive. He'd glance up to see the weatherman pointing out storms and smiling at the cartoon suns that popped up in the five-day forecast, all the future he could manage in the darkness, but for now he held his daughter and swayed with her, trying to be a woman and a man for her, a mother and a father.

"August," said Madeleine, "this is a beautiful place," and he realized that it was, after all, that it was good that Barb would be among such trees.

People stepped up to August and Angie to say their hard-to-say words. "Come back to the house later," Madeleine called, as they waved goodbye, and most took another look back at the marker above the grave. Gray stone, Madeleine thought, why is it gray stone, and left bright feathers on the earth there, and made sure to drop in a deerskin pouch filled with good things for the journey before the earth was shoveled over the coffin. So deep in the ground, so she threw in her scarf too. When she looked up, one of the children was watching her. "That was a pretty scarf," he said. "Why did you throw it in there?"

"The earth can be so cold," she said, and he seemed satisfied with that. She looked past him and wondered how many, how many were buried in the earth out on the prairie, or given in the old way to the air above, and saw the mounds of the dead, endless waves of the forgotten. The earth would hold them all and hush their pain, but the markers, she realized, are for the ones who are left, the ones who need a place to come back to, to remember their dead.

"Come on, Auntie," William came to her when the last friend had left. "Let's go to the car."

She held his arm and they walked, and waited in the car for the man and his daughter who stood still at the grave as the sky turned red.

They stared into the earth, jealous for what it held. "Dear Wife, Beloved Mother," the gray stone said over the dear body she had never simply been, even with its truth of flesh, of passion and birth.

190

Without a word, they walked away, back to the car and then back into the house that was filled with family and friends and food and drink, and talk of Barb, thoughts of her, and deep and fearful longing for the knowledge she was dreaming.

## *Chapter Thirteen*

Ugly woman in the ground,
Make the crops grow green, not brown,
Ugly woman's flesh below,
Make the waters fall and flow,
Ugly woman leave your bones
So crops grow tall, and cattle moans
With birth of baby calves, and more,
Bring pigs and chicks, and at the door
The beauty of the harvest seen
As far as seeing, waves of green.
Ugly woman in the earth,
Give us dreams and give us birth.

Carver kept hearing the shrill voices of children in their mean singsong. Haven't heard that for more than thirty years, he thought. He was driving over to Mopstick's, where the mourners were gathering. The voices of the children kept blaring in his ears. He remembered back to his father's sermons, and all was sermon. He wasn't even a real minister, but a hard man who screamed if there was a spot on his shirt Sunday morning after sleeping in his own foul breath on the drunken table of Saturday night.

Carver kept hearing the man's talk now, and he did talk his way through the years. He remembered his lectures on beauty, and how, when Carver first touched Katie, first saw her full and womanly as her clothing fell away under his hands, there was a pain in his heart that his father had put into him.

When she lay waiting on the bed, uneven in her bones, marked by the sun and the early disease, yet so full of grace, he almost fainted into her body. He believed that if he learned her, he would know why his father was wrong, and so he moved his hands everywhere, and each part of her that he touched, opened and led him to move and sigh and keep on touching her. His father's voice erupted in his ear, "Why this one? Why this girl? Marked by the polio, boy, don't you see that twist in her leg?"

And Carver's protests of his love for her, no matter; his yelling out, "She is a beautiful woman, and there's nothing better I want or need," all this drowned out by the father's voice that aimed to break his dream of making a home with her: "Don't you see that mark on her, that mark of God's Judgment?" Then, more questions that sickened Carver: "How can you touch her? How can you take her for a wife?"

And the voice pounded in his ear as he loved her, pounded like an ax splitting the heart of the rings of time, and Carver trembled and cried out with the pounding, there in Katie's flesh, and she thought, yes, he is mine, when he stopped his riding her and said her name, and he thought, yes, she is good, and she is mine, my own woman. Then his father's voice quieted and her beauty flowed into him, that first night.

He kept driving. He took the long route, the quiet route, and made the turns, dazed and slow. Carver could hear his father's voice, could hear him day and night sometimes, and it was this voice that bestowed upon the things and beings of this world what to call them, according to the Great Namer. The Great Separator. His father, the Measure of All. Discipline was his motto.

He separated the animals. "Here are the cows and there are the horses. Here are the workhorses and over there the riding horses; here the milk cows and there the ones to sell for meat.

"Here are the sickly, the hens that don't lay, the beans that won't sprout. This strain of wheat, the one to be burnt.

"But that strain is the finest, the king, the one we'll be famous for selling. A strain of wheat worth a patent, not a discard. Here are the beautiful seeds. Over there, the warped ones." And the edge of his palm came down straight and hard on the table.

Always and every day, the line was drawn, the wheat separated from the chaff.

"Your brother was a hero, and you're a coward."

"But I had to stay and help you run the farm."

"I could have done it my damn self. You could have found a way to serve. A way to fight. To join up with your brother over there in that hellhole so he wouldn't have to die alone. So you could prove yourself, boy, prove yourself."

The trees would fall to fences, as the Great Voice said. First the ax, then the saw, always the cutting, making smaller and more fine, leaving the cut ends to shine their ringed hearts in the air, marking the boundaries to make it so this crop did not touch that crop, this animal stayed with its fellow.

Heroes separated from cowards.

But the dead, thought Carver as he drove, are always here with the living. No fence can hold them.

He saw one day the massive head of a stray buffalo push at the fence and knock it down in the far field, and he turned away; waited while it fed, and turned back as it raised its dark shaggy head and shook it. Beautiful, Carver thought, and shook his own head, his hair flying about in the sun. He watched the creature until it took off, and then walked away.

Carver pulled up to Mopstick and Barb's house and parked across the street. He put his head down on the steering wheel. Ugly woman in the ground, he thought, God bless you, and he cried there for a few minutes, until the wheel pressed hard into his forehead. "Barb in the earth," he whispered, "bless us. Oh, Mother," he cried, and pushed the car door open, gasping for air.

He had bought a cake, chocolate with a rich frosting, and he picked up the box by the red and white string tied around it. He went up to the door, which was a few inches ajar, and pushed it open. "It's me," he called, and again, "it's me, it's Carver."

# *Book Six*

## *Floor Plan of Paradise*
### *Summer 1997*

"O give the wind a flute to weep for the people
    of this wounded place,
And tomorrow to weep for you.

And tomorrow to weep for you."

—"Speech of the Red Indian" from *The Adam of Two Edens*
Palestinian poet, Mahmoud Darwish, translated by Sargon Boulos, pp. 138-39

# *Chapter One*

Carver and Mary were stunned by the feelings they found for each other. He tried to think what this was like, and he saw the plains when the land was unbroken. She began to look for Carver at the end of his shift, though he told her not to wait on him for dinner. But she loved the emptiness in her belly when he lay on top of her. She could feel him all along her spine, unfolding with her, vertebra by vertebra.

She wondered how she felt to him. She knew her own skin, too well she knew it. How smooth it was, how it drew in a man. How she could let him in. Too often. But then she waited for his disappointment, when he saw her scars from the beating. His disgust.

Now, when Carver touched her in the moonlight streaming in from the windows, all was softened. Even history. She'd once read a story where light became water. She loved that story. She saw her scars swim away in the moonlight. But then she remembered the children in the story. The light kept rising in the apartment until they toppled off their raft and drowned. She could not bear that vision, the children sprawled out and bloated when their parents came home. She could still send off her scars like fish darting away. But could she banish her story? Could she ever dart away from the hand raised, the whip unfurling, the father who wanted to kill her for loving a black boy; or even from Carver, that bitter farmer who might want to kill her for loving him?

She was sick of this story: "You'll amount to nothing. A girl like you."

And these: "Black and white don't mix. Indian and white, that's a crime against history. And don't let me catch you with no Jewish boy. There's some in town. They at your school? You better stay away. I don't know what they are doing out here. This is God's country, not theirs. Somebody should teach them something."

She wanted to show her father, she supposed, but it was more than that. So she went home with Anthony one night for dinner with his family. Of course, she lied about it. Studying with Kim, she'd told them.

"The land, the schools, better than where we were outside Kansas City. Maybe better than anywhere in this US," his father said.

She'd expected them to look at her in a strange way, this white girl sitting at the dinner table, but then she realized they must have expected something like this.

Something like her. It was the numbers. Just the way it was. Land, schools, white girls. Most of Anthony's friends were white.

She wondered if it hurt to look everywhere and see no one that looked like you.

She was glad her hair was dark.

"Beautiful hair, you have," his mother said, and she brushed it away from Mary's forehead, and looked at her. "And beautiful eyes," she said, so that Mary could not blink or turn away, but looked back at her, and was comforted.

"Thank you," she whispered, not sure what else to say, whether to protest, or to believe her.

When she left, after chicken and sweet potatoes and greens, pie and good coffee, Anthony walked her almost home. She trembled in fear that they would be seen in the cool dark evening, but no one veered out of the night, or ran from their homes to stare.

They got to the long driveway up to the barn and looked at each other. "I can go the rest myself. I'll be fine."

"My mama taught me to walk home a girl."

"You know," she said. "Please."

He took her hand and led her under the trees, and kissed her. "I've only once," she began, and as he kept kissing her, she said, "I've never—" She did not finish, could not remember words or the way she should act or what she was told. He did not touch her except to hold her, but the kisses led her into a world that was all breath and warmth and she could not bear to stop, though he moved away after a while and turned around. She stepped behind him and put her hands around his waist. He looked up and she rested her head against his back. Nothing in her whole world was better than this, no moment, no thought, no dream.

They said nothing when he left. She could not sleep, not till morning. If she dreamt then, it was of things she did not understand.

In the kitchen, her father at the table, she saw how ugly the linoleum was with its small phony flowers, how marked the wood, how dry and lined her father was, as if he had never been outside, but was scored by the tail of the dragon of the sun, and by something inside him that he stirred every morning, and drank up every night.

One morning in Minneapolis, as the hands of the clock moved around its black center with the jump of her heart, she pulled out the files from her supervisor's drawer, and read where the heavy marker circled what would be cut from the story by the time she was supposed to look it over. She couldn't make out the name of the chemical the leather company was letting churn in the river, but she knew what it spelled. She knew that it was toxic, and this inky rumor of death would be hidden under white redacting tape, put under the copy machine and spit out like a newborn without name or scar.

When they assigned cases, most of the stories they threw at her were like stories from home.

"Take this one, Mary." A boy who fell into the gears of a tractor and lost his arm.

"And this." Another file came sailing onto her desk. A family dusted with pesticides as they picnicked, the plane pushed off its route.

Even her own accident would have had a place here. She remembered her father's response that night: we'll sue those bastards. Who, she laughed now, the boys, whose fathers let them buy illegal fireworks? The folks, who were too damn busy to notice what their kids were doing, who looked the other way when the kids went off with paper sacks with the sulfured cannons sticking out of the top, plain as some old man's nose?

She still smelled that burning. She still yearned for music to reach her left ear. She still heard it there, but she heard it like a love song, unvoiced. She swayed in the moonlight at her window to what she could not hear. She whispered, and sometimes did not hear her own promises.

But she had promised this, no more lies. She told her boss so.

"Claims Adjuster. Even sounds like a liar should do the job."

"What they adjust is the amount, not the facts, Mary."

"Well, the word 'claims' makes it seem like the party injured is the liar. But my job, a Claims Examiner, sounds like a real scientist, no? Like someone who pores through documents looking for the truth. I thought that's how it would be."

"It is, Mary, that's exactly how it is."

"No, I'm poring through the documents looking to make true the story you tell me. Looking to deny the claim."

"Just because someone was hurt, doesn't make it someone else's fault."

She couldn't argue there. "But that," she said, "doesn't make a lie any less of a lie."

He slammed his hand on the table. He took a step toward her. "I'm done with you, Mary. Get to Data with your things, or get your things and get out of here."

"Yes, Boss," she said, and stared at him until he walked out. A voice in her head said she would soon be free of this.


One evening Mary and Carver fell into a deeper rest than usual, slept longer, and woke up hungrier. Carver stood naked at the fridge and berated her choice of foodstock.

"What's this stuff doing here?" he asked, holding up a tub of tofu.

"No cholesterol. It's made of beans, Carver. Soybeans."

"Not like any I've ever eaten, and I was a farmer, you know, give me some credit here. Sorry to poke around in your personal dietary collection."

"Oh, that's fine, I'm enjoying the view," she laughed, and he loved hearing it.

"Let's go," he said, "and get us some real food."

The bar was noisy, metal spatula ringing against the grill at the take-out window, bursts of laughter from the booths, and from the jukebox a heavy drumbeat beneath a tune he did not recognize. Whenever Carver went to Sonny's, he thought he might get a glimpse of the woman he had danced with the night that Angie almost drowned. But she never again appeared to him in solid form, more like a voice that seemed to follow him. Voice on the Wind Woman, he thought, maybe she'd call herself that.

Mary was fighting with Carver by the time they got back to her apartment. Maybe it was the adrenaline from ducking out of a brawl that broke out at the bar, at least, that's what Carver said, but, no, Mary said, it was something old, something she wanted to forget, but couldn't.

"It was the way you would toss the sheet over me when you were finished. 'Cover yourself,' you'd say. Do you remember? Do you remember that?"

"I remember," he said, his stomach tight.

"Like you couldn't bear to look at me."

"It wasn't you I couldn't bear to look at."

"What's that supposed to mean?"

"It was me, Mary. It was me."

"Then why didn't you cover your own damned self?"

"Mary, please, I don't want to do this—"

"You made me a despised thing." She saw the sheet flung over her body.

"If I could take it back, I would. I was nothing when I did that."

"And who else did you do that to?"

She watched his face turn red and saw him cornered there.

"I said, who, Carver. Who else?"

And he remembered the night when Mopstick had fallen with him into the arms of the girls from off the farm.

"What good will it do to talk about this?"

"I want you to tell me. How you threw a sheet over someone you had just been with, like she was a dead thing. I know it wasn't only me."

"No, it wasn't only you," he said, caught, and in terror that she would leave him.

"Who, then?"

"Some kid."

"Some kid?"

"Someone pretty much younger than me. An adult, you know, but still a kid. And I am so sorry, Mary."

Inside Mary was that constant moment, unfolding now, after her father had seen her kissing Anthony, and took her in that iron grip, and beat her. That moment

199

of the unfurling of the whip, and that breath before, when Martin grabbed it from the great rusted nail, and she saw it coming.

She saw it coming.

"Say something, Mary," Carver said.

She was locked in Martin's grip, the snake uncoiling. Inside Mary was the moment she saw her father could kill her. The moment she saw he wanted to.

"Tell me you don't want to kill me, Carver," she said.

"Never," he said. "Never."

"I'm still so angry at you."

He said nothing more but wept, wept with her. He wept for her. He wept for the girl he had covered in his own ugliness. He wept, finally, for himself.

And that night Carver dreamt of heads bare down to the skulls, of blood pooling into messages, and he strained through the thick night to read them, to know something true about this language of blows, of the beatings regular as rain.

"He's only a child," his mother said. "She's only a woman," his father said. "He's only an Indian," and Carver's heart burned at hearing his own voice say it. He heard the word chanted in his sleep, "Only. Only." And then he heard it as a great and precious blessing, "He is only this, our miracle of boy. She is only that, a gift to us. Not a burden, not an afterthought, not a failed being."

We are each other's true companions, along with the wild-eyed beasts, and the soft-eyed pets who let us name them, he thought in a moment of waking. "She is my one and only," something whispered. "This is our family, our truest mirror, our heaven. This is how we walk into a room. This is how we walk the earth. This is how we come to live within this world, bone against bone, skeletal hands clasped," and he shuddered back into sleep and was glad not to wake yet. He clamped his eyes tighter, then, grateful for the flesh, and held Mary's hand as they lay together with the moonlight, as they would lie together for many nights, perhaps for all of them. And they slept, in the onliness of every moment.

"It's just for a moment," he heard someone say, but made a hushing sound in his new dream, made his body soft in sleep, to fit there, within that moment that kept growing.

## *Chapter Two*

When her latest story came out in *The Planet*, Mary jumped in her car to grab a pile of newspapers from the closest coffee shop, and drove home to meet Carver after his late shift.

"Look! Read it! It's my story. It's out. Under my own name."

"I can't read it now, Mary, I'm too tired for it to make sense." Hansen was still in the hospital, and everything was on his shoulders at the station.

"You have to. It's the story I lost my job for, Carver."

"I can't."

"Yes," she said.

"No," he shouted.

"Yes," she shouted.

No, yes; no, yes; they yelled back and forth, no, yes; and then they forgot which side they were on, which word was theirs to say; who was to speak; who, to finish. They forgot the knot of argument. They were left with laughter, and with the knot of their bodies.

"We do better without words," he said.

"But we're human beings. It's a sign of human life that we talk to each other, that we communicate with words."

He said nothing.

He kissed her. Then he read every letter in her skin.

She let the newspaper lie open on the table, almost flying off in the breeze from the ceiling fan. She forgot to scold him, watched the moon rise, held him.

He talked in his sleep, woke and whispered to her.

He read her story in the morning, as he drank his coffee. He could not stop reading. It brought up face after face of people he'd known, people knocked around and made ill by their labor, and by the companies that made big money off them. She wrote of the farmers and their families, and the small town folks living down river from where the companies dumped their poisons. She explained how the insurance companies were hand in glove with the very companies the people were filing their claims against. He already knew the ending, the denial of their claims by insurance. But Mary had the scoop from inside. And what she wrote, outright and clear, this could make a difference. She was a fighter, his woman, smart and tough.

Mary raced down the steps to the river. Carver was jolted out of the gray sky that filled his sight. She was gone. Just like that. He called her name, then took the steps two at a time. He loved the wind of it, that jump to the bottom that became all wind and landing and leaping onto the trail when he saw her, the red spot of her shirt like a laser tracing the river, and he ran after her. He did not know she could be so swift, she had hung back so much, but there she was, blazing down the path and he in his work shoes like a plough horse, thumping after her.

She stopped and turned back. He saw her hand lift and wave something white, and he laughed. I surrender, he heard on the wind, and thought, what a joke to surrender to someone who can't catch you. What a perfect joke. What a perfect surrender.

"I give up!" Mary said and laughed like water and the river rushed by them. He reached her then.

"It's about time. What were you waiting for, me to have a heart attack?"

She laughed again and he could not help but kiss her neck and they forgot everything, and remembered the one thing they needed to know: what happens when the prison door of the body is flung open for love. What happens when the past glitters and disappears down the way of the river.

# *Chapter Three*

He didn't talk much to Mopstick about Mary, not wanting to remind him of what he'd lost, so he confided in Freddy, who was wise beyond his years, and had already seen Carver at his lowest. Whenever Freddy got up to the city, Carver met him for a beer and something to eat. Some weeks passed, with Freddy needing to study for exams. Carver didn't want to wait much longer, but had to work to get up the nerve to ask him.

The day was a steamy one and nobody was moving very fast, the waitress included. Carver and Freddy sat and talked family in the noise and smoke of the bar, each tracing back their lineage, but Carver had to stop at the ocean crossing, not knowing much of anything about his people before they reached this place and its rich black earth.

He lost all sense of time as Freddy went on. He imagined the Bible coming to life, he saw Solomon and Sheba on their thrones, and the first mixing of Arab and African. Freddy spoke names he had never heard. Cushites. Bantu. Oramo.

"You're making all this up, aren't you, Freddy?"

"Not any of it. It's our history. We Somalis know the names of our ancestors back very far, twenty-five generations maybe, to our beginning. Some clans, many more."

Carver looked into Freddy's green eyes. "Strange," he said, "you've got the ocean in your eyes."

"It's not just the color of ocean. It's the color of crossing."

After the second round of beers, Carver leaned over the table.

"Freddy, I got something I want you to do for me. I want you to meet me at the farm. You know, where you found me."

"Why, Carver? That was such a hard day."

"That's why. I've got to go back and say a proper goodbye. To my land. To my house."

"You sure that's a good idea?"

"I don't know, but I have to do it, and I don't want to do it alone."

"Tell me when. I'll be there."

"Okay, farmer. From sunrise to sunset on Sunday. Like all-day church. Then, dinner's on me."

"I'll save up on my appetite. Should I bring anything?"

203

"Just come, Freddy. Be there."

Carver arrived before dawn and went to Old Redeemer Lutheran. He found where they lay together under the grass in the churchyard. He stood with his back to the old man's grave. "Now when I want you to speak, you're silent as a rusty plow," he whispered, and turned to face them. "There wasn't a damn thing I could have done. You shouldn't have worked so late, old man, gotten so tired."

And it was this daze he returned to, remembering how his own body drove itself beyond all sense, how everything demanded this of him, this very thing, and how he'd learned to do it from his father. No complaining. No hunger or cold could stop him.

But then Carver began to shake. He remembered how little he was, crouched beneath the shadow of the tractor, deaf in the clatter of machinery pulling machinery. He remembered how the wind threatened and then toppled the tractor, and he ran, screaming, right into the hard grip of the man, who struck him for his fear. "See," the man yelled at him, "I got away! That damn thing's not going to get me. So, cut it out."

He remembered the machine that ate up the earth and how afraid he was that it would not be content with the simple grasses, the tough, sheathed corn, but would want him, too, want a boy. Maybe if it took a leg or an arm, he would not have to go back to the fields, not have to worry over the devouring gears of debt he heard about at every meal, a number greater than a man, a good and honest man, could ever pay. Greater than a boy could understand.

He could still hear the scrape of metal sharpening against itself, always hungry, always ugly. He turned from the graves, and went to the old farmhouse to meet up with Freddy. The grove of trees held him again in its magical circle as he entered the blessed shade. Someone was cutting the grass in the path of the wind, timothy grass, sweet in his nostrils.

The windows were dark, somehow, in the blazing light of August, which could not enter. There was the blue door, which he painted in celebration after he'd gotten the silo, the great blue tombstone of the prairie now, a solid storm of emptiness.

He waited outside the door like a stranger. He went up and knocked, and laughed and stood there, where Freddy found him a bit later, holding his grief in his eyes.

"Let's go in," Freddy said.

"Not yet. Let's take a walk."

Behind the barn was a dead field. "Used to be acres of corn here," Carver said. "All the way over to that rise." And they followed the path to where he pointed. No crop, but still the rich black earth gave forth, yellow and blue, purple and whispers of deep red berries tight in the bushes low to the ground.

"Here," Carver said, and stopped a couple of feet south of the shadow of the rise in the earth, where the rusty shanks of an old chisel plow, wired against each other into a cross, were driven into the earth. "This marks it," he said, and knelt to run his finger over the jagged edges. "I put this here."

"What does it mark?"

"This is where my father died. Not at the hospital, not at the place they put his bones. Here. Right here. And my mother died in that house, not a year after he went."

Carver saw again how the sky had gone dark with night and his father had kept working. He heard the old man spitting out the word, "Old."

"I'll show you old," he'd said to his wife, and laced his boots back up, and pushed himself away from the dinner table.

She heard the rumble of the tractor in a while and shook her head. "Old man, that's right."

She went to the barn and saw to the milking of the few cows they had left. It was a soft night, and she stood under the sky to watch the stars and imagine she saw them moving. "Slow as God wanted them to," she laughed, but knew that they were whirling so fast she could never know what their journey meant. She heard the tractor steady, but then it seemed to stick, the sound angrier and angrier. She ran to it and saw it fallen over on its side, the moon eclipsed for him, the stars silent, retreating into the darkness.

She could not budge it. Of course, she thought, and grunted at her own weakness, at the effort she gave, and at how nothing moved. She thought she heard him moaning, but the sounds of the earth were loud that night as she ran to the house, yelling his name back into the wind. "I'll get help," she screamed, but she knew there was none.

Carver rushed there to meet the ambulance from town. His mother was silent as she watched them lift the machine. But she crumpled to the ground when she saw him there, crushed by his pride, and by the grinding work of it.

This is how things grow, she thought.

She walked to the house and lit a candle. She sat and listened to the men shouting and the siren wailing as if it weren't already over.

"Come on, Mom," Carver said at the door, "let's go to the hospital."

"There's no reason to. They can't do anything for him in town."

He came to embrace her, but she was so still. He stepped back, and put his hand on her shoulder. "I've got to go take care of it, then, Ma."

"That's okay, son. I have some phone calls to make," and she turned to the candle and its weak flame.

"That's where she used to sit," Carver pointed, "at that desk, reading or working on the bills." A shaft of light had fallen across the spot, like a transparent, rotted timber. Carver spun around and stepped into the empty space opposite, by the kitchen window. "And my father sat here late at night, after coming in from haying or plowing. Got drunk, many nights. You didn't want to go near him then."

Freddy walked around, stared out through the windows, gazed up at the ceiling. He looked down at the marks in the linoleum, where the refrigerator and stove had sat. Carver looked down, too, and saw the patterns of the furniture at his feet, and how room opened into room like a life-sized floor plan marked by shadow and sunlight.

But there had been no plan. Each part of the house was tacked on as the need arose, or as they could manage. Mom's back porch, abandoned. Every face of the house pointing in a different direction, pulling away from the center into the sun rising or setting, into the winds that howled down straight from Canada, into the flight of birds away from winter. He'd wanted to fly with them, as he walked the frozen path to the barn to milk.

"It must have been quite grand," Freddy said.

"Grand?" Carver was confused, and felt again the small space he'd had to fit into, to keep it all going.

"It's a lot of work, no matter the size of the place, yes? To make things grow. To keep the animals healthy." Freddy looked through the window and saw the rusted old Case with the sunburst grille. He clapped his hands. "That was my father's dream! To have such a tractor. He prayed for one. Thought it would solve our problems. As if it would bring rain."

"That old relic?" Carver laughed.

"Oh, yes," Freddy said. "It's still a beauty. We would fix it up. It would be running through the fields, going strong again."

"That old heap?"

"Yes, old man, that old heap."

"I'm ignoring that. Want to see the barn?"

"Let's look at the rest of the house first."

He could be bitter then, as was his way, but he looked at Freddy in the light from the bedroom window, and saw again the scar that ran from his cheekbone to his chin.

"So, which room was this, Carver?" Freddy asked.

"It used to be my brother's. After he died, it was a spare room. It was going to be my son's room. We'd hoped for a son, or I did, after Rosie was born."

In the room where he and Katie had slept, the furniture lay broken down as for firewood, stacked up in one corner. "I loved that old bed," he said. "Land of ten thousand dreams. Looks like somebody hacked it up for fun."

Freddy ran his fingers across his jaw. "I am thinking," he said, "you might take photos here, many photos, for your memories and for other people, to say to them, look, this is what we lost. This place, where we lived, ate, slept. Worked the earth, early to late. This home, we are losing to the banks, and must leave behind."

"Photos."

"Yes. To tell the story."

"Maybe," Carver said, "might be something." He would know for certain when he had the photographs in his hands, image after image, the brilliant shafts of light, the breath of the cold gone to frost on the machinery, the wind wrestling with the trees. The rusted tractor, its blood orange paint still vibrant in streaks. The bales of hay untouched, the hills above the house, and the great empty house itself; he would have a way to begin to show it.

"The place where the cows slept," Sophie would call the barn.

"A house crazy with add-ons," Angie would say. "I'd love a house like that."

"That wind," and William would shake his head, his finger tracing how the leaves were pulled into dance.

Mop would keep turning the stack of pictures over and over, and arrive at the beginning as if he didn't notice he had already seen that first one. He'd just keep on looking.

All was green that day, it seemed to Carver, except for the seepage of buttery light through the thick old windowpanes, with their sharp edges hidden in the wood, splintering what they drove into. Each thing seemed driven with violence toward another, nail into wood as into flesh, glass scored to fit, shade's face curled into itself and forced down to cover by the demanding human hand. Even the chair leaning against the wall kept wearing away the same spot for years. Waiting for its burden.

Patient, that's what we were, Carver thought. Taking on burden after burden, worn away like the land. Living in the green air, stained by something seeping through, something both harsh and blessed.

He didn't know what to think as he stepped into his mother's porch, but oh how the wood was beautiful, as was her face before she died. And the doorknob, coppery and smooth, cold like the old man, but his color somehow stayed warm, even in the dead white month of January. They had times in there, those two, when they seemed happy, when they sat close, the housecat in his lap; when they leaned into each other, breathing together as the green room fell into blackness.

Maybe there were some things he didn't know about his father, he admitted. Or didn't remember. He sat. He searched, he did, for anything that would make him say, Yes, this was my father and he loved me and wanted the best for me.

There might have been a night when the old man put his head into his hands and cried because he knew for certain that Carver would lose the land, and it wouldn't be any fault of the boy's. Just the way things were going. Debt mounting to the skies, the banks hovering, the new ways of doing things. "Stupid," he might have howled, "stupid, these men, killing the land with their one big crop, fields so big you can see them from the moon. Hungry crops, leeching the soil."

That old man must have ached, as he saw the farm slipping through his fingers—his fingers, not his son's—after a hundred and thirty years. He watched the roads coming, saw the shopping center go up, and the parade of cars trooping in for people to buy what they used to make themselves.

What grief, Carver thought, in the coppery face of that old man. What rage, maybe at himself, too, handing down to Carver a farm that was dying, a sheaf of bills, a mother who'd never had a rest.

No wonder. He would have hated to look at them and see how worn they were, laboring toward the sale they couldn't stop, the sale of their hearts, of their place of burden.

But what if Carver had never had the land? He let himself think about that, and it was hard for him to imagine it. He looked down at his hands and saw how different they were, now that he was off the farm. Even his laundry was different—the green dust no longer shook out of his pants, no longer stained them. The odors of earth were no longer woven into his shirt. And the soil and hay no longer stuck in the treads of his shoes, nor the calls of animals in his hearing.

If he'd never had the land, he thought, he could never stand in front of this porch door and see the shade swinging black in the sunlight. He could never open this door and remember the used and grieving bodies that toiled to bring in wheat and corn. How would that be, to never have been on the land? To eat as if bread were birthed by magic, corn always wrapped in plastic, and milk flowed first from a carton?

He wouldn't know where things came from. And he wouldn't know to keep the land sacred.

He let the door slip out of his hands and clatter back into its frame, where, somehow, through all weathers, it stood with perfect fit. Then he walked over to Freddy, who stared at the line of blood the sunset had painted at the edge of the land.

Freddy sat on his haunches and dug up some earth with his fingers. He held it up to his nose. "So rich," he said. "Black and fertile."

"Used to go down like that, six feet and more."

"We could have made Paradise in this earth."

"I guess we should have."

## *Epilogue*

## **Dream of Home**
*Labor Day weekend, 1997*

"Truth, which existed since the beginning, is sown everywhere."
— *The Nag Hammadi Library,* p.143

"And, Wind, I am still crazy. I know there is something larger than the memory of a dispossessed people. We have seen it."
— *Joy Harjo*

"Grace" from the collection *In Mad Love and War.*
Published in *How We Became Human: New and Selected Poems:1975-2001,* pp. 65-66

Carver dreamt of building a house embedded in the earth, where he would live with his stores of grains, his rutabaga and beans, his old cook stove. He would live underground with a simple roof, one window to peek above the earth, capped by red rocks from the nearby quarry. He would climb up to the window seat, invisible mole of the past, and watch his land transformed to the one crop of money, and there pray for storm, for great winds, for tornado. With his bowl of corn meal mush, his soup of roots and greens, his fresh cold well water, he would watch the twister come to obedient lands that had yielded for each new master, and race over them in a wild crossing that uprooted the orderly planting, and unearthed a memorial to those who had loved the land, watered it with tears and sweat, fed it blood, buried bone in it.

He dreamt such a house. He dreamt such a storm, and was satisfied in his sleep, and woke, and fell back into dreams. Always the voices by the boundaries entered his night, and there laughed, there chanted, and there died, only to swell forward again from death, and laugh and sing, and perhaps, he thought, pray. To what, he didn't know, couldn't think in the turmoil of sleep, but he did know that it resided in the earth, in its trees and rocks and waters. In its animals, too, and fish; in its birds calling out as they rose into the sky to what was holy above that would live together with its sacred bride of earth.

At first, the boundary voices disturbed him, but then it was as if they lived with him, moved along everywhere he went. He knew they were Indian, and had loved the land before he did. He knew they were still here, in their children. He was comforted, a part of something that knew his ugliness and had always lived on the land with him. He dreamt a return to the farm, and stood up not as its owner, but as an exile who still loved his home, and loved to look upon the lands which were not his, but which sang with the prayers of all who had lived there, and dreamt there still. And then, what must grow, did grow, came back in the dream to blanket the land, and grace all that hungered for its ocean of quiet, its prayers of wind, the scent of its embrace.

Blessings, he thought, as he dreamt the earth, and it was there in his sleep, his blessed sleep that sometimes haunted him for the things he had done, but other times sang to him songs of forgiveness, that he saw his life unfolding, along with the lives of those he loved and those he wanted to love, all threaded through the cloth of his dreaming. It was there he saw streams of people in their journeys, crossing the globe times without number, encounters birthed at every road, the crooked and the straight.

He flinched then in his sleep and woke and cried out at the straight rod lifted in his father's hand against his own sons, and the crooked heart he understood the man to have, and the harsh tongue. Then he remembered that his own people had come a long ways from their language, and he missed it, that language he knew by only a few words, that perhaps his father ached to speak as well. He missed, too, that air he had never breathed, that land his feet had never trod, the Black Forest he knew must be filled with song and stories. It hurt him never to have seen the land of his ancestors, but then he thought how much more it hurt for everything to be taken from him, right before his very eyes; to know in his heart he would never hold his daughter again, though others had.

Then it struck him like iron against bone, how much it must hurt to see every day the plowing and mining, the foresting, the raising of cities on the plot of your memory, the fields of your history, the graves of your mothers and fathers. The graves of your murdered infants. And he wept and kept on weeping, and gasped for breath at the thunderous fall of knowledge all about him.

He knew he would never be alone again, and rose and walked through the shadows at play in the room, and the songs of wind that had carried him to this moment. The water he drank then was pure truth.

Then he went to shower and dress, give Mary a call, and drive up to the Iron Range, to the old camp where they were all gathering, Barb's family and friends, to remember her and celebrate, to feel the brilliant end of summer on their faces, to fish and eat together, and to drink in the stars.

"I'm going with you," he said, as he put a few things in a bag. "They invited me, and I'm going."

"In rooms you build,
the dead are already asleep…

O you who are guests in this place,
leave a few chairs empty

for your hosts to read out
the conditions of peace

in a treaty with the dead."

—"Speech of the Red Indian" from *The Adam of Two Edens*
by Mahmoud Darwish, translated by Sargon Boulos, p. 145

## *About the Author*

Anya Achtenberg is an award-winning fiction writer and poet. Her publications include the novel *Blue Earth*, and autobiographical novella *The Stories of Devil-Girl*, both with *Modern History Press*; and poetry books, *The Stone of Language*, published by *West End Press* after being finalist in five poetry competitions; and *I Know What the Small Girl Knew* (*Holy Cow! Press*). Her short fiction has received awards from Coppola's *Zoetrope: All-Story*, *New Letters*, the Raymond Carver Story Contest, and others.

She is at work on *History Artist,* a novel centering in a Cambodian woman born of an African American father and Cambodian mother at the moment the U.S. bombing of Cambodia began. This work received a grant from the Minnesota State Arts Board. She is also writing a book of poetry and short prose, *The Matadors at the Crossing.*

Anya teaches creative writing workshops and classes around the country and online with growing international participation, and offers manuscript consultations and coaching for fiction writers, memoirists, and poets. She also organizes groups of writers, artists, filmmakers and educators to travel to Cuba. Along with her numerous fiction and memoir workshops, she developed and teaches a series of multi-genre workshops on *Writing for Social Change* (*Re-Dream a Just World*; *Place and Exile/ Borders and Crossings*; and *Yearning and Justice: Writing the Unlived Life*), which she has started writing into a movable workshop.

Visit Anya at www.AnyaAchtenberg.com